I0554146

Praise for the novels and storytelling of
award-winning author Catherine Kean

Dance of Desire

"On a scale of 1-5 stars, this is definitely a 6 star book!... Don't miss this one!"—6 stars, *Affaire de Coeur* Magazine

My Lady's Treasure

"Filled with lively characters, a strong, suspenseful plot and a myriad of romantic scenes *My Lady's Treasure* is a powerful, poignant tale."—5 stars and Reviewer's Choice Award, The Road to Romance

A Knight's Vengeance

"Kean (*Dance of Desire*) delivers rich local color and sparkling romantic tension in this fast-paced medieval revenge plot."—*Publishers Weekly*

A Knight's Temptation

"...an entertaining medieval romance brimming with sass, action, adventure, and lots of sexual chemistry."—*Booklist*

A Knight's Persuasion

...stirring adventure, superb characters, and enticing heroes. Ms. Kean continues to snag the reader with her fast-paced tales of heroic knights."—4-1/2 stars, *Affaire de Coeur* Magazine

A Knight and His Rose

"This is an ideal book for those looking for a quick afternoon read that will sweep them off their feet."—*InD'tale* Magazine

Cat's Paw Cove Books

A Witch in Time by Wynter Daniels and Catherine Kean (Book 1)

Her Homerun Hottie by Wynter Daniels (Book 2)

Gambling on the Artist by Wynter Daniels (Book 3)

Meows and Mistletoe: A Cat's Paw Cove Holiday Anthology by Candace Colt, Kerry Evelyn, Sharon Buchbinder, Kristal Hollis, Debra Jess, Mia Ellas, Sue-Ellen Welfonder, and Darcy Devlon (Book 4)

Hot Magic by Catherine Kean (Book 5)

Reimagining Mr. Right by Wynter Daniels (Book 6)

Familiar Blessings by Candace Colt (Book 7)

Magical Blessings by Candace Colt (Book 8)

Christmas at Moon Mist Manor by Kerry Evelyn (Book 9)

Love Overrules the Lawyer by Kerry Evelyn (Book 10)

Fated Kiss by Darcy Devlon (Book 11)

Charlotte Redbird, Ghost Coach by Sharon Buchbinder (Book 12)

Hot Magic

by
Catherine Kean

Published in the United States of America.

ISBN-13: 9781370665952
ASIN: B07YR1RG74

Cover design: Dar Albert, Wicked Smart Designs

Welcome to Cat's Paw Cove!

Dear Reader,

Cat's Paw Cove is a fictional, magical town where anything is possible! It was dreamed up by Wynter Daniels and Catherine Kean and is located south of St. Augustine on Florida's Atlantic coast. The name Cat's Paw Cove is derived from the small islands in the harbor, which look like the pads of a cat's paw.

We are so excited to bring you not only our own stories, but also contributions from an incredibly talented group of Guest Authors. With paranormal and mystery romances, historicals, time travels, and more, there's something for everyone.

We hope you'll enjoy reading the series as much as we enjoy writing it. For more information about the Cat's Paw Cove series, please visit:
http://CatsPawCoveRomance.com.

You are also welcome to join our fun, friendly Facebook group where you can interact with the authors, learn about our upcoming book releases and special events, and more:
https://www.facebook.com/groups/CatsPawCove/

Happy reading!

Wynter Daniels and Catherine Kean

Dedication

For Richard Landells.

Thank you for the laughs we've shared, your insights into intriguing bits of history that have inspired my Muse, and for the tweaks which helped put the polish on this book. I will always believe you have magic.

The Legend

In the late 12th century, Lord Chadwick, loyal knight of the realm, was returning to his castle accompanied by Galahad, his young squire. However, a woman's desperate screams drew them from their horses and into an ancient forest clearing.

To his horror, Chadwick discovered his betrothed, Brigitte, about to be burned alive by a jealous sorceress. Agnes had posed as a servant at his fortress and had tried to seduce him, but Chadwick had rejected her. He loved Brigitte and wanted only her.

His lordship manages to rescue his lady love, and despite Agnes's fiery magic, he and Galahad defeat her. But, as Agnes dies, she curses Chadwick, his squire, and his lordship's bloodline.

For more than eight centuries, Chadwick has lived, died, and been reborn.

Galahad, who was turned into a cat, has survived many more lifetimes than nine.

Chapter One

"I wish that woman would stop moaning."

In the midst of hanging a gilt-framed watercolor on the wall of Black Cat Antiquities, Lucian Lord glanced at the long-haired, orange and white cat sitting nearby—the feline who'd just spoken in a refined British accent.

"The Lady of the Plate can't help it, Galahad," Lucian said, as the feline jumped up onto the upholstered seat of a Victorian chair. The plaintive moan, coming from the shelf toward the back of the store, started up again. "Remember what my grandfather told us?"

Galahad huffed. "Yeah, yeah, she cries when there's a change in barometric pressure."

"Yes, and—"

"Since it's summer in Florida and the rainy season, she'll be wailing a lot. Lucky us."

Lucian fought not to smile. So, Galahad *had* been listening to the conversation, even though at the

1

time he'd been wild-eyed and attacking a pink toy mouse filled with catnip.

"We should have gone on that cruise to the Bahamas with your grandfather and his lady friend. But, no. You agreed to mind the shop. How chivalrous of you."

Lucian returned his attention to the painting. As Galahad well knew, Lucian had agreed to look after the store because he owed his grandfather, and not just for his help with Lucian's recent work crisis. William Lord had taken twelve-year-old Lucian in and raised him after the horrific car accident in which Lucian's parents had died.

Galahad excelled at complaining, but to be fair, he hadn't always been a cat. In truth, he was a reincarnated twelfth-century squire, a lord's heir, whose ancestors had hailed from Nottinghamshire, England.

Hard to believe some days—not just the reincarnation part, but that Galahad was really fifteen years old and not four.

"If I'd known about the Lady of the Plate, I might have stayed in Boston," Galahad muttered. "I wouldn't have moved with you to this humid, alligator-infested, mosquito-breeding swampland."

"Hey, that's not a fair description of Cat's Paw Cove."

"Alligators live in the lake down the road. Your grandfather said so."

"He did." Lucian straightened the painting.

"And the mosquitoes—"

"And the Sherwood cats." Lucian stole a glance at Galahad. "You got quite excited about meeting female kitties who have ancestral ties to

Nottinghamshire, as you do."

Galahad growled.

Lucian grinned. "Admit it, you were as intrigued to start afresh here as I was."

Indeed, moving to the seaside tourist town, with a long-term goal of taking ownership of the antique shop once his grandfather had retired, had sounded ideal weeks ago, when Lucian's life had gone to hell from one day to the next.

The moan came again from the rear of the store. The sound of a soul in torment, the wail started softly and then rose in volume. "Ooooooooooo...."

"That cry gives me the creeps." Galahad's puffed-up tail, swishing to and fro, resembled the fluffy duster stowed under the store counter.

Shaking his head, Lucian took a few backward steps and studied the watercolor in relation to the other artifacts around it. Sunlight, streaming in through the shop's long front windows facing Whiskers Road, shifted as people outside walked past.

Thankfully, the passersby wouldn't be able to hear the Lady of the Plate's cries. Even if they caught some of Lucian and Galahad's conversation, they'd just hear a man talking to his cat, who'd responded with meowing. Only the few gifted—or in Lucian and Galahad's case, cursed—with ancient magic could hear sounds made by magical items or understand what the feline was really saying.

"Ooooooooooo...."

Galahad's ears flattened. "Can't you shut her up? Cats *do* have a far superior sense of hearing to humans."

That could well be true. However, Galahad was always claiming ways in which felines were far superior to their human masters.

"Grandfather said she doesn't cry for long." Moving forward, Lucian nudged the painting's right edge a little higher.

Galahad growled again. "Make her stop, or I might report you for torture of a Familiar."

"*What?*" Lucian frowned. "Don't be ridiculous."

The feline's eyes gleamed. "I'm quite serious."

"You are *far* from tortured. I spoil you rotten. I feed you that expensive, organic cat food you like twice a day. You can eat dry kibble—"

"That looks like rabbit poop—"

"—whenever you like." Lucian scowled. "And I clean your litter box several times a day and brush you every morning."

Galahad started washing a front paw.

"You haven't puked up a single hairball since I started the brushing. And, as far as I know, you haven't had any more diarrhea or digestive issues—"

"God, Lucian!"

"—since you ate the ribbon around that stack of old postcards a few months ago and I had to take you to the emergency vet."

The cat averted his gaze. "You know I couldn't help what happened with the ribbon."

"You just *had* to gobble it down."

"Yes! It looked *so* enticing." Galahad sighed. "I wish I could explain how it called to me like a lusty siren, seducing my willpower and—"

"Yeah, well, surely my rushing you to the clinic and paying the four-hundred-and-fifty dollar vet bill showed I care about your wellbeing?"

Galahad grumbled. "You're never going to let

me forget that unfortunate incident, are you?"

"Nope. And, you are never getting the chance to eat ribbon again."

"Sometimes, I can't stand to think that you and I are cursed to be together *forever*."

"Oooooooooo...."

"That's it!" The cat leapt down from the chair. "I'm going to break that damned plate. Then, she will be quiet."

"All right." The soles of Lucian's brogues squeaked on the hardwood floor as he swiveled to face the shelf and lifted his right hand, palm up. He focused his thoughts upon the exquisitely hand-painted Wagner plate portraying a beautiful, young woman with flowing brown hair and wide blue eyes.

"Shh," he silently commanded and curled his fingers inward, as though to catch and contain the sound.

The lady's mouth closed. Caught in Lucian's spell, her gaze became lifeless, as though there was no more to her than layers of paint on porcelain.

"Ahh," Galahad groused. "Finally."

Lucian retrieved the etched wine glasses and figurines he'd moved from the shelf near the watercolor and set them back in their places. To be honest, the Lady of the Plate *had* gotten on his nerves, but because he pitied her. Like the gallant knight he'd once been centuries ago, before he'd been cursed, he hated to hear a woman in distress. The antique, like many others in the shop, bore the ghostly fragment of what had once been a flesh-and-blood person who'd died under tragic circumstances.

"I have an idea. Let's wrap up the plate and ship it off to your brother's antiques store in London,"

Galahad said.

"You know we can't do that." Lucian picked up the hammer he'd used earlier. "Rules, remember? The curse became attached to the item here in Florida. So it belongs here in this store, with us."

Galahad stomped across the Persian carpet. "Well, thanks to Little Miss Moaning, my hopes of a much-needed afternoon nap have been destroyed. I'll be cranky for the rest of the day. *Not* my fault."

Lucian brushed cat hair off the Victorian chair. "Even if I could send the Lady of the Plate away, I wouldn't. Grandfather has a fondness for the young lady."

"Unfortunately," Galahad muttered.

Days ago, Lucian's grandfather had taken the plate from its lacquered display stand and had handed it to Lucian. "She's one of my favorites among our long-term guests. I got her from a guy who'd bought her shortly after Hurricane Andrew. Remember that storm back in 1992? It caused lots of damage in South Florida. Killed quite a few people, too."

As soon as Lucian had touched the plate, its provenance had flashed like snippets of film in his mind: the shrieking winds of a hurricane; an oak tree crashing through the roof of an upscale Florida home and crushing the screaming woman inside; and the plate, knocked from her hands onto the rug on the floor, intact but a silent witness to the tragedy.

When the woman had died, a piece of her soul had become connected to the antique. Most likely, she'd had a strong sentimental attachment to it.

The older man had returned the plate to its assigned spot next to the Steiff teddy bear that had belonged to a mass murderer from Orlando; the box holding the desiccated pinkie of a former trapeze artist for the Ringling Brothers Circus; and the Ancient Egyptian scarab beetle purchased in the 1920s by a late Sanford resident during a visit to the Valley of the Kings. Upon Lucian's arrival in town, a gold and lapis lazuli box inlaid with the Eye of Horus and holding an ancient cat collar had joined the collection. So many tagged and catalogued items of dark magic lined the shelves, his grandfather could claim to have a small museum.

Lucian's grandfather had then carried out a pattern of movements with his fingers to reinstall the field, complete with hallmarks that identified him as the sorcerer who'd cast the spell, around the plate. The magical barrier not only made the antique invisible to non-magical visitors to the store, but prevented the dark energy from influencing anything—or any*one*—in the normal world. The Experts required that all antiques tainted by evil magic brought into the store had to be contained in that manner.

Lucian's gaze shifted to Galahad, now sitting in one of the front windows. "Next time, try to be patient with the Lady of the Plate, okay? She isn't to blame for her curse."

"Like you and I, my lord."

Galahad rarely addressed Lucian that way anymore. The formality between them had become irrelevant long ago.

How Lucian wished he could recall the battle with the sorceress that had made him and Galahad into who they were today. But, he had no memories beyond his lifetime as Lucian Lord.

Galahad, though, remembered everything. He'd said the fight had taken place when Lucian was a medieval lord and Galahad his squire. Lucian had rescued his betrothed from being burned alive by the jealous sorceress, but before the evil bitch had died, she'd placed a curse upon Lucian's bloodline.

Immediately after she'd perished, he'd been confronted by The Experts. This secret society, originating from the era of the Ancient Egyptians, was dedicated to good magic and had given him one choice: swear allegiance to them, or die. They wouldn't allow him to fall under the influence of the ambitious, evil Dealers of Darkness. Fearing he'd never see his lady love again, Lucian had taken the oath to serve The Experts.

For eight centuries, Lucian had lived, died, and been reincarnated. Each of his lives had been connected in some way to his original lifetime. Most often, he'd been a private collector or antique dealer who'd specialized in artifacts from the Middle Ages.

Galahad, who'd somehow been transformed into a cat when the sorceress tried to kill him, had also lived numerous lifetimes. To be fifteen forever, trapped in a feline's body with all those raging teenage hormones....

Maybe Galahad had a right to be grouchy.

The cat sprawled in the sunshine, and Lucian crossed to the store's oak counter and put away the hammer. Earlier, he'd started sorting through a box of silverware his grandfather had bought at auction and stored until he had time to tag the pieces. As his grandfather had done before purchasing the lot, Lucian had confirmed by running his hand over the silver that none of the pieces held dark magic and therefore could be sold to the general public.

Lucian set an ornate serving spoon on the

counter and thought of the gleaming cases of antique silver at the New England store. Until two months ago, he'd been the East Coast Representative for The Experts: a prestigious position. He'd screwed up, and had lost all that he'd worked for.

His jaw tightened on a flare of anger and disappointment while he tied the string of a white price tag around the spoon's handle.

"Now *there's* a lady I'd like to hear moan."

Lucian glanced up. A young woman wearing sunglasses stood outside the shop window, looking in.

He knew quite a few people in Cat's Paw Cove, but he didn't recognize her.

Wavy, blond hair brushed her bare shoulders. She wore a sleeveless white sundress, and as his gaze slid down her shapely curves, he saw the open cardboard box tucked under her left arm.

Was she a potential customer? He hoped so.

Heat tingled in Lucian's gut.

"I saw her first," Galahad said, sounding petulant.

"True, but you're a cat."

To get a better look at Galahad, meowing and gazing up at her, she leaned closer to the window. The shift in posture brought the shadow of her cleavage into view. Lucian's hand curled against the counter's cool surface, for he longed to see more.

Reining in his stirring of interest, he forced his attention back to the silverware. She might be on her way to another downtown shop—not bringing items to his grandfather's store for a free evaluation. Lucian didn't want to be caught ogling, no matter how much her hourglass figure appealed to him. She might think him one of those antique dealer geeks who were starved for a woman's attention.

He wasn't starved. Single, yes. But, he'd never had a problem getting a date when he wanted one.

As he fastened a price tag around another piece of silver, though, he couldn't resist looking at her again. Shifting the box, she tapped on the glass and smiled at Galahad, who promptly rose to all fours and stretched to the tip of his tail.

Show off.

The woman's smile widened with delight.

How lovely she looked—

As she cooed to Galahad and leaned down even farther, something in the box shifted. Panic swept her features, and her free hand flew to keep items from falling out. Her sunglasses slipped from her nose.

Before Lucian realized he'd sprung into motion, he was halfway to the door.

"You *would* play chivalrous knight to the rescue," Galahad groused.

"Of course." Lucian pulled the wooden door open. A small bell attached to it chimed, a musical sound against the noise of traffic on Whiskers Road.

When he stepped outside, ninety-nine-degree heat washed over him. In the air conditioned store, it was easy to forget just how scorching hot it could be in Florida. A shock-like tingle also raced through him, a sign he'd passed through the magical barrier his grandfather had set up around the premises—added protection in case a Dealer of Darkness decided to infiltrate the shop, or any of the dark magic artifacts tried to cause trouble.

Lucian went to the young woman. She crouched on the sidewalk, her skirt brushing the dirty concrete, the box in front of her. With careful hands, she felt the newspaper-wrapped items, as though checking nothing was broken. In the brilliant sunshine, her hair looked even more golden.

Either she hadn't heard the door open, or she was too concerned about breakage to acknowledge him right away. Looking down at her, he found himself in the perfect position to see what had been denied to him before. The shadowed valley of her cleavage was framed by the lacy trim of her bra—

No. He was a gentleman. He wouldn't ogle.

A thudding noise intruded: Galahad, up on his hind legs and pawing on the other side of the glass.

A timely interruption.

"Is everything all right?" As Lucian crouched beside the woman, he caught a hint of her citrusy perfume.

Her shoulders—slopes of fair, satiny skin—tensed. Either she was reluctant to answer his question, or she'd only just become aware of him. Her long lashes flickered then she glanced up at him. Her blue-eyed gaze held his before she looked back down at the box. "Oh, damn it," she muttered.

Lucian fought a jolt of surprise. Most women, when he talked to them, smiled. Many tried to prolong the conversation by flirting and touching his arm. Not once had a woman answered him by averting her gaze and cussing.

"Sorry. I didn't mean to be rude." She peered down at the box again. "I lost one of my contact lenses yesterday. It went down the bathroom sink, and I haven't had a chance to buy more." Her hand slid to the right. "My sunglasses are prescription. I know they fell in here somewhere—"

"Bottom right corner," Lucian said, just as her

fingertips hit the tortoiseshell plastic frames.

Her shoulders dropped on a relieved sigh. "Thank you."

"My pleasure."

She pushed the sunglasses onto the bridge of her nose. Perspiration glistened on her face, and Lucian became aware of the sweat trickling down the back of his neck and under the collar of his polo shirt.

Be a gentleman. Invite her in.

When she picked up the box and rose, he stood as well.

Their gazes met again. As though seeing him for the first time, a pretty blush stained her cheekbones. Her gaze darted over his shirt that fit snugly enough to show off the muscles he'd built through intense workouts—the only way he'd kept his sanity through the turmoil of the past few months.

"Well." She sounded a little breathless. "Thank you so much for your help."

Lucian ignored the *thud* of Galahad's paws on the window again. "It's very hot out here." Good God, couldn't he have come up with something more inspiring to say?

"Yes, it is." Her expression turned rueful. "It's supposed to be a heat index of one-hundred-and-five today. I'm not used to such temperatures or the humidity."

Was she was a visitor to Florida? To Cat's Paw Cove? He must find out.

As she wiped her brow with the back of her hand, Lucian managed his most charming smile. He gestured to the shop's open door. "Why don't you come in for a moment and cool off?"

Chapter Two

Molly Hendrickson adjusted her sunglasses on her slick nose and discreetly studied the hero who'd rushed to her rescue: a tall, dark-haired man.

An unbelievably *gorgeous* man.

Her gaze darted down to his expensive-looking yellow polo shirt straining over his broad shoulders then back up to his face. He appeared to be around her own age—late twenties. With his unruly beard and wavy hair that needed trimming, he looked a bit scruffy and untamed. She could easily imagine him in chain-mail armor, wielding a sword and battling villains in the latest epic television series or movie.

Maybe he *was* a star of the big screen. He could be doing research for a role. Universal Studios wasn't that far from Cat's Paw Cove.

That would be just her luck, to meet a hot movie star while sweating like crazy and being extraordinarily clumsy.

Face burning, she snapped her gaze back to the box under her arm and adjusted several items. *Stop blushing. You're looking even more of an idiot than when you almost dropped the antiques on the sidewalk.* But, Molly sensed the man's gaze wandering over her, and somehow that made her cheeks flame even more.

Ugh.

After being very busy but accomplishing very little that morning, she should have known her afternoon would go awry. Despite the urge to turn on her heel and hurry away, she *was* going to follow through with her visit to Black Cat Antiquities.

A few days ago, she'd spoken on the phone to a man at the shop. While clearing out her late mother's home to get it ready to sell, she'd found items that might be of value, and had called to see if she could have them appraised. The man had asked her to bring them to the store.

He'd sounded older than the guy beside her, though. Maybe her cell phone had distorted his voice?

He was still gesturing to the open doorway, still smiling…and what a smile. It softened his features, defined by dark eyebrows and strong cheekbones. His brown eyes gleamed with humor and a trace of mischief.

She'd read historical romance novels about heroines swooning over men. She'd wondered if that kind of extreme reaction was even possible…until now.

Say something! He invited you into the store, remember?

"Thanks." She managed to smile at him in return. "I'd like very much to cool off—"

"Good."

"—and to meet your adorable cat."

The man's gaze flickered. Had she said something wrong?

"He *is* your cat? Or does he belong to the

store?"

"No, he's mine. He and I have a long history together." As Molly walked past the man and into the cool interior, he added: "I got him when he was a kitten."

Her rescuer shut the wooden door; the bell attached to it jingled.

"Your kitty's a rescue, then?" she asked.

"Of sorts." Somehow, inside, the guy seemed even taller and broader through the chest. The cat left the window and sauntered toward her, fluffy tail pointed straight up in greeting. "Galahad turned up on my doorstep one rainy day."

"Galahad," she echoed. "An old-fashioned name."

The man shrugged.

"Wasn't Galahad one of King Arthur's knights?"

"Yes." Admiration glinted in the man's eyes before he looked at the approaching feline. "I think the name suits him. After all, in many ways, he and I are kind of old-fashioned guys."

How cute, that he thought of his pet as a guy; as though Galahad was human and not an animal. But, her late mother had loved her four cats as dearly as if they were people, too.

With a twinge of anguish, Molly reminded herself to contact the airline later that afternoon. She needed to find out how much it would cost to fly the cats to Seattle when she returned home; also, what paperwork she'd need from the local vet. She couldn't bear to surrender her mother's pets to an animal shelter, so they'd be moving to live with her in her small, two-bedroom apartment.

"Would you like to put down the box?" The man motioned to an oak side table.

"Actually, I've brought items to be evaluated. Who do I need to speak to about that?"

"I'll be glad to take a look at them."

"Oh. Thanks. I don't mean to be disrespectful, but you are?"

His mouth curved in a sheepish grin. "Where are my manners? I'm Lucian Lord. My grandfather, William Lord, owns this shop."

Grandfather. That explained the gravelly quality of the voice she'd heard on the phone.

"May I ask your name?" Lucian asked.

"Molly. Molly Hendrickson."

He nodded, as though making a mental note of her name.

"I think I must have spoken to your grandfather when I called last week."

"He usually takes the calls when he's in the store."

Lucian's answer implied William wasn't at the premises all of the time.

"Sometimes he goes to clients' homes to do appraisals," Lucian added, "especially if there's an estate to settle or the customer wants evaluations on large pieces of furniture."

Molly did have some large pieces to sell, and an in-home appraisal would be convenient. However, the thought of Lucian wandering about her late mother's home sent an icy-hot shiver racing through her.

If she was so unsettled by him, maybe she shouldn't work with him. "Is your grandfather here today? Since I spoke with him...."

Disappointment tinged Lucian's gaze. "He's

on vacation. He won't be back for another eight days."

"I see. Well—"

"I'm a trained antiques specialist too. I managed a store in Boston before moving here."

A couple days ago, she'd emailed pictures to several dealers at the big antiques mall in Mt. Dora, and the replies had given her a rough idea of value. If Lucian gave a fair evaluation and wanted to purchase the antiques, she'd be willing to sell them to him. "That would be great. Thank you." Molly handed him the box. As their hands lightly brushed, awareness skittered through her, a physical acknowledgement of his nearness and masculinity.

She drew a quick breath, for she'd never experienced that zing of sexual attraction before—not even with her ex-fiancé. Why would she feel so strongly about a guy she'd known for less than ten minutes? The sweltering heat must have affected her brain.

As Lucian strode to the counter, his butt looking oh-so-fine in his snug, dark-wash jeans, she curled her hands at her sides. Either she had heat stroke or, as her girlfriends back home had insisted, she *had* gone too long without a date. She'd resisted joining online dating sites or agreeing to blind dates her friends had wanted to set up for her, because she just, well, hadn't felt up to it, not once since her non-wedding day last September.

Molly struggled to tamp down welling anguish. Right now wasn't the time to revisit her heartache.

Standing at the counter, Lucian started removing newspaper-wrapped bundles from the box. Molly had found plenty of newspaper in the house, including stacks of old issues of the *Cat's Paw Cove*

Courier. Her mother always had been a bit of a hoarder.

Tucking damp hair behind her ear, Molly glanced about the store. Shelves of china, glassware, books, and ornaments ran along the walls. Groupings of furniture and rich-toned rugs encouraged shoppers to linger and browse.

The store had an intriguing smell: a blend of things old, musty, and timeworn. Her mom would have loved it.

The ache within Molly deepened.

"Meow." Galahad brushed against her bare calves.

Glancing down, she murmured, "Hello, handsome."

"Push him away if he bothers you," Lucian said over the crinkle of paper.

"Oh, he's fine." She leaned down and stroked the feline's back. Purring, he brushed against her again, this time wandering between her legs and rubbing his face against her brown, Gladiator-style sandals.

Lucian unwrapped a hobnail glass bowl. "If you don't mind my asking, where did you get these items?"

"They belonged to my mother. She recently died." Molly swallowed hard. "It was very sudden. The doctors think she had a heart attack."

"I'm sorry for your loss. Did she live in Cat's Paw Cove?"

"Yes, for more than thirty years." Painful childhood memories blended into Molly's grief. "My parents divorced when I was seven, and she moved to this town after accepting a job offer."

"Might I know her?" Lucian asked. "I spent some of my childhood here."

So had Molly, although most of the time, she'd lived with her dad in Miami. Her parents had thought she'd be better off staying in the house where she'd grown up, and attending school with her friends, rather than starting over in Cat's Paw Cove. "My mom's name was Betty."

He stilled. "Betty Hendrickson?"

"Yes. She taught English—"

"—at Lancaster High School," Lucian said, "just a few blocks from here."

Molly couldn't hide her surprise. "That's right."

"I remember her well."

Lucian had known her mother? Had he been one of her students? Drawn by what he might remember about her parent, Molly took a step forward.

"Mrrrowww!"

Gasping, Molly tottered sideways. The feline shot across the floor, hid under a side table, and glowered at her, his ears flattened to his head. "Galahad, I'm sorry. I didn't mean to step on your tail."

Lucian snorted and set out a blue-and-white cup and saucer. "Serves him right."

That wasn't a very nice thing to say. Molly frowned. "Stepping on Galahad was entirely my fault."

Meeting her gaze, Lucian said firmly: "No, it wasn't."

"Why would you say that? I should have looked before I took a step."

Setting aside wadded newspaper, Lucian shook his head. "Galahad has a habit of getting too close, especially to beautiful women."

The reply forming on Molly's lips froze there. Lucian thought she was beautiful?

Heat crept into her face again. *Don't be stupid. Don't read more into his words than is really there. You're not interested in a relationship, especially not right now.*

Focused on the plate in his hand, Lucian turned it to study the pattern, tilted it to view the markings on the bottom then set it beside the other items on the desk. The residual pleasure of his compliment faded on a memory of a hot summer afternoon long ago.

Her mother sat cross-legged on a blanket spread out in the shade of an oak tree, one of several that shaded the front of the home. She poured lemonade from an elegant blue and white teapot into four cups. She handed one to Molly, pushed one in front of the rag doll and the plush beagle, and took the last cup for herself.

Sticking out her pinkie finger, she said in a posh voice, "What a delicious cup of tea. Don't you think so, my dears?"

"Three teacups and a teapot?" Lucian was saying.

Molly blinked away the sting of tears. "Yes. There used to be four cups. The fourth must have gotten broken."

He nodded and resumed the unwrapping. When she glanced back at Galahad, she saw the cat was grooming his tail. Was he trying to lick away his pain? Poor thing. She *had* trod on him quite hard.

"I really am sorry," she crooned while crossing to him, her sandals clicking on the wood floor. "Will you forgive me?" Crouching, she stroked him again, marveling at the silkiness of his fur. When he responded by rising and brushing against her knee, as if to say she was forgiven, she scooped him into her arms. Purring, he relaxed against her. "What a nice kitty you are."

Galahad's purrs grew louder. She carried him over to Lucian, who appeared to have finished unwrapping all of the antiques. "Your cat is so sweet," she said.

In her arms, Galahad stared up at her and meowed.

Lucian slanted a glance at the feline and then his gaze returned to her. Molly's breath froze, for no man had ever looked at her as he did now. His narrowed gaze captured hers—as though he wanted to get hold of every secret she'd ever kept. And that was just for starters.

Unease crawled along her spine. Her heartbeat sped up and echoed with a hollow thud in her ears. She wanted to back away, but her legs refused to work.

Slowly, his gaze slid to her mouth. Her belly tingled, for she saw hunger in his eyes. She easily imagined his mouth crushing down on hers, almost tasted the earthy essence of his lips....

What *was* she thinking?

A sigh rattled in her throat, and the sensual spell—or whatever it was between them—broke.

Frowning, he looked back down at the desk.

"Do you...see anything that interests you?" she dared to ask.

Did he see anything that interested him?

Hell, yeah.

Lucian clenched his jaw on a silent groan while he fought to control his inappropriate stirrings of desire. He gripped the rounded edges of the desk and pretended to be contemplating the items in front of him. Far better than what he really wanted to do: walk around the counter, pull her into his arms, and kiss her.

Regardless of her perfect, cherry-red lipstick.

Regardless of the fact they'd only just met.

Regardless of the fact she was a client, placing her trust in his professionalism.

What was wrong with him? Sure, she was a beautiful woman, but he'd known many beauties. Something about her, though, intrigued him and sent anticipation tingling through his veins: The slightly wry curve of her mouth, or the kindness he sensed within her, or the intelligence in her bright blue eyes.

He'd never been tempted so intensely before. Not even by his ex, Stephanie, a successful model with a wicked sense of humor and a passion for running marathons. His heart constricted as a memory flashed though his mind, of Steph wheeling her suitcase out of their apartment and slamming the door behind her.

Bitterness gnawed, because her leaving wasn't entirely his fault. Of course he could have done a few things differently in their relationship, but his duties for the Experts had created the rift between them. Those same duties would stand between him and a less-than-superficial relationship with any woman.

They always would.

"Don't look so grumpy, Lucian," Galahad mewed from Molly's arms. How smug the squire sounded, as though he'd guessed how much Lucian liked her. The squire *would* know Lucian's taste in women, though, after more than eight hundred years spent together.

"What was that meow for, Galahad?" Molly

cooed.

"She likes me," the feline said. "Ohhh, but she knows how to pet me juuuust right."

Lucian's fingers tightened on the desk.

"You are cheeky, with all that kitty talk." Molly nuzzled the cat's head.

Lucian silently groaned. If only she knew what the hormone-driven teenager she cuddled was really saying. Thankfully, she'd never find out.

As the cat shifted in Molly's arms, Lucian straightened away from the desk. "Thanks for your patience. I've given your items some thought, and—"

Galahad started kneading Molly's left breast.

"Boob," he purred.

Lucian gritted his teeth. He and the squire would have a talk later.

"Sooo soft and plump," Galahad said.

Hissing a breath, Lucian glared at the feline then looked up at Molly, who seemed a little startled. "Maybe you should put Galahad down. I wouldn't want him to scratch you."

"He's fine. Really." Molly beamed down at the cat. "Look at him. He's so happy."

The feline was positively grinning, his paws going at a furious pace. Next, he'd get one of his claws stuck in her dress, on purpose, and then—

"Did I tell you she's wearing white lace panties?" Galahad meowed.

"Shut *up!*" Lucian snapped.

Molly frowned. "What?"

Damn.

"I didn't say anything," she insisted.

"I know," Lucian said quickly. "I didn't mean you. I meant Galahad. I want him to shut up."

"He's only kitty chatting."

"Yeah, Lucian," the squire shot back.

Lucian managed a tight smile. "I still think you should put him down."

"If she sets me on the floor, I'll have another peek up her skirt," Galahad said. "Maybe I'll even see some sweet, round butt cheek."

Lucian pinched the bridge of his nose. He was sorely tempted to take the cat and shut him in the storage room for the rest of Molly's visit. Meeting her gaze, he said: "When Galahad meows like that, he usually needs to use the litter box."

In the midst of scratching the cat's chin, Molly went still. "Oh."

"Liar." Galahad huffed. "Liar, liar—"

"Sounds like he really needs to go." Molly set Galahad on the floor, the movement giving Lucian a prime view once again of her cleavage and all its generous promise.

He forced his attention back to the feline.

"Litter box?" the squire groused. "My furry ass—"

Lucian picked up the cat.

"Hey!" Galahad yowled. "Put me down."

Lucian tucked the struggling feline under his arm, carried him to the back room, and shut him in.

"We'll talk about this later, Lucian." Galahad yelled through the door.

Molly brushed off her hands. "He does talk a lot, doesn't he?"

"I think he's part Siamese. They're known to be rather vocal. Now, as I was saying about your items…."

She moved to the opposite side of the counter.

Her nearness, her scent, teased him and caused a light sweat to dampen his palms.

"What you have here is a nice collection of vintage pieces," he said.

Her lips curved in a charming grin. "But."

Lucian chuckled.

"I sensed that word on the tip of your tongue."

"I'm afraid so," he agreed. "Some clients think because a piece is a hundred or more years old, it has to be worth lots of money. That's not necessarily true. So much depends on the condition, whether it's decorated with a pattern that's highly sought after or not, whether it's mass-produced or a one-of-a-kind piece."

She nodded, her expression thoughtful. "It must be tough sometimes, when you know the pieces you're appraising hold a lot of sentimental value for a client."

Sadness underscored her voice, and he sensed she was thinking about her late mother.

"Well, before I give you a dollar figure, let me tell you what you have here. The three teacups and teapot are what we call Blue Willow. It's a pattern that was first featured on Chinese porcelain and imported into Europe in the late sixteenth and seventeen centuries. The English pottery manufacturers soon began to make their own versions of Blue Willow, which became extremely popular. These are by a well-known company named Spode, and date from the late nineteenth century." He moved on to the turn-of-the-century plates and the hobnail bowl. As he talked, he turned each item over to point out the factory markings and condition issues, including several small chips and cracks that would affect value. "For everything," he said, "I could give you one-hundred-and-twenty-five dollars." A more generous offer than he should make, but the Blue Willow pieces would be an easy sell and one of his uncle's long-time clients collected vintage plates.

Molly sighed.

"You're disappointed."

"A little. I'd hoped they would be worth more."

A pang of sympathy trailed through him. Selling the antiques was obviously hard for her. "You don't have to accept my offer. If you prefer, I can refer you to other dealers."

"No." She smiled, as though despite her dismay, she was determined to see the negotiations through. "One-hundred-and-twenty-five dollars is fine."

"Is it okay if I write you a check?"

Molly nodded.

He took a ring of keys from his pocket and unlocked the drawer under the counter that held a small amount of cash and the check register. As he opened the checkbook, she said, "The items are just old belongings, after all. It's not as though my mother is in any way attached to them."

Chapter Three

C arrying a paper bag of groceries and a bag of dry cat food, Molly climbed the steps of the porch that fronted the single story home. Her mom had bought the house, built in 1907 and located on the outskirts of Cat's Paw Cove, for a bargain price after its previous owner had moved into an assisted living facility.

Molly set down the cat food, and her keys clinked as she looked for the right one. She couldn't help smiling, because she'd never forget her mother's excitement about the purchase. Her mom hadn't been put off by the damaged wood floors, peeling exterior paint, or overgrown garden. The house, she'd said, had just felt right—like home—the moment she'd stepped inside.

Renovating the place had taken most of her mom's spare time and money, while she'd had a new roof installed, the floors restored, upgraded the two-and-a-half bathrooms, and turned the neglected yard into a lush garden of pentas, bougainvilleas, and perennials that attracted songbirds and butterflies. She'd created her own little piece of paradise.

Regret tugged at Molly, for she would have liked to keep the charming little house, maybe rent it out. But, with her finances as tight as they were, it seemed most practical to sell it.

She pushed the key into the lock. The door opened with a *creak*, and shutting her eyes, Molly sighed. She'd remembered to buy contact lenses, which she'd put on in the car before getting groceries, but not WD40. Thanks to Lucian, she'd forgotten.

Just recalling his name made her stomach flutter. How ridiculous, to get wound up over a man she'd only met once.

But, *something* had happened between them: Something thrilling, unfamiliar, and enticing. Not that she intended to pursue her feelings. There was still *a lot* to do at the house, and when she was still healing from her ex's betrayal, life would be a lot less complicated if she stayed single.

Besides, a man as intriguing and hot as Lucian had to have a girlfriend or even a wife and kids.

As she crossed the threshold into the shadowed house, a loud "meow" came from across the room, followed by a higher-pitched mewl.

"Hello, girls." Molly elbowed the switch on the wall by the door. The dusty overhead fixture came on, casting light on the worn but cozy green upholstered furniture, shelves of ornaments, books, and glassware, as well as the mounds of papers, magazines, and even more books she needed to sort through and either sell in a yard sale or donate to charity.

Two tabby cats—one sleek and gray, the other plump and ginger—padded across the hardwood floor toward her. A golden and white feline and a fluffy calico, curled together on the sofa, watched her with sleepy eyes.

The gray tabby meowed again. "Hi, Rose." Molly nudged the door closed with her heel. "Did you miss me?"

"Meow."

"You know, you sound a bit like Galahad, the cat I saw today."

The ginger feline yowled as she brushed against Molly's calf.

"Yes, Marigold, I know. You're hungry. I did remember to buy more food. Let's go fill your bowl."

Molly headed across the room. Sunlight streamed through a row of windows into the spacious kitchen, crowded at one end with boxes of clutter Molly had swept off the counters to carry out a long-overdue cleaning.

Housekeeping had never been one of her mother's strengths. There were far worse things, though, to be guilty of. Her mom had never once failed in her generous love for Molly or for the homeless cats that had found their way to her yard. Rose, Marigold, Petunia, and Daisy had all been strays. They all happened to be Sherwood cats. Each had the breed's tell-tale mask marking around their eyes.

"Robin Hood cats," her mom had called them. A fitting name, since the breed had originated in Nottinghamshire, England, many centuries ago and had arrived in Cat's Paw Cove by the same shipwreck that had brought the town's founders. Since the cats were protected by law, there could well be as many Sherwood felines in Cat's Paw Cove as residents.

After filling the cat food bowls, Molly stashed the groceries in the pale blue fridge that had to be older than she was and then quickly checked texts and emails on her cell phone. Nothing urgent, thankfully. Setting the device aside, she ran water into the kettle to make tea. Earl Gray. Strong. The best kind.

Leaning back against the sink to wait for the kettle to boil, she folded her arms and watched the four felines jostle each other for room at the bowls.

From this angle, the bowls looked like they might be antiques. Treasures to take to Lucian?

He'd offered to look at more of her mom's items, right after he'd written her the check. His swooping handwriting, authoritative but also elegant against the plain gray paper, had held her focus as he'd torn the check from the ledger and handed it over.

"As I mentioned earlier, we do handle entire estates," Lucian had said, drawing her attention up from the slip of paper in her hand.

"I remember."

"If you like, I could come to your mother's home, look over what you want to sell, and give you estimates." His charming smile had caused her pulse to quicken. "It might be more convenient than bringing boxes to the store."

"I'll keep that in mind." Glancing down at her purse, she'd stuffed the check into the side pocket. "I'd need to sort through more of Mom's belongings before I'd be ready for that kind of appraisal."

"I understand." Kindness warmed his voice— as though he really did understand how hard it was to go through her late mother's possessions. He'd picked up one of the shop's business cards, featuring black and gold ink printed on sumptuous, cream-colored stock, and handed it to her. "If I can help in any way, you can reach me at this number."

The boiling kettle clicked, automatically

switching off and drawing Molly back to the sun-drenched kitchen. She straightened away from the counter, poured hot water over a tea bag in a mug, and leaving the cats to finish eating, headed into the master bedroom.

Sadness weighed upon her as she set the mug aside then dropped down on the edge of the queen-size bed. A fine layer of dust covered the perfume bottles, framed photos, and knick-knacks on her mother's dresser. How vividly Molly remembered her mom leaning into the mirror to adjust the hand-painted scarf she'd tied at her neck. Molly had been home from college for fall break, and they'd been on their way to see a local theater production of *Twelfth Night*.

Molly dried her damp palms on her skirt. Going through the dresser drawers would be hard, but she mustn't put it off any longer.

She pulled over an empty cardboard box and drew open the top right drawer. It slid toward her with a *squeak* and held a black shawl fringed with jet beads, rolled-up leather belts, gloves, and folded scarves.

Molly's hand lingered over the closest scarf: her mom's favorite and the one she'd worn to the theater. Notes of floral perfume still clung to the silk.

"Oh, Mom." Tears burning Molly's eyes, she set the scarf to one side then looked through the rest of the items in the drawer before putting them in the cardboard box.

When she tugged on the dresser's left top drawer, it didn't budge. She wiggled and pulled until it finally opened.

Inside were jewelry boxes of various shapes and sizes. She went through each one, setting a few pieces aside with the scarf, until only a lacquered box of costume jewelry remained.

She set the box beside her and sorted through the sparkling pins, strands of fake pearls, drop earrings, and gold and silver-toned chains, adding a few more items to the pile of things she'd keep. Some of the baubles had been her grandmother's. She'd read in a magazine a few months back that vintage costume jewelry was highly collectible.

Anticipation skittered through her. She had a reason to visit Lucian again. Tomorrow, if she had enough items to justify a trip into town.

She sorted the remaining jewelry. Near the bottom of the lacquered box, her fingers brushed another one made of wood. She pulled out the container that covered her entire palm but didn't have a lock or clasp.

How odd.

Even more curious, there wasn't a single scratch in the dark-grained wood, even though the box looked very old. Its simple, stark design hearkened back to more primitive times.

Maybe Lucian could tell her when the box was made, and by whom?

Even more reason to see him tomorrow.

With an inquisitive "brrtt," Rose landed on the bed.

"Come to help me?" Molly asked.

The feline brushed against Molly's arm then noticed the box she held. Her ears went back. She yowled and leapt away.

"You're scared?" Molly chuckled. "Silly cat. This can't hurt you."

Searching for a way to open the box, Molly turned it over. Rose meowed again, but Molly ignored the feline.

A loud *thud.* The gray cat had jumped onto the TV stand. Front paw raised, she was about to bat the remote onto the floor.

Molly shooed the cat away from the TV then focused again on the box. How strange, that there was no obvious lid. Had whoever made it intended for it to stay sealed?

Fabric rustled. Glancing up, Molly saw Rose dragging her late mother's scarf to the end of the bed.

"*Rose!*"

The feline raced out of the room, taking the scarf with her.

"Stop! Come back." Even as Molly shouted, she acknowledged yelling was pointless. Rose wouldn't understand a word she said.

After setting the box on the dresser, Molly hurried out of the room. She could only hope the scarf wouldn't get damaged—

She stumbled, desperate not to tread on Ginger, Petunia, and Daisy lying like feline speed bumps in the hallway. As soon as she passed Daisy and Petunia, they darted past her, turned, and blocked her way again.

Rose was nowhere in sight.

Molly exhaled a harsh breath. If she didn't know better, she'd think the cats were conspiring against her.

Late afternoon sunshine slanted through the

antique shop's windows as Lucian set the cordless phone back on its base and jotted a note in the journal his grandfather kept near the cash register: A representative from the *Cat's Paw Cove Courier* had called to offer a special discount on ads. Lucian had taken down the details in case his grandfather was interested.

Setting down the pen, Lucian rolled his shoulders to ease knotted muscles. "Almost time to close up shop," he said to Galahad, lying on the end of the counter. On weekdays, the store usually closed at six—in just under ten minutes.

The cat sniffed and stared toward the opposite side of the room.

Lucian stifled a sigh. The squire had ignored him from the moment he'd been let out of the back room several hours ago. "You're *still* giving me the silent treatment?"

"You deserve it for the next month, for shutting me away when Molly was here."

Lucian fought not to grin. He'd love to point out—but wouldn't—that Galahad had just nixed his silent treatment by answering Lucian's question.

"If you'd shown some manners, I wouldn't have had to remove you from the room."

The cat glared.

Lucian folded his arms across his chest. "You *know* you were out of line."

"What I *know* is that I am very good at holding a grudge."

"Indeed you are. But—"

"When you least expect it, I'll get you back for locking me in that room." Galahad licked a front paw, as casually as if he'd just mentioned a long afternoon nap. "Remember when I peed on your favorite T-shirt while you were in the shower? Well, my revenge this time will be just as epic."

Lucian would rather not have a repeat of the cat pee incident, or anything else biological and unpleasant. "What else could I do while Molly was here? You refused to behave."

Galahad growled.

"My grandfather entrusted me with managing this store. I have a responsibility—a duty—to him and to the customers who come into the shop."

"I wasn't hurting Molly. I didn't scratch or bite her."

"You were disrespectful."

The squire blinked slowly. "I was in character."

"Hold on—"

"All she heard was meowing: My way of telling her I enjoy her attention. That's what normal cats do, right?"

Lucian frowned.

"How else am I to convince people I'm just an ordinary kitty? I have to get up to at least *some* cat mischief. I was only having a bit of fun."

"If you were my son, you'd be grounded for your antics this afternoon."

"Yeah, well, I'm *so* damned lucky to be a cat then, aren't I?"

Anguish threaded through Galahad's words. Suppressing a sigh, Lucian walked around the counter to stand in front of the feline.

"Look," he said. "If you mind your manners from now on, I will not shut you in the back room again."

Galahad muttered under his breath.

"Well?" Lucian asked.

The squire's gaze shifted past him to the front windows: a clear attempt at deflection. But, Lucian wasn't going to back down. Not when there was a chance Molly would come back to the store. His gut heated at the thought of seeing her again. Maybe he'd ask her out for coffee—

The bell on the door jingled.

Could she have returned already?

He turned, to see a slim woman with cropped white hair and scarlet lipstick step into the shop. She was carrying a foil-covered casserole dish.

She beamed at him. "Lucian."

"Hi there." A twinge of dread raced within him. From the looks of things, widowed Cora Johnson had brought him yet another supper—the third in less than a week.

Her bright gaze shifted from him to Galahad. "I saw you talking to your cat. I hope I didn't interrupt anything important?"

Ignoring the feline's huffed breath, Lucian chuckled and crossed to her. "How are you?"

"Fine, thanks." She offered the casserole dish. Light sparkled off the large rings on her fingers; baubles that might have been gifts from her late husband, who had managed several Orlando jewelry stores. "I made Beef Stroganoff last night for my Bridge club. I made too much, as usual, so I thought I'd bring you some."

"That's very kind of you." Lucian thought about saying he'd gone grocery shopping and had dinners for the next few nights, but decided to accept the dish. She had, after all, made a special trip to bring him a meal she'd made from scratch.

"I don't imagine a busy man like you has much time to cook." She winked. "I did promise William I'd keep an eye on you."

Lucian's grandfather had warned him about Cora, a wealthy resident who frequently shopped at the store. She'd taken several much younger lovers since her husband had died and had expressed an interest in Lucian. While Lucian didn't want to create problems for his grandfather, he'd turned Cora down gently three times so far. He'd do so again if necessary.

"Believe it or not," he said, "I am reasonably good at cooking."

"Really?" Acting surprised, she pressed her hand, tipped in glossy red nails, to her throat.

"I'm nowhere near as good a cook as you, of course," he added. "But, I have watched the Food Network." Stephanie, who'd once thought about starting a business making and decorating cakes, had loved watching baking shows.

"I love the Food Network." Cora's eyes sparkled. "That's something you and I have in common."

"Yes, well—"

She touched his arm. "Maybe one night, you can make dinner for me."

Oh-kay. Time to squash any expectations on her part.

Refusing to let his smile slip, Lucian held her gaze. "As you said, I am a busy man."

"Who still needs to eat supper sometime," she murmured.

Lucian shrugged, and as he'd hoped, caused her hand to drop from his arm. "My grandfather left me with some tasks to tackle for him. If I don't get them done by the time he gets back from vacation...."

She wrinkled her nose. "Don't worry. I've known William for years. He'll appreciate however much you get done while he is away."

Yeah, he would.

Cora Johnson was certainly persistent.

Galahad meowed: a loud, demanding wail.

The older woman glanced at the feline, who leapt down from the counter and walked toward them.

Lucian chuckled and silently thanked the squire for the timely interruption. "He's reminding me it's his dinnertime."

"Is that so?" The older woman's lips formed a coy smile. "Does that mean you speak the language of cats?"

"Can't say that I do." Even if Lucian were to admit he understood every word Galahad said, she'd never believe him. "But, since I normally feed him after locking up the store, I'm pretty sure that was a demand for food."

Cora glanced at her diamond-inlaid watch. "You close at six?"

"Yes, on weeknights."

"As it happens, I don't have any plans now." Her smile broadened. "We could heat up some casserole...?"

Hell, no.

"As nice as that sounds," Lucian said, "I really must get some paperwork done."

"I won't stay long."

"I'm sorry, but I have a *lot* of paperwork. I need to finish it tonight." He hated to lie, but it was for the best.

"Okay." She sighed, disappointed. "I'd better

be on my way, then."

Whew.

"Thank you again for the dinner."

She turned to leave, but abruptly turned back again. "My casserole dish."

"I'll get it back to you safe and sound. I promise."

"I'll hold you to that promise, Lucian."

No doubt she would. He might be wisest to put the meal into another container now and she could take the dish home with her.

"By the way, the Cat's Paw Cove Paranormal Society has their monthly meeting tomorrow. It's at the community center. If you'd like to join us, you could bring the dish back then?"

Nope. "It sounds fascinating, but—"

"My friend, Roberta Millingham, will be there. She's a good person to know in town, since she volunteers for a lot of organizations, like the Historical Society."

"I appreciate the networking opportunity. However—"

"Let me guess. You don't believe in spirits and such like."

Ha! If only she knew.

Galahad sat down beside Lucian. The feline was perfectly behaved for the moment, although Lucian recognized devilment in the cat's expression. "I can't commit to tomorrow evening, I'm afraid," Lucian said. "It will depend how things are here at the shop."

"Of course. If it turns out you're free tomorrow, give me a call and let me know you'll be at the meeting. You have my number?"

How clever of her. "You gave me your card last

time you brought me dinner. Grandfather also has your information on file."

"That's right; I remember now." She smiled. "You *could* add my number to your cell phone contacts, just in case."

He could, sure, but he'd rather not. "Mrs. Johnson—"

"Cora. Mrs. Johnson is too formal and makes me sound so, well, *ordinary*." Before he could attempt to reply, she added: "The paranormal society meeting should be a good one. We're going to see if we can contact one of the town's founders. You know, one of the people who were shipwrecked here in the seventeenth century."

A frisson of unease tingled at the base of his skull. Probably no reason to be concerned, but still…. "How are you going to do that? Hold a séance?"

She giggled. "I'm not telling. If you want to learn our group's secrets, you'll have to come to the meeting."

He dared not ask more. He didn't want to seem too curious. Their efforts to summon the spirit should be unsuccessful.

She waved her bejeweled fingers. "I hope to see you tomorrow. Good night."

"Good night, Cora."

The door jingled then closed behind her.

"Did she just ask you out on a date?" Galahad asked.

Lucian dragged his fingers through his hair; he really should get it cut. "It wouldn't be a date. And it really doesn't matter, because I'm not going to the meeting." Lucian walked back to the counter and put down the casserole. He reached for the key ring, beside his cell phone, on the counter shelf under the cash register.

"What if the society really does connect with one of the founders?" asked the feline.

"It's unlikely." The spirits in the area knew the rules about engaging with non-Magicals and the consequences for disobeying. So did the local fortune tellers. His grandfather, on behalf of The Experts, had ensured they did.

"But if the paranormal society does connect—"

"I will handle it, as is my responsibility."

"*We* will handle it," Galahad said firmly.

Lucian's brows rose. "I thought you were holding a grudge."

"I am. But, let's get real here. Keeping Cat's Paw Cove safe takes priority over being mad at you."

Warmth spread through Lucian's chest. "I'm glad to hear it."

"Yeah, well, don't go all mushy now. It must be after six, and you still need to lock up."

Lucian shook his head and grinned. Turning the keys in his fingers to find the right one, he crossed to the front door, flipped the Open sign to Closed, and turned the key in the lock. He made his way around the shop, shutting off main lights and ensuring all was in order for the night, including casting a barrier spell that encompassed the whole store. After taking the money out of the till and retrieving the casserole and his phone, he headed for the rear door that opened into a parking lot, where he could access the private entrance to his grandfather's apartment above the store.

"C'mon Galahad." Lucian had bought beer along with his groceries. He'd enjoy one while he watched the news and tucked into the stroganoff.

"Just a sec." The cat ran into the storage room and returned with his favorite toy mouse in his mouth. "Mffg mffgh mmtt."

Lucian reached for the door. "That made absolutely no sense—"

Briiinnnng: The ring of an old, rotary-dial telephone.

The cell phone alarm meant only one thing.

At the same instant, clicking, flashing, and the crackle of a vintage radio.

Galahad dropped his mouse. "Uh-oh."

"Un-oh is right." Lucian put down the items he'd been carrying, hurried into the room, and shielded his eyes against the blinding flash of an old Olympus camera.

He might not get to enjoy that beer, after all.

Molly looped the scarf around a hanger and hung it in the closet. Thankfully, the scarf was fine, but Rose hadn't wanted to give it back. Molly had chased her all though the house, with two of the other felines getting in the way, until at last Molly had cornered Rose behind a pile of boxes and had snatched the scarf.

Molly shut the closet door, just as Rose bolted into the room and jumped onto the bed. Was the feline going to cause more trouble? Maybe she'd calm down and take a nap while Molly finished emptying the dresser.

Molly returned to the furnishing, even as shock

rippled through her.

The wooden box was gone.

"Rose," she said, drawing out the feline's name. "Brrrttt."

"Where's the jewelry box?"

The feline blinked. "Mrrrow."

Molly shook her head. She must be losing her mind if she thought the cat could tell her what had happened.

Could someone have stolen the box while she'd been distracted?

No. She kept the doors and windows locked.

Maybe the box had fallen on the carpet?

She retrieved the flashlight from the bedside table and shone it under the bed.

Lots of dust bunnies, but no wooden box.

Her confusion deepened. She shifted the flashlight to shine underneath the dresser. Relief washed through her, for close to the wall, she saw the box. "Thank goodness."

How strange, though. It wouldn't naturally have fallen in that spot. Had one of the felines somehow pushed it underneath?

After fetching a long-handled wooden spoon from the kitchen, she retrieved the box.

All four felines were now in the room. They brushed against her, wanting attention, but she'd given them plenty of cuddles and chin-scratches earlier.

Picking up the wooden box and the costume jewelry she wanted to try on before deciding whether to keep the pieces, she crossed to the ensuite bathroom. The felines hurried after her, but she shut them out.

The cats pawed at the closed door. Geez,

couldn't she have five whole minutes to herself?

Molly put the glittering jewelry on the bathroom counter and picked up the plain box again. It was so unusual, she *had* to know what was inside. The smooth wood, though, refused to divulge how to open it.

Bang. Bang.

"Stop it, girls," Molly called. Irritation gnawed as she moved closer to the window over the bathtub. There! The thinnest trace of lighter grain, where the box lid met the base.

She pushed her thumbnail against the join.

Bang. Bang.

Molly pushed her nail harder against the wood. It had to open.

"Meow. Meow."

What on *earth* was wrong with the cats? She'd never known felines to make such a racket.

Molly studied the join again then pressed her index finger against it. "Come on—"

With a faint grating sound, the lid slid off.

A folded piece of light-brown cloth lay inside. The coarsely woven fabric looked very old. Was it linen?

"Meow. *Meow.*"

The continued cacophony from the cats faded to background noise as excitement whipped through Molly. She set the box lid down beside the other baubles. Her fingers seemed to move before she'd even made the conscious decision to draw aside the fabric and toss it onto the pile of other jewelry.

"Oh, wow," she whispered.

The box had protected a necklace, wrought from three delicate gold strands entwined like vines.

Linked to the necklace was a gold pendant set with a reddish-orange stone the size of her thumbnail.

Her hand trembling, Molly lifted out the necklace. A thrill raced through her, so strong, she got a little dizzy. She'd never seen a more beautiful piece of jewelry, feminine and yet bold.

The stone reminded her of fire. Its coloring shifted in the light, as though flames burned within.

The barest whisper of sound registered in her mind.

She brought the stone closer for a better look—

The sound again.

A voice?

Couldn't be. She had to be imagining—

The faint voice spoke again; words of an ancient-sounding language.

What was happening?

"*Meow. Meow!*"

Molly moved to put the necklace down. But, even as she did so, she experienced a surge of curiosity.

How would the necklace look on her?

No. She didn't care to know. She was going to put the necklace away.

Curiosity, headier this time, flared once more. It really was an exquisite piece.

If she put it away, she might not be able to get the box open again.

Since she had the jewel in her hand now, why *not* try it on?

Yes.

Molly unfastened the clasp.

"Meow! *Meeeoowwwww.*"

Mentally shutting out the cats' howling, she

slipped the necklace around her neck. With a soft chime, it brushed her collarbones and settled against her skin. The pendant rested at the top of her cleavage.

Why, it was such a perfect fit, it could have been made for her.

Molly studied her reflection in the mirror. Maybe her imagination was running wild, but she'd swear the necklace made her complexion look smoother. Her eyes, too, seemed brighter. And the elegant lines of the jewel made her cleavage look, well, tantalizing.

Her fingers trailed over the gold, and delicious heat wove through her body. She'd never owned a piece of jewelry that made her feel *sexy*.

She smiled at her reflection, for the necklace was definitely a keeper.

She'd never sell it to Lucian.

Not ever.

Chapter Four

"What's going on?" Galahad yowled, peering at the satellite image on Lucian's laptop. After jumping up onto the storage room table moments ago, the cat had positioned himself by Lucian's left arm.

"Damn," Lucian muttered. The dark magic was dissipating: Strong one instant, and fading away the next.

The old camera slowed in its flashing and clicking.

Situated behind the computer, the art-deco-era radio was quieting, as though an invisible hand were turning off the volume. The thin needles of the radio dials were dropping back toward zero.

Now, every second counted. Lucian must pinpoint the location of the dark magic before its residual energy evaporated.

He skimmed the incoming data from his grandfather's system as well as the state-of-the-art machines invented by the Experts. The Experts' technology had long ago made William Lord's system obsolete. But, William had insisted his set-up worked fine and had kept it as a backup.

"Imagine if The Experts' machines should stop working," he'd said. "It's a long shot, I know, but I won't risk being responsible for a catastrophe in this town or anywhere else."

To help protect Cat's Paw Cove, Lucian's grandfather had installed numerous magic-detecting devices in the area, including at the cemetery, the waterfront, the train depot and its underground tunnels, and at the historic Sherwood House.

Today's dark magic, though, hadn't come from any of those places.

Lucian pulled up another satellite image. With a few clicks of the mouse, the wide view narrowed to a residential area past The Cove on Sherwood Boulevard. A see-through, reddish circle covered several streets, but as Lucian zoomed in again, the red hue disappeared altogether.

"At least we have a rough idea of where to find it," Galahad said.

Lucian frowned. "It's strange it would show up for less than a minute and then disappear."

"Maybe the magic belongs to an object that was unearthed? Someone might have dug it up doing yard work but then buried it again."

"That's possible." Lucian pulled up a graph on the computer and whistled.

"What?" Galahad demanded.

"According to this information, the magic's very old."

"How old? The era of the Spanish Conquistadors? The ones who built the castle at St. Augustine, or—?"

"Older than that," Lucian noted. "It's also not native to Florida."

"Where's it from, then?"

"From what I'm reading here…Western Europe."

"Imported magic, then," Galahad said, "like you and I."

"Mmm." Lucian's frown deepened. "Strength-wise, it was also close to a Category One." Whoever had created the dark magic scale for Florida—Categories One through Five just like hurricanes—obviously had had a warped sense of humor.

"Well, hopefully, just like a bad storm, the magic's over and done with," the squire said.

Lucian continued scrolling. Nothing he was seeing explained why the magic would show up and then quickly vanish, unless…it had been taken out of a container designed to suppress magic and then put back in.

Such vessels were rare, though. They'd become close to obsolete by the end of the Victorian era, when steel, steam, and machine production had replaced hand-crafting items out of natural materials like stone and wood. For magic to be attached to an object, the item had to be at least partially made, decorated, or finished by a living, breathing human.

Galahad arched his back in a lazy stretch and faced Lucian. "Since the excitement seems to be over, I say we call it a night."

"The excitement's over for now," Lucian said, not taking his gaze from the laptop, "but the dark magic could show up again."

"Tonight, you mean?"

"Yes, tonight. I'm going to wait here for a

while, in case there's another spike."

The cat grumbled. "I'm hungry."

As he'd done every evening when locking up, Lucian had put away Galahad's bowls of food and water. "I can pour you some more crunchies—"

"I don't want boring kibble. I want the good stuff: canned duck dinner in gravy."

"Then you're going to have to wait."

Galahad swatted at a pen lying beside the laptop—no doubt planning to knock the writing implement onto the floor just so Lucian would have to pick it up. "Your phone *does* send you dark magic alerts."

As if Lucian needed a reminder.

"If after dinner you happened to get an alert, we'd come back to this room right away."

Lucian snatched up the pen, seconds before it was about to tumble to the floor, and tossed it into a pen holder. "I'm going to stay. Why don't you chase your mouse?"

"I'm too hungry to chase my mouse."

"Take a nap, then."

"I'm too hungry to—"

Lucian shook his head. "You of all people should understand my duty to—"

"Yeah, yeah."

With an impatient sigh, Lucian focused again on the laptop. Galahad, thankfully, stopped gabbing and making mischief and lay down, his paws tucked under his chest.

Lucian's sense of disquiet deepened. He'd seen plenty of dark magic spikes through the years, but this one…. His gut-instincts warned him this was different.

"You're worried," the squire said.

"Of course I'm worried. We just detected very old dark magic."

"I mean, icy-chill-in-your-bones worried."

Lucian hesitated, because he hadn't wanted to share his concern yet, but then nodded.

Galahad did not say more, obviously waiting for Lucian to explain. "The magic tonight.... I don't quite know how or why yet, but something about it is...wrong."

"It's not what your grandfather told us to expect," the squire agreed. "Do you think you should call in some help?"

"No." Not yet, anyway. Lucian would do his utmost to secure the dark magic himself; to make sure The Dealers never got to the magical item first and then twisted its powers to their own nefarious exploits. If Lucian excelled, he had a chance of regaining the respect of his superiors and salvaging his professional reputation. "It's my duty to handle such situations. I don't want to get The Experts involved unless I have no other choice."

"I get that your pride recently took a beating," Galahad said. "But, if this magic has *you,* an experienced professional, worried, maybe it would be better to—"

"—go check out the area where it appeared? Excellent idea."

Galahad grumbled. "That's not what I was going to say."

With clicks of the mouse, Lucian closed files on the computer. "We should, though. We'll go as soon as we can, since night will fall soon."

The feline visibly shuddered. "Do we have to?"

"Are you scared of what we might find?"

The cat scowled. "I'm no coward, as you well know. But, it means a trip in the *car*."

"Oh, come on. You love riding in the Mini Cooper."

"No, I hate it—and don't you dare put me in the cat carrier. That's like being in jail."

"Fine, no carrier, but you need to stay put in the passenger seat. If we get out of the vehicle to look around, you're to stay by me at all times." Lucian scowled. "No chasing after hot girl cats or starting fights with stray toms."

"I can't have any fun, you mean," the squire muttered.

"I don't like rules either, but you've caused mischief in the past—"

"Hey!"

"—and I'm responsible for your safety," Lucian said firmly, as he shut down the laptop.

Galahad snorted. "Maybe I should stay here. I'd for sure be safe."

A wry laugh broke from Lucian. "Nice try. You're coming with me."

The feline rose to all four paws, determination in his golden eyes. "If I *have* to go—"

"You do. A squire always accompanies his knight, remember?"

"—then I get two cans of duck dinner in gravy when we get home."

Lucian's brows rose. "Now who is setting rules?"

"You owe me," Galahad insisted, "after shutting me away this afternoon. *And* I saved your ass with Cora Johnson."

True. "All right. It's a deal."

After taking off the necklace, Molly wrapped it in the linen again and put it back in its box. Thank goodness the cats had stopped crying outside the bathroom door. They'd fallen silent and had finally given up on trying to get in.

Her fingers trailed over the box, the antique wood dark against the light-colored, modern countertop. Disappointment lingered, for she hadn't wanted to take off the beautiful piece of jewelry, not when it looked so nice on her and made her feel good, too. But, it was too ornate for everyday wear. It was best kept for special occasions, like the annual gala at her favorite art gallery or a fancy Christmas party.

Or a date with Lucian.

A wicked little shiver trailed through her. Yes, she'd wear the necklace if she had a date with him. But, he hadn't asked her out and probably wasn't going to—and she'd sworn off relationships anyway, at least for the time being.

Remembering the jobs she'd wanted to tackle that afternoon, Molly quickly tried on the costume jewelry and decided to part with all but two pieces. Then she picked up what she'd brought into the bathroom and opened the door. The four kitties were waiting outside.

Her mother had told her about the felines being by her side all day, no matter what she was doing. With her mom gone, the cats had obviously decided they must stick by Molly.

She dropped the baubles she planned to give

away on the bed then headed to the guest bedroom she was using. The felines fell in behind her.

She'd ask Lucian, when she found a good opportunity, if the cats' behavior today had been normal: the meowing outside the bathroom door; the following her everywhere she went. She had a lot to learn about kitty behavior, if they were to all get along in Seattle.

Upon reaching the guest room, she put the box and the jewelry she was keeping in the long inside pocket of the suitcase she'd brought to Cat's Paw Cove. Pushing aside the cats trying to climb into the case, she zipped it shut before stowing it back in the closet and shutting the door.

"You won't be able to hide that special box now," she told the felines then crouched to scratch each of them under the chin. She still couldn't explain how the box had gotten underneath the dresser, but the cats had to be responsible...unless the house had a ghost.

There were plenty of weird stories about Cat's Paw Cove. Some folk claimed to have seen spirits; others said they'd experienced magic. But, Molly didn't believe in such things. Her late mother, as far as Molly knew, hadn't believed in them either.

The kitties seemed much calmer now. They purred, and when she rose and went to the living room, only two of them followed.

Hands on her hips, Molly studied the daunting piles of magazines and papers. "Where to start?" she murmured. Deciding she'd just have to choose a pile and get to work, she sat on the floor, pulled over a trash bag, and began sorting and tossing.

Ugh. The dust was terrible.

"Achoo!" Ignoring her watering eyes and scratchy throat, Molly pressed on.

One stack dealt with at last, she started on another. It contained several years' worth of *National Geographic* magazines as well as some letter-size files.

She looked at the file tabs and recognized her mother's neat handwriting. "The Cat's Paw Cove Paranormal Society?" Had her mother been a member?

After sneezing again, Molly opened the thick folder and began to read.

Lucian steered the Mini to the curb in the modest but well-maintained subdivision. Trash bins and brimming boxes of items for recycling sat at the ends of driveways of some of the houses. Tomorrow must be pick-up day in the neighborhood.

Lucian put the car in park. The engine purred, its low rumble underscoring the hiss of the air conditioning.

According to the magic-detecting equipment on his dashboard, there was no significant trace of dark magic for miles around.

Residual but inconsequential energy remained from earlier, as he'd expected. Lucian had also found faint traces of dark energy dating from different years through the centuries, right back to when the first humans had settled in the area. But, dark magic existed everywhere in the world, and finding a low level of it was normal.

Galahad's eyes gleamed in the car's shadowed

interior. "Are we done yet? We've been driving around for hours."

"Actually, thirty-eight minutes." Lucian picked up his cell phone for a quick check of text messages and emails. Thankfully, nothing urgent.

"I am not just hungry now, I'm starving," the squire said.

Lucian returned his phone to the console in the car. "All right. If there was something important to find, I think we'd have found it by now."

"Yesss." Galahad grinned. Turning his head, he rose up on his back paws and peered out the passenger side window at the nearby houses along the street.

Just as Lucian readied to drive away, his phone buzzed. Lucian picked it up and read the email he'd just received. His superior in The Experts had responded to the quick report Lucian had submitted before leaving the antiques store.

Lucian's brow knit with a frown.

"Stephanie?" Galahad asked.

"No. Julius."

"Uh-oh. What does the bastard want?"

The squire shouldn't call their superior a bastard. Except the guy *was* one of the most obnoxious people Lucian had ever dealt with. "Julius directed us to further investigate the dark magic we saw tonight," Lucian said.

"No kidding." The feline growled. "Are you going to tell him we're way ahead of him on that plan?"

"No, I'm going to confirm I've done as he ordered. It's what he'd expect from a team player."

Galahad snorted and returned his gaze to the street.

Lucian sent a quick reply to Julius. When he looked up, Galahad was back up on his hind legs, staring intently at the sidewalk.

"What?" Lucian's hand moved to the driver's side door. On occasion, the cat had sensed dark magic right before it had shown up on the devices.

"Roll down my window," the squire said.

Urgency sharpened the cat's tone, so Lucian immediately depressed the button to lower the window. Before he could ask again what had captivated the squire, a cat meowed outside.

The tension that had gathered between Lucian's shoulder blades eased a little. "You made a friend," he said, just as the feline outside mewled again.

"Shhh!" Hot, humid air wafted into the car's interior as Galahad stretched his head out the window and meowed back at the other kitty.

"Will you please tell me—?"

"Quiet!" the squire said. "I'll explain later."

Lucian waited, his hand resting on the cool door. A moment later, a gray kitty ran across the nearby lawn and disappeared under a white fence.

Galahad dropped back down to the passenger seat. "Damnit! I need to go after her."

"Her?" Lucian shook his head. "Not tonight."

"I have to. She's a Sherwood Cat."

"I get it. You liked her," Lucian said, "but—"

"I understood her."

Why did Galahad sound startled? As Lucian rolled the window up, he said, "You *would* understand her, right? You're both cats."

"No," Galahad said firmly. "She's no ordinary kitty. I understood all that she said; the same way I understand every word you speak."

"That's never happened before?"

"Nope. Never."

A chill crawled across Lucian's nape. The readings on the magic-detecting devices right now weren't unusual. The cat wasn't connected to the dark energy spike, and she didn't, according to the special instruments, pose a threat to the local population or the town at large.

But, what—or who—was she? Had she once been human but had been cursed and reincarnated as a feline, just like Galahad?

While Lucian knew about the reincarnation curse upon his bloodline, he didn't recall ever meeting other cats who had previously been people. That didn't mean there weren't any.

The squire exhaled a heavy sigh. "Do you want me to get out of the car and try to find her?"

Lucian heeded an inner cry for caution. "We'll come back another night." Since they had no idea what they were dealing with, they'd be wise to do a bit of research. Maybe there would be answers in past reports that Lucian's grandfather had filed.

As Galahad settled down on the passenger seat, Lucian glanced over his shoulder then pulled the Mini away from the curb. Regardless of what he and Galahad found, though, there could only be one explanation for the cat tonight: Magic.

Chapter Five

S tanding behind the store counter, Lucian stifled a yawn with the back of his hand. He downed more of the coffee he'd bought at Devon Rex Desserts, a bakery a short distance down Whiskers Road, then continued reading. He'd transferred some of his grandfather's files onto his laptop so he could access them whenever and wherever he liked, and had stayed up until the wee hours reading at the apartment's kitchen table while Galahad had snoozed on the sofa nearby.

Shortly after 2 A.M., however, Lucian had called it a night and had gone to bed, since he had to open the store by nine. But, he intended to get through all of the files by lunchtime.

As he downed another mouthful of the flavorful, French-roast java, the doorbell chimed. It was too early for any package deliveries, so the person entering must be a customer.

"Good morning," he called, not looking up from the computer.

"Good morning."

Molly. His whole body zinged alert.

Last night, while trying to fall asleep, he'd thought of their meeting, how he hoped to see her again, and what he'd say if he did. His fingers tightened around the paper cup, and he carefully set it where he or Galahad, lying like a sphinx on the counter, wouldn't accidentally knock it over.

Across the store, Molly stood in profile, bracing a box on her left hip while she shut the door.

His mouth went dry. He hadn't thought she could look any more beautiful than the last time he'd seen her, but she'd put her hair up in a sleek ponytail that showed off her graceful neck. His gaze slid down to the fuchsia-colored top she'd paired with dark-wash skinny jeans and heels.

Did she have any idea how long her legs looked in that outfit? He silently groaned in appreciation.

"Mee-owww," Galahad drawled.

Anticipation hummed in Lucian's blood as he closed his laptop and went to meet her. Galahad jumped to the floor and followed.

Turning to face Lucian, Molly smiled. "Hi."

"Hi." She wore shiny gloss that accented her full, pretty lips. Desire tingled in his veins; he tamped it down. "It's nice to see you again."

"Yeah, it sure is," the feline said.

Laughing, she looked down at the cat. "Well, hello to you, too, Galahad."

"God, she has the most gorgeous legs." Purring loudly, the squire brushed against her.

Shifting the box, Molly tipped her chin at the feline. "Still as chatty as ever, I see."

"He won't be a rascal like he was yesterday, though." Lucian shot the squire a meaningful glare.

"You know, I think yesterday was just one of

those days for cats and mischief," Molly said.

Every day was a mischief day for Galahad. Indulging his curiosity, Lucian asked, "Why do you say that?"

"One of my mother's kitties ran outside last night when I put out the trash. She's a housecat, and I spent a good half-hour in a panic, searching for her."

"I hope you found her?"

"She wandered onto the front porch just before dark, perfectly fine and wanting a snack."

Could that have been the cat Galahad had spoken to last night? Possibly, but they'd seen several other felines during their drive around that neighborhood.

"I'm glad she returned home safely," Lucian said.

"Thanks. So am I."

"That makes three of us," Galahad meowed.

Molly smiled. "You know, I could swear your cat is trying to take part in our conversation; like he's responding to what we say."

Yep. Exactly right. "He's been a talker ever since he was a kitten," Lucian said with a wry chuckle. "I hope he won't scare you away?"

She laughed. "Nah."

Lucian liked the sound of her laughter. He ached to reach out and brush his fingertips down her cheek, to touch her. But, even as he acknowledged the longing, part of him shut it down. The events of the past few months had taught him he should avoid meaningful relationships. His gut had already warned him that if he got involved with Molly, their affair wouldn't be a brief, casual fling.

He'd end up hurting her. There was no

alternative, when he couldn't tell her about his work for The Experts. He didn't want to have to keep secrets from her, or to see anguish and disappointment in her eyes when she asked for the truth and he couldn't give it. For all of those reasons, he'd ignore his attraction to her and keep their interactions strictly businesslike.

He gestured to the box. "What have you got for me today?"

"A few vases and some costume jewelry." She tilted her head. "I forgot to ask last time, but you do appraise vintage costume jewelry, right?"

Either his imagination was teasing him, or her tone held a hint of flirtation.

He forced himself to release the breath lodged in the center of his chest. He could well be misreading her. But, she did seem a little different today. More confident.

Sexier.

She was waiting for him to answer her question. What was it, again? Something about costume jewelry. "I must admit, jewelry isn't my specialty," he said. "I do, however, have plenty of contacts in the antique business." If Julius and his underlings couldn't help Lucian out, The Expert would know someone who could. "I can take pictures of what you've brought and send them on for an evaluation."

"That sounds good."

"Good." Now he sounded like a damned parrot. "May I take the box?"

"Oh. Sure."

As she shifted it into his arms, he noticed perspiration glistening on her forehead and nose. Yesterday, she'd mentioned she had a hard time tolerating the high temperatures. Even early in the morning, as he'd discovered from his jogs along the beach, the heat and humidity were stifling. "How about a cold drink?" he asked. "Water?"

Her expression softened with gratitude. "That would be wonderful. Thanks."

"My pleasure."

Lucian set her box on the counter then walked to the storage room, took a bottle of spring water from the fridge, and headed back into the store, to find her dabbing her forehead with a tissue.

"I'm sorry to be such a mess." She laughed, the sound tinged with embarrassment. "I am just so *hot.*"

"Don't we all know it," Galahad rumbled, sitting at her feet and gazing up at her.

Lucian handed her the water. "I promise, you don't look a mess."

"Liar." When his eyes widened in surprise, she grinned. "I'm pretty sure I do."

Whoa. She'd definitely flirted that time.

As Lucian mulled how to respond, Molly twisted off the cap of her bottle, tipped up her chin, and took a long drink. Lucian tried not to stare at her mouth, pressed to the top of the bottle. Her slender throat moved with a swallow, drawing his attention down to her cleavage—

Refocus, idiot. Now.

Lucian turned on his heel, went to the desk, and pulled over the box she'd brought.

Molly sighed. "The water was just what I needed."

"I'm glad." Would she sigh like that after she'd been kissed? Frowning, he pulled an item out of the box and noisily crinkled the paper while he unwrapped it. Still, he couldn't help imagining his mouth settling over hers, the warmth and softness of her lips—

"Is it okay if I sit here?" She pointed to an Edwardian chair his grandfather had gotten back from the restorer last week. "If it's not okay, I will completely understand."

"It's fine. A chair is a chair," Lucian added, "and meant for sitting."

"Yes, but not all chairs are refinished *antiques.*" Even as he registered her coy tone, she sat, leaned back against the upholstery, and crossed one shapely leg over the other.

The throne-like chair suited her. She could have just been crowned Queen of Cat's Paw Cove.

She brushed her hand over the velvet-covered seat. "The chair's comfortable. An oldie, but a goodie."

"Just like you, Lucian," Galahad piped up.

After scowling at the cat, Lucian looked back at Molly. Determined to keep the conversation business-related, he asked: "So, how are things going at your mother's house?"

"Fine."

"You made progress yesterday?"

"Not really." She sipped more water then grimaced. "I ended up with two bags of trash, but there's still a lot to sort through. I'm afraid of throwing out something important, so of course, I'm going through every box, drawer, and file."

He set down the glass vase he'd unwrapped. "I'm sure you're doing a fine job. And, of course, my offer to come to the house and look at items still stands." He pulled the protective paper from another item: an etched bowl.

"It's strange," she murmured.

"Mmm?"

"I thought I knew my mother. I mean, she was my mom. But, going through her things…."

Lucian lifted out a lacquered box that rattled when he set it on the counter. It must hold the jewelry she'd mentioned. "You found a few surprises?"

She nodded. "Quite a few, actually."

"Tell me more."

"Why?" Her eyes narrowed in mock suspicion. "You don't write for the local paper, do you?"

He chuckled. "No, but I'm definitely intrigued now. The Mrs. Hendrickson I remember was fairly…well, conservative."

"She was," Molly said. Galahad had ambled over to the chair, and she leaned down to scratch his back. "I remember when I called and told her I was moving in with my boyfriend."

Just about to open the lacquered box, Lucian stilled. Dismay settled like a stone in his gut, but he should have known she would be taken.

"Nooooooo! She can't have a boyfriend," the squire wailed.

"Is Galahad okay?" Worry in her gaze, Molly added: "Did I pet him the wrong way?"

"He probably wants you to scratch behind his ear," Lucian said. "That's his favorite."

"Oh. Okay." Her fingers shifted to the feline's right ear. "My boyfriend…. Well, actually, my fiancé, since we got engaged and almost married last fall."

Almost married. That meant—

"Howard and I split up six weeks before our wedding date," she quickly added. "Just in case you were wondering, or curious, or…whatever." Her cheeks turned pink.

Lucian fought not to smile.

"Anyhow, Mom went quiet on the line after I broke the news about moving in with him. Even though he and I had been together for more than a year, she obviously didn't approve." Molly moved her hand to scratch the back of Galahad's neck. "I thought she was going to try and talk me out of it, to insist Howard and I should be married before we lived together, but instead, she said, 'If that's what you want to do.' I think she knew he wasn't right for me, but she chose to let me find out on my own."

"She probably realized you'd do whatever you wanted anyway, regardless of what she said."

"Yes. I was twenty-five, after all. I can be pretty stubborn."

According to his grandfather, so could Lucian.

His attention once again on the lacquered box, Lucian opened the lid. Gold and silver-toned necklaces, beaded brooches, and rhinestone bracelets sparkled—

The faintest chill skimmed his nape, as though someone had trailed the tip of an icicle across his skin: A warning of dark magic.

His phone hadn't sounded an alert, and the devices in the back room hadn't gone off. As he'd realized in a split-second, the energy wasn't very strong. Still….

What wickedness had Molly brought him?

"Anyhow, the secrets I mentioned? I discovered my mom was interested in genealogy. She'd been tracking down our ancestors…."

Blocking out Molly's voice, Lucian set his right hand, palm down, upon the glittering jewels. He shut his eyes, focused on the steady rhythm of his own breathing to clear his mind, and sank into the mental quietude that allowed him to tap into the magic connected to the jewelry.

Multi-colored lights glimmered in his mind. He found vibrant imprints of good memories: dinner parties; bridal showers; lively meetings and afternoon teas. But skirting the edges of those happy remembrances was a wisp of darkness.

Sharpening his focus, he sifted through the ephemeral layers of magic and memories. *There.* He mentally grabbed for the inkiness, but it eluded him. He pursued. As soon as his mind attempted to hone in again, the magic vanished and reappeared as a shadow behind another recollection.

Frustration gnawed, and reluctantly, he began to surface from his trance. He wouldn't catch the murkiness, no matter how hard he tried. The object possessing it wasn't in the box of jewelry. The item hadn't come into direct contact with the other baubles, either.

What *did* hold the corrupt magic? Even more worrying: to leave such a resonance, the energy had to be highly potent—

"Lucian," Galahad urged.

Lucian opened his eyes.

Now standing in front of the Edwardian chair, Molly stared at him, her eyes wide. "What just happened? Are you all right?"

While telling Lucian about her mother's genealogy project, Molly had sensed he was only half-listening. She hadn't wanted to bore him, so she'd stolen a quick glance, to gauge whether she should change the subject...and her words had unraveled in her throat.

He stood very still. *Too* still. He wasn't intently analyzing an item in front of him, but appeared frozen, as though he'd been paralyzed from head to toe. Or, as she'd seen in TV shows and movies she'd watched with Howard, caught in a spell.

Not possible. Spells only existed in fictional worlds, not real life.

Was Lucian having some kind of medical crisis?

"Lucian," she said, pushing Galahad aside and rising to her feet.

Lucian didn't blink, exhale, or otherwise stir to acknowledge he'd heard her. He remained at the counter, eyes closed, his features set in an expression of intense concentration.

Could he be asleep? He might have an undiagnosed sleep disorder. Whatever was going on, she'd take a picture of him to show him once he was awake again. Then she'd call 911.

She reached for her cell phone.

Galahad yowled. She startled, because she hadn't touched or stepped on the feline. Why, then, had he cried out?

She glanced back at Lucian, and his eyelids flickered. A sound between a sigh and a growl broke from him.

Oh, thank God.

As Lucian's gaze sharpened on her, a tremor raced through her. She'd never known a man with such a piercing stare.

"What just happened? Are you all right?" How she wished her voice hadn't wobbled.

"I'm fine." He didn't look fine. His dark brows had knitted together in a frown, and she sensed his thoughts had been far from the appraisal of her items.

Maybe he was too proud to admit he'd just experienced a health issue in front of her. Howard, too, had never wanted to be seen as vulnerable or weak. But, the last thing she wanted was for Lucian to collapse and get hurt while falling to the floor.

Molly crossed to the counter. "Maybe you should sit down for a minute."

The barest smile curved his lips. "Really, I'm fine."

"No, you're not. You blanked out."

"I what?"

"You…." Struggling to find the right words, she waved her hand. "You weren't here for a while."

Amusement touched his expression. "Did I leave the store?"

"Not physically, no. But mentally, yes."

Lucian glanced over at Galahad, who meowed again. "He says I seem fine to him."

Annoyance warred with her concern. "Don't try and bring your poor cat into this conversation. He can't tell you what happened. I know what I saw."

"Molly—"

"I still think you should sit down, at least until we're both sure you're okay."

Lucian exhaled a deep breath. "Look, it's sweet of you to be concerned—"

"Maybe I should call 911 and ask what to do."

"No."

"Yes." She turned to get her phone.

"*No.*"

Howard had spoken to her that way before; the tone of a commander giving orders to his subordinates. Her spine stiffened.

"Hey." Regret softened Lucian's voice.

She glanced back at him, her jaw tight.

"I'm sorry. I didn't mean to sound harsh, but I don't need medical attention."

She crossed her arms. Why did she get the feeling a lot more was going on than he was telling her? "Explain to me what happened, then."

A muscle ticked in his cheek. "What you saw…. It's part of my process when doing appraisals."

She drummed her fingers on her arm while considering his words. She shook her head. "I need more detail than that."

"Why? With respect, how I go about my work isn't really your concern."

Refusing to back down, she held his gaze. "With respect, I don't think you've been honest with me yet. I'd like the truth."

Galahad meowed several times, and Lucian's attention shifted to the cat. Lucian brushed his thumb over his bearded chin, as though struggling with an inner debate, then said: "Very well. I didn't 'blank out,' as you called it. I was….meditating."

"Meditating?" she echoed, unable to hold back disbelief.

Lucian nodded once. "Meditation is an excellent way for me to focus my mind."

Had he told her the truth this time? She didn't know much about appraising antiques. She didn't know much about meditation, either, except what she'd read in women's magazines. The articles had usually been accompanied by photos of people sitting cross-legged on the floor, not standing. "Why didn't you tell me about the meditation before?"

"It's a little...personal."

"I would rather have been forewarned." When he shook his head, she added, "Seeing you frozen like you'd been turned to stone was creepy."

Mirroring her defiant posture, he folded his arms. With the movement, hewn muscles rippled under his shirt, teasing her with imaginings of how he'd look bare-chested. Deliciously tempting thoughts, but she would *not* be distracted from the discussion.

"If I'd told you the truth earlier," he said quietly, "would you have believed me?"

Ha. Fair point. Even now, she wasn't convinced what she'd seen was meditation.

Lucian's brows rose. "Well?"

She shrugged. "I might have."

A rough laugh broke from him. "You don't believe me now, do you? Even after I just divulged one of my deepest, darkest secrets."

"The fact that you meditate is a deep, dark secret?"

His lips formed a roguish smile. "If other antique dealers heard about my process, everyone would start doing it. I'll no longer be special."

She rolled her eyes and fought a smile. "Now you're teasing me."

"Yep." He chuckled, uncrossed his arms, and flattened his hands on hands on the counter. "Now that we've got that matter straightened out, I have a few questions about this jewelry."

He spoke mildly enough, but she sensed a note of concern in his voice.

"Did you say these pieces belonged to your mother?"

"Yes," Molly said. "She inherited some of them from her mom."

"Is this all of the jewelry? Are there any other items?"

She thought of the gold necklace she'd put in her suitcase. A warm glow rippled through her, swiftly followed by a pang of caution. She didn't want to tell him about her wonderful find. There was no reason to, since she wasn't going to sell it.

"I kept a couple of pieces I liked. Why do you ask?"

"Some of this jewelry looks like it belongs in sets." He picked up a dangling pearl earring and a necklace with a similar pearl-drop pendant. "These, for example. Also, these." He held up a sparkling bracelet and matching necklace. "I suspect there are earrings to match."

"The items I kept aren't from either of those sets," Molly said. "I didn't finish going through my mother's dresser yet. I might find the missing pieces you pointed out."

He nodded, but his expression hardened a fraction, as though she hadn't told him what he'd wanted to hear. "Did you find any old boxes? Even empty ones?"

I'm not telling you about the special one I found. "Boxes are important?"

"Vintage jewelry is often worth more if it's presented in its original box. More still if it belonged to someone famous and there's proof of that ownership."

"Proof? What kind of proof?"

"Well, ideally, photographs, drawings, or

paintings of the person wearing it. The original receipt from the store where the jewelry was purchased would also help establish provenance, or mention of it in journals or letters."

"I see." Apart from the unusual wooden box, all of the other jewelry containers she'd found had been modern and mostly from department stores. "Unfortunately, I think the original boxes were thrown out long ago. Are you still able to get me an estimate on what I've brought?"

"Of course. Would it be all right for me to keep the jewelry for a few days? That will give me a chance to take good photos of the pieces as well as contact some associates."

"Sure," Molly said. Why not? She wasn't going to be leaving Cat's Paw Cove for a while.

"Good," he said. "There is one more thing I need to know, though."

"Yes?"

"Would you like to go for coffee with me?"

Chapter Six

"Y ou're lucky she believed that crap about meditating."

Lucian put the lacquered box of jewelry on the storage room table. After casting a silencing spell to ensure Molly wouldn't hear what he said, he nodded to the squire. "It was a good suggestion. Thanks."

"Once again, I saved your ass."

Lucian scowled. "Don't get carried away now."

Galahad's smile was entirely too smug. "Just being truthful."

"I'm sure I could have come up with a convincing explanation for the trance on my own." Ignoring the cat's indignant snort, Lucian added, "Whatever made you think of meditation?"

The feline sauntered over to bowls filled with dry kibble and water that were sitting on the floor to the right of the fridge. "Your grandfather's lady friend talked about it a couple of weeks ago when she came to the store. An instructor at her gym had mentioned it in Yoga class."

"Well, it was timely you remembered the

conversation."

Reaching his food, Galahad sat and studied Lucian. "What's going on? You've never risked a trance in front of a non-Magical before."

"No." Sitting back against the table, Lucian gripped the edge with his hands. "I sensed dark magic in the jewelry."

"The same energy as we detected last night?"

"I don't know. I couldn't tell." Unease crawled down Lucian's spine. "That's why I'm holding onto the jewelry and why I asked Molly out for coffee. I need to learn more."

Galahad noisily crunched some kibble. "What if she refuses to talk?"

"I'll convince her she needs an in-home appraisal."

"What if she doesn't agree?"

Lucian's fingers tightened on the table. "She has to. I'll make it happen."

"You mean, you'll seduce her."

"Yes." Lucian's sense of honor rebelled at the thought of leading Molly on, of giving her false hope that a romantic relationship would blossom between them. But, his responsibilities took priority—not just his duty to the Experts, but to her. He couldn't let her fall victim to dark magic.

To think of her corrupted by wickedness, enslaved to the Dealers of Darkness—

No. That must never happen. While he'd only known her a short while, he cared about her too much to let her endure such a fate.

If the object holding the dark magic was in Molly's late mother's house, especially if it was the energy detected last night, he must find it. He'd either secure it in the shop's collection of corrupted artifacts or deliver it to the Experts to keep under lock and key. Then he'd break Molly's heart. He might even leave town—not because he was a coward, but because it would be best for her, when his life was and always would be ruled by magic. She'd hate him, just like Stephanie, but there was no other choice.

The wretchedness of the situation forced a sigh from Lucian. "I'll be back this afternoon." Leaving Galahad to his kibble, Lucian undid the silencing spell and walked out into the main part of the store.

Molly turned away from a 19th century oil painting hanging on the wall. The glass items he'd bought from her earlier remained on the counter, waiting to be priced and put out on sale. None of them bore any trace of dark magic.

Lucian smiled at her. "Ready to go?"

Molly averted her gaze. "I've been thinking...."

She was going to turn him down.

"I'd love to go for coffee—"

"Great. I'll lock up on the way out." Lucian reached under the counter for the keys.

"—but I have so much to do at the house. Maybe another day?"

Don't let her go. You can't.

"The coffee at Devon Rex Desserts is very good."

"I've never been there. I'm sure the coffee's great, but—"

"Half an hour. Surely you can spare that?"

"I wish I could, but I really do have a lot to accomplish today." She glanced at the door, clearly readying to leave.

He must sweeten his persuasion.

"Do you like Key Lime Pie?"

She blinked. "Well, yes, but—"

"What if I told you the bakery serves the best Key Lime Pie in Florida?"

As he'd hoped, interest registered in her expression.

"It has a perfect graham cracker crust. The filling is tangy, creamy, and melt-in-your mouth amazing."

"It does sound delicious," Molly said.

"The sisters who own the shop breed Devon Rex cats. That's how the bakery got its name. They've also won awards for some of their pies, including the Key Lime. I swear, one bite, and your taste buds will explode with pleasure."

"Explode?" She laughed. "That pie sounds dangerous."

He'd intrigued her. But, he wouldn't relent until she'd said yes.

He turned the keys in his hand, the metal cool against his palm. If she wouldn't go with him willingly, he'd persuade her by using a little of his magic on her. Disgust flared within him, because he didn't want to have to use his powers to coerce her. While magic controlled his life, and not by his choice, he'd rather she remained free of it.

But, he did have to find out all he could about the corrupt energy.

"So?" He forced a teasing note to his voice. "What do you say?" He'd give her one last chance to agree of her own free will. "You're not going to turn down such an incredible culinary experience, are you?"

Her smile tinged with sadness. "I've already had the best Key Lime Pie. No one's can ever compare to my mom's."

Molly's words stirred thoughts of Lucian's own mother. He treasured the small stack of photographs and the few memories he had of her, and understood all too well the grief in Molly's expression. He'd never ask her to choose between her mom's dessert and what she'd experience at the bakery. "With luck, what you taste today might be a close second to your mother's."

"Maybe."

How he admired the fierce loyalty gleaming in Molly's eyes. "There's one way to find out," he said. "Come on."

Molly thanked Lucian as he held one of the bakery's swinging glass doors open for her and she stepped inside. Before she'd glanced around the crowded premises, tantalizing scents assailed her—cinnamon, peach, and lemon, and the sweetness of freshly baked pastry.

A teenage couple holding hands ahead of her moved aside after checking in with a hostess at the reception podium. Molly took a step forward and her gaze shifted to the refrigerated glass case of desserts nearby. Pies filled the three shelves, each kind identified by handwritten cards featuring a silhouette of a shorthaired cat with overlarge ears: a Devon Rex.

"Buy our pies by the slice," read a larger sign inside the case, "or take home a whole one. Made from scratch every day."

Each dessert looked perfect. Not a single

decorative pecan, crest of meringue, or swirl of whipped cream was out of place. Molly's mouth watered. She'd probably blow her day's quota of calories on one piece of pie, but considering what Lucian had told her about the awards the owners had won, such indulgence would be well worth it.

Lucian's voice rumbled behind her while he chatted to someone who'd come in after them. As the buzz of conversation and laughter cocooned in around her, doubt also crept in. What *was* she doing here? Each hour she procrastinated meant more of a rush to wrap things up before she returned to Seattle.

And Lucian…. There were so many reasons why spending time with him was a very bad idea: above all, that for the first time in a long while, she'd felt stirrings of desire. For him.

Her stomach swooped as he moved past her, powerful masculinity emanating from him. She couldn't deny it. He made her ache inside; tempted her, regardless of the consequences, to explore outside of the safe, predictable life she'd settled into since being dumped last fall.

"Lucian. Couldn't stay away?"

His easy laughter carried over the other noises in the café as he embraced the tall, black-haired woman wearing beige cropped pants, a white blouse, and a red-and-white checked apron. The woman looked like she hadn't indulged in one fattening bite of pie in her entire life.

"Hi again, Diane," Lucian said, stepping back.

"Have you come back for more of our Granny Smith Apple Pie? I know that's your favorite." Diane winked. "Or will you try the house special today: Blueberry Cobbler with Vanilla Ice Cream?"

At Molly's side now, Lucian motioned to her. "Actually, my friend has never tried one of your famous pies."

"What?" Smiling, the black-haired woman came around the podium and extended her hand. "I'm Diane Thompson. My younger sister and I co-own this bakery."

"Molly Hendrickson."

As they shook hands, Diane's asked, "You're Betty's daughter?"

"I am."

"She used to buy pies from us now and again for Historical Society events. I was so sorry to hear about her passing."

"Thank you."

Diane picked up two menus. "Let's get you to a table right away. Follow me." She strolled down the restaurant's main aisle, past rows of booths and tables filled with customers.

Lucian gestured. "After you, Molly."

A hot shiver raced through her as she followed Diane. Molly sensed Lucian's gaze upon her back. Was he checking out her butt? Her body tingled with awareness.

Diane set the menus down at a booth next to a window looking out onto Whiskers Road.

Molly slid into the dark-brown-colored seat, the vinyl creaking as she scooted toward the window. Lucian sat opposite, folding his hands on the beige tabletop. He didn't pick up a menu, just smiled in that oh-so-handsome way that made Molly feel a bit lightheaded.

"What would you like to drink?" Diane asked.

"Coffee, please," Molly said. "With cream."

Lucian nodded. "Same for me."

"I'll find your waitress—who happens to be my daughter—and let her know." Diane walked away, talking to customers as she went.

Molly picked up a menu, laminated and printed on white paper with black ink sketches of cats at the corners. "I take it you already know what you're going to order?"

"The apple pie."

"That did sound good."

"What? No Key Lime?"

"Well...."

"Not up to the challenge?"

Molly smiled. "I haven't decided yet. I *am* allowed to change my mind."

He chuckled. "Fair enough."

Molly's stomach growled, the sound drowned out by the rowdy giggling of four gray-haired women seated one row over.

"If you'd like something other than pie, I can recommend a few other desserts on the menu." Lucian unfolded his hands to brace his elbows on the table.

The shift in his posture stirred a memory: Howard, sitting in just that way at the trendy Seattle restaurant overlooking the Pacific Ocean. He'd proposed that night. He'd arranged for their waiter to bring the ring, tucked into a clam shell she'd found on the beach earlier, with their dessert. When Molly had discovered the glittering diamond, she'd been so thrilled, she'd burst into tears. And then, after saying "yes," she phoned her mom and cried some more.

Molly mentally shoved aside the recollection and put down the menu. "I'm going to get the Key Lime Pie after all."

"Good."

More laughter carried from the table of women. Lucian glanced over his shoulder and two of them beamed and wiggled their fingers at him. He raised his hand in greeting before his attention returned to Molly.

"Friends of yours?" she asked.

"Clients. They visit the store fairly regularly."

A red-haired waitress of high-school age approached their table. She set down glasses of ice water then placed coffee mugs and small cream jugs in front of Molly and Lucian. "Have you decided what you'd like, or do you need a few more minutes?"

Lucian motioned to Molly. "I'll let the lady answer first."

Lady? Hardly. But, Molly couldn't deny a flicker of pleasure. "I'd like the Key Lime Pie, please."

"Great choice. That's my favorite." The waitress beamed. "On your next date, try the Lemon Meringue."

Molly shook her head. "This isn't a date."

"I hope not," said the woman wearing scarlet lipstick who approached the table. Molly recognized her as one of the ladies who had waved at Lucian. "If he's going to date anyone," the newcomer added with a saucy grin, "it'll be me."

Lucian set down the spoon he'd used to stir cream into his coffee. "Hello, Cora." While he smiled at the woman, Molly discerned a trace of annoyance in his eyes.

Cora set her age-spotted hand on the back of Lucian's seat. Molly had never seen so many big rings worn together. Were the gemstones real? If so, Cora must be very wealthy. "What a coincidence to meet you here," the woman said, her full attention on Lucian.

"Not a coincidence," he said easily. "I eat here quite often."

Cora elbowed the waitress. "To have a body like yours, you're not eating pie."

The young woman blushed.

"Actually, I do eat pie, but I'll go for a longer run the next morning." Lucian pointed to Molly. "She's new in town and a client, so I thought I'd introduce her to this place."

The older woman's gaze shifted to Molly, pouring creamer into her coffee. Molly tried to keep her shoulders from tensing, but Cora's stare was more than a little intimidating.

"You're visiting Cat's Paw Cove? That must be why I don't recognize you."

Seriously? Did Cora know everyone in the area? "I have visited in the past," Molly said, "but never for very long."

"What brought you to town?"

That's none of your business, a little voice within Molly answered. But, to be fair, the woman might just be trying to include her in the conversation. "My mother recently died," Molly said. "I'm here to get her house ready to sell."

"Oh. I'm sorry for your loss. What was your mother's name?"

"Betty Hendrickson."

Recognition flickered in Cora's eyes. "She and I volunteered for some of the same groups—"

"Excuse me for interrupting." The waitress appeared flustered. "I didn't finish taking the order, and folks need me at another table. If I could just ask him—"

"I'll have the apple pie," Lucian said, "with ice cream."

"Okay." The waitress hurried away.

Cora tittered and her focus returned to Molly and then Lucian. "Well, I should get back to my friends. It was great to see you, Lucian, and nice to meet you, Molly." The woman's hand dropped to Lucian's broad shoulder. "Don't forget the meeting tonight, if you're able to make it."

Her painted nails trailed over his arm before she wandered away.

Molly stared down at her coffee while fighting not to laugh. She couldn't stand it any longer and raised her lashes, to meet Lucian's gaze. He appeared thoroughly disgruntled.

"Don't," he muttered.

Molly couldn't help it; she giggled.

Shaking his head, he drank more coffee.

"Cora is quite a character." Molly pulled a tissue out of her purse to dry the corners of her eyes.

"She is," he agreed. "Just so you know, I'm *not* interested in dating her. Not in the slightest."

"I understand. Your girlfriend would get upset."

"What girlfriend?"

Oh. Judging by his tone, he'd gone through a break-up, and fairly recently.

Her pulse should not have quickened at the fact he was single.

Determined to lighten the mood, Molly teased, "You don't want to be a rich woman's toy boy?"

"I don't want to be anyone's toy boy." He clearly found the idea repugnant. His reaction implied that at some point his life had been controlled by someone else—perhaps his ex—and he'd resented it.Molly didn't know him well enough to ask what had happened, but she couldn't deny she was curious.

When he looked out the window, obviously caught up in his thoughts, she stowed the tissue back in her purse. Best to change the conversation.

He and his grandfather clearly knew a lot more people in town than she did, and that might be helpful to her in coming days. "If you don't mind my asking," she said, drawing Lucian's attention back to her, "what is the meeting that's happening tonight?"

"The monthly get-together of the Cat's Paw Cove Paranormal Society."

Molly's heart jolted.

"You look shocked," Lucian noted.

"My mom belonged to that group." Molly glanced over at the table of women, who'd risen from their chairs and were readying to leave. Longing flared; a need to talk to Cora about her mother, to learn about the final weeks of her parent's life. Entwined with the longing was the sense of loss that had haunted her ever since her mom's death.

Warmth enveloped the back of her hand.

Molly sucked in a quick breath, for her expression must have given away her torment. Lucian had reached over and cupped her hand in his.

His touch.... A callus on his palm lightly grazed her skin. As her body acknowledged the comfort he offered, heat spread like slow-running honey from her fingers down into her palm and into her wrist.

Stronger heat also kindled, the promise of what could start between a man and a woman with the barest touch. A promise she shouldn't pursue, but oh, how she wanted to.

"I have Cora's card, if you want to get in touch with her," Lucian said.

Nodding, Molly struggled to control her emotions. How crazy to be so affected by a touch. A kiss, maybe. But just his hand against hers?

Panic fluttered. She couldn't pursue her feelings; especially not right now, when she was grieving and dealing with her mother's estate.

She should pull her hand away. But, Lucian had been kind to comfort her. If she did move her hand, he'd assume she didn't like him touching her, and that wasn't the situation at all—and trying to explain why she'd drawn away would reveal to him just how vulnerable she really was.

How did she break contact without offending him?

He squeezed her fingers then withdrew his hand from hers.

A sigh of relief broke from her. Embarrassed he might have noticed, she coughed, as though bothered by a tickle in her throat, and then drank some coffee. As she set the mug back down on the table, she curled both hands around it. "I would like Cora's contact information. Thank you."

He nodded, but didn't reply. Tilting his head, he studied her; an assessing look that made her wonder if he was trying to read her thoughts. Again, she experienced that sense of lightheadedness. Geez. Maybe she should go to the restroom and hang out there for a few minutes, so she could collect herself?

"Why are you interested in the society?" he asked.

Molly brushed her thumb against the mug's

cool handle. "I'm curious to know what my mom did in her free time."

"That's all?"

"Yes. Why?"

After the barest hesitation, he shrugged. "I've heard some pretty wild stories about Cat's Paw Cove. Since you've visited before, you probably know them."

"Do you mean the stories about local houses that are supposedly haunted?"

Grinning, he scratched his bearded jaw. "Those, as well as ghost sightings. Weird happenings. Tales of pirate treasure."

"There are stories like that about a lot of towns in Florida."

His grin slowly broadened, tinged with mischief. "Okay, Molly. Fess up."

With him looking at her like that, she could hardly think straight. What did he expect to hear from her? "I don't know what you mean."

He leaned farther forward, and his smile turned sly. "You can trust me. Just between us…. Did you have a strange experience in this town that you can't explain? An experience you'd describe as paranormal?"

What had happened at the house earlier with the cats was kind of unexplainable, although it probably didn't fall into the realm of paranormal. "Umm…."

"Did you see a spirit? A zombie pirate? Is that why you want to connect with the society?"

"Nope, no ghosts or pirates." Wiping away a drop of coffee running down the side of her mug, she asked, "Do you know what time the meeting is tonight? Is it open to the public?"

"I'm not sure."

"I'll look it up online later," Molly said.

Lucian's dark brows rose. "You're planning to go?"

"It would give me a chance to speak to Cora."

His expression hardened a fraction, as if he didn't like that idea. "She's a board member and will be busy running the meeting. If I were you, I'd call her and set up another day to meet, when you'll have plenty of time to talk."

That did sound like a better plan. But, other people in the group would have known her mom, and she might have the opportunity to speak with them, too.

Besides, while Molly had never paid much attention to the stories that provided fodder for the town's haunted tours, the topic of the meeting could be interesting.

Lucian continued to study her, as though waiting to hear her final decision on the evening event. She had to wonder: Why was he so interested to know if she'd had a strange experience or seen a ghost? Had he witnessed something unusual in Cat's Paw Cove?

One way to find out.

She smiled at him. "Okay, Lucian. Your turn to fess up."

"My turn?"

"How about you? Did you ever see a ghost or have a strange experience you'd describe as paranormal?"

Chapter Seven

Had he ever seen a ghost or had a strange experience he'd describe as paranormal? Every single day.

While he couldn't tell her the truth, he wanted to. He'd do it just to keep the fascination in her gaze, because she was so beautiful. In the sunshine coming in through the window, her blue eyes sparkled, and her face glowed with a genuine excitement that touched deep inside his chest. And her mouth....

His focus shifted to her lips, and heat gathered in his groin. He ached to press his lips to her sweet, pink mouth and hear her sigh because she'd loved the way he'd kissed her.

And he wouldn't stop with just one kiss—

"You *have* seen something unusual."

Molly's voice pulled him back to the clink of silverware, clatter of crockery, and buzz of conversation in the restaurant. The lies came easily after years of practice. "Nope, I haven't."

"Yeah, right." She mock-frowned. "What did you see? Or was yours a bump-in-the-night kind of experience?"

Lucian simply couldn't let that one go. He winked. "That question's kind of personal, when we barely know one another."

As he'd intended, her face turned red.

"Lucian!" she murmured, clearly embarrassed but also trying not to giggle.

"I couldn't resist." Teasing aside, minutes were ticking by and he still hadn't gotten any leads on the possible source of the dark magic he'd sensed. Molly had only promised him half an hour. Resolved to return the focus of the conversation to her, he added: "By the way, in the store, you never finished telling me about your mother."

Molly looked puzzled. "My mother…?"

"Something about a genealogy project."

"Right. Yes. She was researching our family tree."

The Experts had recorded Lucian's family tree in a special leather-bound book, starting from the day he'd gained his powers in the Middle Ages through to the present day. Details of every lifetime he'd ever had were in that tome. Anyone with even a trace of Lucian's DNA was named in the book and monitored by the organization.

"I imagine genealogical research could be fascinating," Lucian said, sipping more coffee.

"She spent many hours on it. She kept notes on where she went and how much time she'd spent researching."

A waiter with a carafe stopped at their table and refilled their coffees. After murmuring his thanks, Lucian said: "In the store, you mentioned surprises. Did your mom discover some family secrets?"

Molly tucked hair behind her left ear. The

strands gleamed where they curved against her shoulder. He'd enjoyed the feel of her soft skin against his palm. How he yearned to touch her again...but he wouldn't.

"...were a few things," Molly was saying.

"There have to be salacious secrets. Every family has them."

"Even yours?" she asked.

If only she knew. "Yep, even mine."

"How far back have you traced your family?"

"A long ways." Before she could pursue that tangent, he asked, "Is your family originally from Cat's Paw Cove?" The founding families had survived a shipwreck during a terrible storm in the mid-seventeenth century. Folk related to the founders still lived in the area.

"One of our relatives was on the ship that sank in 1645—the boat that was restored and is now the Shipwreck Museum."

"The Guinevere?"

Molly nodded.

"How fascinating. Man or woman?"

"Man. He was a cook." Her expression thoughtful, Molly poured more cream into her coffee. "Mom went to the local museum and requested copies of documents from the archives. One of them was a list of some of our relative's belongings. I think officials at the time were trying to match items washed ashore with the shipwreck's survivors."

The back of Lucian's skull tingled. The fear and horror of the shipwreck could have created the perfect conduit for dark magic. "What was on the list?"

"I only skimmed it, but—"

"Here we are." Their waitress set a slice of pie

topped with an elegant, whipped-cream swirl in front of Molly, and then a piece mounded with vanilla ice cream in front of him. "Enjoy, you two."

"Thank you." Molly's eyes widened. "This is a huge piece of pie."

Impatience gnawed at Lucian, but he managed a smile. "You must have looked hungry."

"I am now that I've seen this dessert. Yours looks amazing, too."

He could almost taste the tart apple and creamy sweetness of the ice cream, and he hadn't yet taken a bite. As he picked up his fork, he said, "The list you mentioned?"

"I'd have to look at it again." Using her fork, she broke off a small bit of pie. "I do remember one thing on it—"

Lucian's cell phone buzzed.

If it wasn't important, he'd send the call to voice mail. After putting the first bite of pie into his mouth, he glanced at the phone.

Julius.

The delicious dessert suddenly tasted as bland as cardboard. Julius didn't like being ignored. Lucian swallowed, wiped his mouth with his napkin then picked up the buzzing phone. "I'm sorry, but I have to take this call."

"That's fine." She set her fork down on the edge of her plate.

"Don't wait for me." She'd have to be a saint to sit with that dessert in front of her and politely wait until he returned to eat it. "I'll be back as soon as I can."

"Okay."

He left the booth. Stepping aside to avoid a

waitress delivering food to a table, he answered the call. "Julius."

"Lucian." Julius's voice rumbled on the line, and Lucian easily pictured the stocky, gray-haired man with blue eyes who always wore an expensive suit. "Enjoying your dessert?"

Of course Julius would know where Lucian was right that very moment. Striding toward the restaurant's swinging doors, he said, "I'm kind of busy right now."

"I'm sure you are. But, this is important."

Lucian scowled at his superior's uncompromising tone. "Can I call you back in half an hour?"

"Not this time."

Lucian walked out onto the sidewalk. Heat rose from the sun-scorched pavement, and he headed for the shade of a nearby store's awning.

"I saw your report from yesterday," Julius said.

"I intended to update my progress, but—"

"I'll watch for that update."

Lucian wiped away the sweat beading on his forehead. "I was going to say, I don't have anything more to report yet."

Silence carried on the line. Lucian imagined the older man's expression hardening with disapproval. Perspiration dampened the back of Lucian's neck.

"I trust you realize, as well as I, that the magic you noticed is an anomaly?"

Lucian struggled not to growl. "I know."

"I trust you also realize that, while it registered below a Category One, it might not stay at that level?"

"I do remember what you taught me." Quite frankly, Lucian would never forget his teenage years being mentored by Julius. The guy had run his training program like a haunted-antiques boot camp.

A clicking noise sounded; a pen engaging and retracting several times. "From all I've seen in your report, there's no reason for alarm right now. Hopefully, there never will be. But, while the chance is slim, there is the potential for disaster."

Lucian pinched the bridge of his nose. Did he bother to point out that this wasn't his first anomaly, and that statistics proved ninety percent of such instances ended up being non-events? Also, if Julius wasn't keeping him on the phone, he could be working on tracking down what held the dark magic.

"You'll understand why I want you to make what you saw yesterday a priority, until we've determined it isn't a threat."

Lucian struggled to keep annoyance from his voice. "I assure you, I'm on it."

More clicks of the pen. "I will expect that update soon, then."

"Fine." Without waiting to hear Julius say goodbye, Lucian ended the call.

Molly tried to eat slowly, but the pie was good. Very good, actually. As she downed another scrumptious bite, her gaze settled on Lucian's dessert. He hadn't been gone long, but the ice cream was already starting to melt.

He hadn't been happy to get the call. As soon as he'd seen who was phoning, his demeanor had changed. The twinkle in his eyes had vanished, his shoulders had tensed, and he'd walked away with brisk, almost angry strides.

Was he talking with a client? Or his ex?

Molly pushed down a pang of jealousy. He might not have a girlfriend, but he could be casually dating.

Maybe he'd argued earlier with his date, and she'd called to continue or finish their discussion.

The caller also could be a client unhappy with a purchase from the shop.

How Molly wished she could watch Lucian's body language while he had his conversation, or even read his lips, but he wasn't in sight.

Molly ate the last of her pie then washed it down with coffee. That deliciousness had definitely been worth a delay in returning to her mom's house, although she needed to be on her way soon.

Behind the group of people standing in the restaurant aisle, she saw Lucian, on his way back to the table. When he slid into the booth, she caught lingering tension in his expression. The phone conversation hadn't resolved whatever he was upset about.

"Sorry about the interruption." He set aside the phone.

"Everything okay?"

"As okay as it can be."

His deliberately vague answer told her he didn't want to talk about the call. Maybe that was for the best, since she needed to leave shortly. She'd wait until he'd eaten, though.

He gestured to her empty plate. "That awful, huh?"

"Yep. *Really* awful."

Lucian grinned, and she savored the warmth inside her, stirred up by his teasing. Howard had liked to tease, too. She'd enjoyed their banter until his remarks had become subtle criticisms of her weight, her clothes, and her dedication to her students and teaching career. He'd known her well enough that with just a few choice words, he'd been able to wound her deeply.

She shoved thoughts of Howard aside, because she'd moved on from that part of her life, and it really wasn't fair to compare Lucian, a guy she'd only known for barely a couple of days, to her ex, whom she'd known for years. There were also more pressing things to consider, such as when to list her late mom's home for sale. The real estate agent coming to the house that afternoon would best be able to make that decision.

Lucian's fork clinked against his plate as he scooped up a mouthful of dessert. As he chewed, a groan of pleasure broke from him, the sound only just audible over the rattle of dishes as a busboy cleared off a nearby table.

Geez, Lucian even looked and sounded hot when he ate.

His gaze flicked up to meet hers. "My pie's *really* bad too."

"I'm guessing you'll make yourself eat every bite?"

"You guessed right."

After a moment's pause, she said, "Thanks for twisting my arm and bringing me here."

"Happy to." He wiped his lips with his napkin. "I have to ask: How did the pie compare to your mom's?"

He looked so eager to hear her answer, she

couldn't help but smile. "It was almost as good."

"A close second, then? Yes? No?"

"Yes, I'd say so."

His grin broadened. "Told you. Next time we come here, you can try a different pie."

A startled laugh broke from her. "Next time?"

"Sure. Why not?"

He'd decided for her that there would be a next time? That was pretty bold.

"It would help me out," he added, as though aware of her astonishment. "When customers ask me where they can get the best pie in town, I'll be able to draw upon firsthand knowledge—"

She laughed. "Firsthand knowledge?"

"I'll be an expert in fine art, antiques, and pies."

Molly rolled her eyes.

"It's a worthy quest, my dear lady. Unless, of course, you have a suitor who'd object?"

She forced down excitement, because she wasn't going to—couldn't—get involved with Lucian.

Aware he was studying her and waiting for her reply, she said, "I don't have a suitor—"

"Ah."

"—but I also don't want one."

Surprise etched his features. "Now I'm curious to know why, although I realize it's none of my business."

"The short answer is that I just don't have time for a relationship right now. By the way, most people nowadays call suitors boyfriends. It's the twenty-first century, after all, not the Middle Ages."

She'd spoken in a light-hearted tone, but his eyes narrowed, as though she'd offended him. "No, it's definitely not the Middle Ages." His mouth curved in a roguish smirk. "If it was, I'd already have tossed you over my shoulder and carried you off to my castle."

Oh.

Her imagination easily pictured him as an alpha knight from one of her favorite romance novels, doing whatever he wanted, taking whatever he wanted.... Her face grew hot. No man had ever shown that thrilling but also kind of intimidating interest in her before.

He winked. "I think I scared you."

Yep. "Nope," Molly said firmly and reached for her glass of water.

"You'd be okay with me tossing you over my shoulder then?"

What kind of trick question was that? He had to be teasing her again. She sipped her water as she tried, and failed, to come up with a brilliant, kick-ass reply. "Would you be okay with me kicking, screaming, and calling the police?" she finally said.

"All at the same time?"

She squinted at him. "What?"

He pushed his empty plate away. "If I have you slung over my shoulder, and you're kicking and screaming, how are you going to call the cops?

"I'll use my phone."

"When you're upside down?"

She hesitated. How did she know if she could use her phone while upside down?

His lips parted.

"Before you say 'Are you sure you can phone while upside down?', I expect some of the other customers in this restaurant would call 911, hit record on their phones, or even tackle you before you reached the exit," she said. "Once the video hit the internet, you'd become the world's most famous antique dealer, and not in a good way."

"Good points."

"Besides, as we've already agreed, it's not the Middle Ages. I'm sure you're far too civilized to ever toss me over your shoulder and carry me off."

Call him crazy, but he really did want to throw her over his shoulder, just like he'd said.

With defiance gleaming in her eyes and strong in her voice, the temptation was almost too much. He'd never felt this way about a woman before; she obviously appealed to whatever medieval DNA was left in his character.

But, he wasn't stupid enough to act on the impulse. If he did, his life would become very complicated very fast. He'd never get another chance to get close to her and find the item of dark magic he'd sensed, and once The Experts learned he'd screwed things up yet again…. Well, that was too unpleasant to think about.

Lucian curled his hand on the tabletop; focused on the inward turn of his fingers instead of reaching for her.

"Right?" she said.

He tried to recall what she'd said: Something about him being civilized, which drew a rough chuckle from him. "I'd say I'm civilized most of the time."

Smiling, she shook her head. "At least you're honest."

"Was that a compliment?"

Her smile turned wry as she reached over and drew her phone out of her purse. "Call it whatever you like." She glanced at the phone screen and tapped on it several times. While she read the new messages, her expression sobered with the weight of responsibility.

A sense of urgency gathered inside Lucian. Their half an hour had to be up, and she was going to leave. But, he had to keep her connected to him. He had to find a way to be invited to her late mother's house—although that might be a bit more difficult after his recent teasing.

She picked up her purse and set it on the table in front of her then tucked her phone in a side pocket. "This break has been lovely," she said, "but I really must go now."

"Of course. I'll let you know as soon as I hear back about your jewelry," he said. "The phone number you gave me at the store is the best number to reach you?"

"It is." Molly took out her wallet. "I'll leave money for my pie."

"I've got it."

Her lips pressed together, and he sensed her debating whether to allow him to pay for her dessert.

"I'll pay," he insisted. "I did, after all, twist your arm."

"Well, thank you. As long as you remember this wasn't a date."

"Don't worry, I remember."

She slid toward the end of the booth.

The sense of urgency within him intensified. He had only seconds before she was gone. Seconds to think of a way to keep her tied to him.

He picked up his cell and opened up the web browser. "So. The meeting tonight."

"Mmm?"

"Are you still interested in attending?"

"Yes, I think so."

He typed Cat's Paw Cove Paranormal Society into the search bar and opened the first link in the results. "It starts at seven," he said, reading from the society's home page. "It's at the community center, not far from the boardwalk on Sherwood Boulevard."

"I know the one."

"How about if we go to the meeting together?"

Molly's fingers tightened on the edge of the table. "You want to go? Even after Cora hit on you?"

"I can handle Cora. Since I only returned to the town a short while ago, the meeting would give me the chance to do some networking."

"Well...."

She's going to turn you down.

Lucian bestowed on her his most charming smile. "If you come by the store, I'll drive us both to the meeting. I'll also help with introductions, since I'll know some of the women there."

"That would be a help."

"Good. Why don't you come by the store about fifteen minutes before the meeting is to start? That should give us plenty of time to get there."

As he watched Molly's car join the midday traffic on Whiskers Road, Lucian turned the sign on the shop's door back to Open.

Galahad, who'd been asleep on the Edwardian chair, was now sitting up, bright-eyed. "Don't make me wait for the sordid details. How was coffee?"

Lucian crossed the store. "It went fine."

"Fine?" The squire huffed. "Fine doesn't equate to sordid."

Frowning, Lucian stowed the keys under the counter. "Why would you expect sordid things to happen at a crowded bakery?"

"You were a rogue more than once."

So Lucian had heard. "Many lifetimes ago," he pointed out.

"Yeah, but for all I know, 'coffee' and 'pie' could be trending naughty words."

"They're not." Lucian raked his fingers through his hair. He hadn't realized until now how much he disliked it being long. He was getting tired of his beard, too. "Since I know you'll keep pestering me for an update—"

"Yep."

"—I didn't make as much headway as I'd hoped."

"With Molly, or with figuring out whether her dark magic is the energy we saw last night?"

"Both."

The squire covered his face with his front paw. "Lucian!"

"Molly *did* agree to come by the store tonight, though."

"Okay, I am a *tiny* bit less ashamed of you."

"We arranged to go to the Paranormal Society meeting together. At least, that's how we left things before she went home."

The feline's paw dropped back to the chair seat. "That's a terrible idea."

"Let me explain—"

"Cougar Cora will be there. She'll have her claws in you the second you walk in the door."

Lucian inwardly sighed. Cora was starting to monopolize his every waking moment.

"She'll also expect more than the return of her casserole dish. Unless, of course, 'returning the casserole dish' is kinky Cougar code for hooking up?"

Good God. Lucian had no idea if the words were code, but he and Cora were never going to hook up. "As far as I'm concerned, 'returning the casserole dish' means 'giving back the empty dish that once held casserole."

"Whatever you say." Galahad yawned then jumped down from the furnishing. "You're the knight-in-command. I'm just the lowly squire."

"Not lowly," Lucian said. "You're a lot more important that you seem to believe."

"Yeah, yeah." The cat trudged toward the right front window.

"Tonight, you're going to help make sure Molly and I never get to the meeting."

"Whaa...?" Pausing, Galahad looked back at Lucian. "I'm confused."

Lucian leaned both arms on the counter. "As I tried to explain a moment ago, I've reconsidered going. We still don't know whether the dark magic I sensed in the costume jewelry and the almost-Category-One energy are from the same object or two different ones. I'd rather solve that mystery this evening."

"Okay. No meeting. How are you—we—going to keep Molly from attending?"

"I'll offer an alternative she can't resist."

Galahad's eyes glinted. "Seduction."

Lucian shook his head. "I'm still building her trust. She *has* to grow to trust me. It's the surest way to be invited into her late mom's home."

The feline's whiskers twitched with excitement. "Shall I brush against her calves again? Distract her with my cuteness and sass?"

"You've done those things already."

"Cuteness and sass *do* work, you know."

"Mmm." Lucian eased away from the counter and reached for his laptop, his mind already mulling a plan. "Molly was going to attend the meeting to learn more about her mother—"

"Ha! I'll be a bad kitty. Can I bring her a big spider and drop it on her foot? Or, I could nip outside, mangle a frog, and present it to her?"

Lucian grimaced. "You'll give Molly nightmares."

"That means no." Galahad sulked. "I really want to be a bad kitty."

The computer whirred as Lucian started it up. "If I can't locate what I want tonight, I might be willing to compromise—"

"Yesss!"

"—but my grandfather's files may have just what we need."

Chapter Eight

olly smoothed the cream-colored top with flared sleeves she'd put on a short while ago along with beige trousers and studied her reflection in her bedroom mirror. She'd redone her ponytail but had pulled out wisps of hair to trail down by her cheeks. Neutral beige eye shadow, rose-pink blush, and a shimmery pink gloss finished the look.

Distant thunder rumbled while she tidied a few stray hairs with hairspray and a comb. Dark clouds had been rolling in when she'd driven home, so she'd put the radio on and, at the house, had switched on the TV to check the local news and weather updates. Heavy rain and wind gusts were forecast for early evening, but with luck, the worst of the storm would happen while she and Lucian were in the meeting. The tempest should have subsided by the time she and the other attendees needed to drive home.

Studying her reflection again, Molly wrinkled her nose. While she looked neat and polished, her outfit was uninspiring and, well, kind of boring. It needed…something.

She picked up gold hoop earrings and put them on. Better.

What about the antique necklace?

Unease flickered, because she still couldn't explain the weird language she'd heard yesterday when she'd worn the jewel. Honestly, though, she couldn't be sure she *had* really discerned a voice. She'd been busy, tired, and her imagination could have been running wild.

Still, she'd liked wearing the necklace. More than she'd ever expected.

After her split from Howard, she'd gone to a therapist who'd encouraged her to listen to her gut-instincts and rediscover her authentic self. Maybe she'd found pleasure in wearing the jewel because its design appealed to her true nature.

Her hand rose to trace where the pendant had touched her skin. The sense of feminine power rekindled within her.

Why shouldn't she wear the necklace if she wanted to?

She took off the earrings. Stepping around the four cats lying in front of the closet, of all places, she laid her suitcase flat on the floor and unzipped it. All four felines clambered on top of the case, making it difficult to open.

"You are the craziest kitties." She pushed them off. They returned.

When she tried to shoo Marigold, the cat bit her sleeve and hung on tight.

"Marigold!"

The feline growled, but didn't let go of the fabric.

Tucking the cat under her arm, Molly carried

her to the kitchen then opened a bag of treats. No doubt hoping for a snack, Marigold let go of the sleeve. The other cats had followed, and after scattering treats on the floor, Molly hurried back to her bedroom and shut the door. She took the necklace out of its box.

A thrill raced through her, because the jewel was even more exquisite than she'd remembered.

As she fastened it around her neck, thunder growled. At the same time, several cats cried outside the door.

Bang, bang.

Not again!

She mentally shut out the racket and eyed her reflection. When she touched the pendant, its inner fire seemed to brighten. The brightness couldn't be due to sunlight, because the sky was overcast.

Her imagination must be tricking her again, but still....

Her hair appeared silkier, her figure more voluptuous. How was that possible?

Mrow. Mrow!

Ignore them. Focus on yourself, a little voice within her whispered.

She frowned. That voice—

Doesn't it feel good to be beautiful?

Heady fire spread through her. Never before had she felt so feminine. Confident. *Powerful.* If only she could feel this phenomenal every day.

Thunder boomed again, even as misgiving scratched at the back of her mind.

Meow. Meee-owwwr!

Could the cats somehow sense that she was feeling a bit odd? She'd been fine until she'd put on the necklace. Maybe she was having an allergic reaction to the metal. She should take it off—

Keep it on.

With effort, she forced herself to concentrate. The pendant did look nice, but it *was* too fancy to wear to the meeting.

Keep—

She reached to the back of her neck and undid the clasp.

As the necklace clinked and settled in her palm, craving gripped her. She wanted the weight of the jewelry around her neck once again. She *hungered* for it, as though she couldn't exist without it.

What a strange thing to think. Of course she could exist without the necklace.

Fear brushed Molly's heart as she swiftly dropped the jewel in its box, closed the lid, and returned the box to the suitcase.

The cats had gone quiet. How very bizarre.

She picked up her cell phone to check the time, half-wondering whether she should look up weird cat behavior—

Yikes! She needed to leave in five minutes.

She must remember to grab an umbrella on the way out, because it might be pouring by the time she got to the antique shop.

Looking in the mirror again, she frowned. Thank goodness she still had time to change.

She went to the closet and pulled out a turquoise-colored crossover top and curve-hugging jeans. After putting them on, she applied black eyeliner and plum lipstick and slipped on black heels.

Molly winked at her reflection and sashayed out of the room.

"Is the dark magic in the same area as last time?" Galahad asked, his voice competing with the crackle of the radio and the clicks of the camera. Without waiting for a reply, the cat jumped up onto the back room table.

Assessing the incoming data, Lucian frowned. "It's in the exact same area."

"Ooooooooo."

"Great. Now the Lady of the Plate's moaning again," the squire groused.

She'd started wailing when the afternoon sky had turned overcast. Lucian had silenced her with a light spell, but then the alarms had gone off, and her cries somehow had become audible again—a puzzling development.

"Could she have tapped into the dark magic?" Galahad asked, as though attuned to Lucian's thoughts.

It was possible, since he'd used only a mild spell, but unlikely. "I don't believe so. I think we're in for a strong storm."

Whatever had roused the Lady of the Plate, he couldn't dwell upon it now. Just like before, the corrupt energy had appeared all of a sudden. "The readings are the same as last time," Lucian said, "but the magic's a strong Category One now."

Galahad's eyes widened. "Why is it intensifying? How?"

"I don't know." The dark magic object was obviously drawing power from a source. Not an ancient source—the detectors would have picked it up last time and it would have been evident in the data streaming in now—but a modern-day one.

What, though, could be the source?

"Oooooooo...."

"We need to go. Right now." Lucian shut his laptop and picked it up.

"What about Molly? Isn't she going to be here soon?"

Halfway to the door, Lucian stilled. "You're right."

The dials on the radio suddenly began to slide to the left, toward zero. The camera clicks, too, slowed.

"It's disappearing, just like before," Galahad said.

"Oooooooo...."

Damn. They hadn't gleaned any new information, and Julius would demand an update.

"We'll investigate. It's not far." Lucian reached the doorway.

"And Molly?"

"I'll make sure we're back in time."

"You'd better. It wouldn't be chivalrous to stand her up."

"No, it wouldn't. The sooner we leave, the sooner we get back."

The squire leapt down from the table and headed for the rear of the shop while Lucian locked up. When he stepped outside, humidity enveloped him like an invisible cloak, and the air held the earthiness of imminent rain. With Galahad running alongside him, Lucian hurried to and opened the driver's side door of the Mini. The feline jumped in.

Droplets of rain landed on Lucian as he slid in behind the wheel. Lighting flashed in the distance, followed by peals of thunder. The car's tires squealed as he sped out of the parking lot.

Despite it being rush hour, in less than twelve minutes, Lucian had reached the area of town where the magic had briefly appeared. Rain was falling steadily. Through the downpour, he studied the very normal-looking houses while he drove slowly down the very normal-looking streets. As before, the magic had disappeared.

Lucian stopped the car but kept the windshield wipers on and the engine running. In his grandfather's records, he'd found Molly's late mother's address. He'd intended to look it up on a map of Cat's Paw Cove, but had been waylaid by the report he'd filed—a preventive measure, since he'd rather not have Julius pester him during his evening with Molly—as well as answering the phone and helping customers in the store.

Lucian pulled up the address on his GPS. "Bloody hell."

"Details," Galahad said.

"Molly's mother's house is a few blocks away."

"Uh-oh. That means...."

"The anomaly's what I sensed in the costume jewelry."

Switching on his turn signal, Lucian pulled away from the curb and followed the audio directions to the residence. Through the pelting rain, he studied the single story house shaded by several oak trees. A white-painted fence separated the front and back yards.

"The cat I saw the other night," Galahad said. "The female who talked. We saw her on this street, didn't we?"

"Yes."

"Geez, Lucian. We've gotta find out what's

going on around here."

Lightning flashed. "We will," Lucian said.

An incoming phone call.

Cursing under his breath, Lucian pressed his steering wheel. "Julius."

"Almost a Category Two." The Expert's voice resonated inside the car. "What's causing the magic to strengthen?"

"Not sure. We're near the location—"

"Good. I've elevated this matter to several Archivists. They're going to delve deeper into the data."

Julius had enlisted Archivists? He'd never done that to Lucian before. Did he not have faith that Lucian could resolve the situation? Fighting to keep his voice steady, Lucian said, "I'm more than qualified to deal with a Category Two."

"I know, but I have better resources at my disposal. The Archivists will try to find a precise date of origin. Hallmarks, even, although that may be difficult, since the data has some modern contamination."

"Modern contamination?" Lucian frowned. "What do you mean?"

Muffled voices sounded in the background. "We'll speak again later," Julius said. "As I've said before, make the anomaly a priority."

Pouring rain hammered the roof of the car as Molly parked in front of Black Cat Antiquities. Water streamed off the awning covering the antique shop's front door, causing a small river to flow down the sidewalk.

During her drive to the store, the wind had at times forced the rain sideways, turning the road ahead into a murky blur. The wind continued to gust. She had an umbrella, and had worn one of her late mother's raincoats, but getting from her car to the door without getting soaked would be next to impossible. She'd end up wet and bedraggled; not the way she wanted to look when seeing Lucian.

She switched off the car and listened to the drumming of the rain. Maybe if she waited, the deluge would slow and she could make a run for the door. That seemed the best plan for now. Lucian would surely understand.

She checked her phone. *Five minutes late.* She hated being late for anything. Always had. She'd texted him to let him know, but still.

The deluge continued. Glancing over at the store, she couldn't see Lucian inside, but the lights were on. He might be at the back of the shop, waiting for the bell on the door to chime.

Seven minutes late.

Ugh.

She drew a steadying breath, dropped the phone into her purse, and picked up her umbrella. She was going to have to suck it up and brave the foul weather.

Opening the driver's side door, she snapped open the umbrella before getting out of the vehicle. The wind almost tore the umbrella out of her hand, but she hung on tight, slammed the car door, and hurried to the sidewalk. She stepped up onto it…and her right heel twisted.

With a sharp cry, she pitched forward. The wind snatched the umbrella and sent it sailing down the sidewalk.

She landed on her side. Her purse hit the sidewalk, and a comb and pen tumbled out. Rainwater soaked the leg of her jeans and ran down the back of her neck as she snatched up the fallen items, struggled to her feet, and tottered to the shop's entrance.

Locked.

"You're kidding me." With a groan, she knocked on the door. When Lucian didn't appear, she knocked louder. He might be in a part of the store where he couldn't hear her, although he'd been expecting her ten minutes ago now.

The wind howled again, driving rain and runoff water under the awning. Fingering damp hair from her cheek, she knocked again, praying Lucian would finally answer. She'd give him one more knock—

Lucian appeared, keys in hand, striding toward her from the back of the store, with Galahad trotting beside him like a small dog. Lucian and his cat were soaked, too.

The door clicked as he unlocked it and pulled it open. "I'm sorry," he said, before she could utter a word. "I meant to be back before you got here."

"Back?" She stepped inside, woefully aware she was leaving a trail of water on the wood floor. "You left the store?" Rather odd, when he'd asked her to meet him at the shop.

"I did." He shut the door on the storm outside, and a muscle ticked in his jaw. "I needed to...run an errand."

Molly sensed he'd done more than run an

errand and taken Galahad along. He obviously didn't want to tell her where he'd been—although surely after leaving her out in the rain, she deserved a truthful answer. "An errand? In this weather, with your cat? It—or she—must have been important."

"It," he said firmly. "And it was."

She wished he'd just tell her where he'd been…unless he couldn't, because of confidentiality agreements with his clients?

Thunder boomed, the sound so loud, she startled.

Pausing mid-wash of his front paw, Galahad meowed.

"Fine. I went to get cat food," Lucian said.

That had been so important?

"The special canned stuff he likes," Lucian added with a smile. "Otherwise, you and I wouldn't have a moment's peace and quiet to talk."

"Okay…." That was a somewhat plausible reason for his tardiness.

"Part way back here," Lucian added, "we came upon a car stopped in the street. A tree branch had fallen, and a woman was trying to move it out of the way. I took over and pulled it to the side of the road. You might know the lady: Roberta Millingham."

"I know of her." Molly had seen her name in the Historical Society papers.

Mentioning Roberta though—someone Molly could easily contact to cross-check his story—meant Lucian hadn't lied about his whereabouts.

She could hardly stay upset with him when he'd been doing a good deed.

Molly removed her raincoat and shivered as water slid into her bra. She must look a wreck. Lucian, with his tousled hair, damp skin, and shirt plastered to his muscled chest, looked like he'd just come from a wet modeling shoot.

She doubted her clothes would be dry by the time they needed to go to the meeting. The knit fabric of her top was glued to her skin, and her poor shoes—

"I really am sorry. Let's get you dried off and warmed up."

How? She hadn't brought a change of clothes, although in hindsight, that would have been really smart.

Lucian shifted the key ring to his left hand, beckoned for her to follow him, and headed for a doorway toward the back of the shop.

Thrills of excitement and unease trailed through her. Galahad looked up at her expectantly, as though waiting for her to willingly follow Lucian to part of the store that wouldn't be visible from the street—not that anyone would be window-shopping during the storm.

As she stared back at the feline, another shiver rippled through her; a curious sense that something was going on that she hadn't figured out yet. The cat's gaze seemed so very *aware*. Intelligent, even.

The hairs at the back of her neck prickled. Between the tempest that could be the backdrop of a horror flick, the vibes she was getting from the cat, and being surrounded by a store full of possessions from people who were long dead, her whole situation suddenly seemed off.

"You know, I should head home."

Lucian halted and faced her. "You just got here."

"I can't go to the paranormal society meeting

in these wet clothes."

"The meeting's probably been cancelled."

That would make sense. Even more reason for her to return to the house.

"It's no problem, though," Lucian continued. "We can talk—"

"Let's reschedule for another day. Tomorrow, even."

"No."

She blinked hard. "No?"

With brisk strides, he started back toward her. "Stay." A bit more gently: "You have to."

Her pulse pounding against her breastbone, she took a backward step. "I don't *have* to."

His strides slowed. Raising his hands, palm up, he said, "I'm not trying to frighten you."

"You don't," she said firmly.

Liar.

As though attuned to her thoughts, he smiled faintly. "If you leave now, I can't show you what I found in my grandfather's records."

Molly glanced out at the street, the rain still pouring down. Lucian was almost upon her now. On her next backward step, her bottom bumped the door handle.

The skin across her breasts tingled, because Lucian stood in front of her, so close, she could reach out and touch his shirt. The smells of wet cotton, fresh air, and spicy aftershave taunted her, coaxed her to listen to the part of her that yearned to stay and see what he had to show her.

"Molly," he murmured.

"W-what?" She could hardly breathe with him standing so near.

"I won't let you drive in this storm."

The authority in his tone warned his decision wasn't negotiable.

Her attention snapped up from his damp beard. "You're telling me what to do?"

"Yep."

"You don't have that right."

His brows rose. "You are in my store."

"Your grandfather's store," she amended. "Once I open the door and walk two steps, I will be on the public sidewalk."

"My grandfather made me the manager of this shop, meaning you now are in my premises. I am responsible for your safety. Your wellbeing." Lucian reached up and tucked strands of sodden hair back behind her ear. "*You.*"

Another shiver ran through her.

His fingers glided in along her cheekbone to wipe away rainwater dripping from her hair. He lightly flicked the water away then returned to carefully brush away more droplets.

She'd never experienced a touch like his: as light as the touch of a feather and exquisitely, thoroughly controlled.

Heat and yearning sparked inside her, tempting her to lean her face into his touch, to see where his fingers would go next. The voice of reason, though, urged her to fight the longing. If she was going to leave, she must do it now.

Lightning sizzled outside, followed by loud thunder. She swallowed hard. "I'm sure I will get home just fine."

His fingers glided again. "You'll stay here."

"I don't have far to drive—"

CATHERINE KEAN

His fingertips touched her mouth, stopping her mid-sentence. "No."

Again, his voice held that steely authority. While his alpha male demeanor was kind of hot, she shouldn't let him order her around. "You can't stop me from leaving." If only her voice hadn't wobbled.

"I *can* stop you from leaving." He stared down at her, his expression unyielding. "I will."

Her mouth gaped, dislodging his fingers. If he was trying to freak her out, he was succeeding. Was she stupid to have ever trusted him?

As though aware of her thoughts, the corner of his mouth ticked up. "As I said before, I don't mean to scare you. I'm trying to protect you."

She shuddered, uncertainty heightening her awareness of her soaked clothes and wet hair. Galahad brushed back and forth against her calves. The feline was between her and the door, and with him there, she couldn't yank the door open without it hitting him; she'd never hurt an animal, not under any circumstances.

"I can't risk you getting hurt." Lucian stroked her cheek again. "I'd never forgive myself if you were involved in an accident."

The tenderness of his tone melted some of her defiance. Why did he have to say such wonderful things?

Triumph glinted in Lucian's eyes. "You'll stay."

She would. But, she wasn't going to just give in. "Do I have a choice?"

He winked. "Nope."

She rolled her eyes.

His fingers settled under her chin and tilted her head back, leaving her no option but to stare up at him.

"Just so we're clear…. If you opened the door and walked out, I'd bring you right back inside."

"Bring? As in…?"

"Before, when I threatened to toss you over my shoulder? Well—"

"You wouldn't!"

"I would."

His glower warned he'd be more than happy for her to test him by opening the door and racing outside right now.

Of all ridiculous things, she wanted to. A thrill tore through her, urging her to accept the challenge, grab the door handle, and run. But, knowing her luck, she'd twist her ankle again and do a face-plant on the sidewalk, and her show of bravado would end up being rather pointless.

"I won't need to get all medieval on you, though, will I, since you're going to stay put? I do, after all, have information to share with you," Lucian said. "You must be curious about that."

"I am," she managed to say.

"It's settled then." He released her chin, stepped past her, and locked the door. Then he caught her hand, frowning as their fingers linked. As chilled as she was, her skin no doubt felt like ice.

He towed her toward the rear of the store and she hurried along to keep up with his strides. Thunder roared outside like a feral beast. The lights in the store flickered.

Lucian stowed the ring of keys then picked up a leather laptop bag and continued on toward the rear door.

"Where are we going?"

"Somewhere more comfortable."

Her anxious stomach gurgled. "Where, exactly, is that?"

"My apartment."

Chapter Nine

Molly had to be freezing. Her fingers were as cold as if he'd pulled her hand out of a snow bank.

When she'd glanced out the window earlier, Lucian's gaze had slipped lower, to the round beads of her nipples outlined by her wet top. Such perfect breasts. He'd have loved to gently warm them with his hands, but thankfully, common sense had overruled his desire. He needed to get her warm and dry. If he didn't, she could get sick—and he'd be to blame, because she'd been out in the tempest until he'd let her inside.

Her heels clicked on the floor behind him; two of her footfalls to one of his. At least she'd agreed to go with him of her own free will. She still believed she had choice.

While she was cooperating, he'd made sure she couldn't drive away as soon as he left her alone for a minute. While brushing the rain from her face with his fingers, he'd immobilized her vehicle with a spell, preventing it from starting until he'd removed the enchantment.

Their conversation moments ago had revealed her stubborn streak, and if she wasn't able to drive the car, she might run down the sidewalk to get help and put herself in danger from wind-blown debris. That meant he'd take other magical measures, too, to keep her with him.

He had to—because *he* didn't have a choice. He needed to find the source of the dark energy as soon as possible, before it increased even more in strength. He'd already determined she hadn't brought the object with her tonight.

"Your apartment," she said, sounding a bit breathless.

"Mmm?"

"Is it far?"

"Not far at all."

"You won't let me drive in this storm, but you're willing to?"

"Neither of us is going to drive." Lucian led her outside, the hiss of rain pouring down on the parking lot hindering further discussion. Galahad darted outside, and Lucian locked up without releasing Molly's hand then followed the cat down the covered sidewalk. Lucian typed his code into the electronic keypad to open the door on his left, and the squire bounded ahead up the carpeted flight of stairs.

"I get it now. You live above the store," Molly said.

"It's my grandfather's place, but for now, I'm sharing it with him."

Molly didn't answer, but Lucian felt her tremble. He squeezed her fingers, hoping to reassure her, as they reached the top of the stairs and he drew her down the hallway to the apartment.

Once inside, he let go of her hand, flicked on the lights, and set his laptop bag on the hall table. He took her umbrella and raincoat from her, hung them on the coat stand then pushed the door shut.

Molly's gaze roamed over the modern-style, brown-leather sofa and chair and comfortable recliner in the living room, as well as the big screen TV and the assorted bronze sculptures, Art Nouveau lamps, and other antiques that made up his grandfather's private collection.

He knew the moment she found his grandfather's most prized possessions. "Wow," she murmured, crossing to the rows of swords, daggers, and several shields displayed on the wall next to the kitchen. "What era are these from?"

"The Middle Ages, mainly. Some date to the 17th and 18th centuries." Lucian had his own collection of weapons, most of them in storage. However, he kept his favorite sword and dagger on display in his bedroom in the apartment. His grandfather had insisted that Lucian keep them in easy reach. While it was unlikely a Dealer would try and steal from the shop, or that Lucian would face an uprising of artifacts in the store's dark magic collection, he still had to be prepared for those possibilities.

"They're beautiful." Molly studied a sword with a cross on its pommel. Warmth bloomed within Lucian, for he'd wielded that blade many lifetimes ago. "Where did your grandfather get them?" she asked.

Lucian tore his focus from the light shimmering on her hair. "Private collectors. Auctions."

"I'm surprised these weapons aren't in a museum."

"They're worthy of a museum display, but they

have a good home here." He could hardly tell her that The Experts had documents in their archives that traced the provenance of all of the weapons. They'd all, in one lifetime or another, belonged to him.

Hugging herself, Molly glanced at him. "Do you collect anything?"

"I have a few antique weapons of my own. Most are packed away until I get my own place."

"Are you going to buy a house in Cat's Paw Cove?" she asked.

"I expect so. I haven't found a place that feels like home yet."

She nodded then rubbed her arms with her hands. The movement reminded him why he'd brought her to up to the apartment, and he silently scolded himself for not taking care of her sooner.

"Stay there." Without waiting for her to reply, he crossed the apartment, discreetly reinforcing the locking spell on the front door as he went. He headed to his bedroom, to the oak chest of drawers holding his clothes, and took out a white cotton T-shirt and a pair of gray sweatpants. He didn't have any women's undies, but hopefully, she could make do with what she was already wearing...or go without them. The thought made his blood run a little hotter before he regained his composure.

He grabbed a clean towel from his ensuite bathroom and returned to the living room. She'd stayed by the weapons, although her expression had turned uneasy. Her gaze dropped to the items he was holding.

He held them out. "The clothes aren't high fashion, but they're clean."

She didn't take them. "That's very nice of you,

but—"

"If you stay in your wet clothes, you might catch a chill. You don't want that, do you?"

Molly shook her head. "That's the last thing I want."

"The bathroom is down the hall," he said, pointing. "On the left. There's a hairdryer in the cupboard under the sink if you need it."

"Okay. Thanks." She stepped out of her shoes and took the towel and clothes from him. Lucian waited until he heard the lock on the bathroom door engage then returned to his bedroom, stripped out of his wet garments, and dried off. He pulled on a fresh pair of black jeans and a hunter-green polo shirt and ran a comb through his hair before heading to the kitchen. As he passed the bathroom door, the hairdryer switched on, its high-pitched hum competing with the noise of the storm still raging outside.

"What's the plan tonight, Lucian?" Galahad asked from the leather chair, where he'd been washing his ruff. "Tell me before she turns off the hairdryer."

"Same plan as before: Get close to her to find out what holds the dark magic."

"When you say close…?"

"I mean, get her to—"

"Lock lips with you? Then carry her off to your bedroom?"

Enticing thoughts. Clearing his throat, Lucian opened the fridge and looked over the assortment of food and beverages. "I was going to say, for now, continue to win her trust."

The squire growled. "How totally lame."

Lucian got a lemon out of the crisper drawer, closed the fridge, and met the feline's gaze. "I think you mean sensible."

"Sensible? Must I remind you that in the store, you threatened to go all medieval on her? Also, you were once a bad-ass who wooed ladies all over England. So, yeah, for you, the plan's lame."

Lucian sighed, for it was tough to compete with the legend he'd once been. "I threatened to go all medieval on her in order to protect her, since she seemed determined to put herself in danger. Thankfully my threat worked."

"This time," Galahad said dryly. "Next time? Probably not."

"Well, she's here now, and she won't be leaving until I allow it. I have many hours to work on her trust."

"You'd better succeed. Julius's orders…"

Lucian took a knife from the block on the kitchen counter. "Regardless of what he's ordered me to do, I'm not going to treat Molly as though I'm a noble lord and she's a common wench to do with as I please."

The cat smirked. "That could be one of her bedroom fantasies."

"Galahad!"

"What? I'm just trying to help. You said before you were thinking about seducing her."

"That's still an option. But, given a choice, I'd rather have her trusting and willing."

Mischief lit the squire's eyes. "Do I get to be a bad kitty now? Please?"

"No," Lucian said firmly.

"But—"

"Thanks, but I can handle the situation myself."

"Fine, but if I were you…."

The squire was clearly going to give advice whether Lucian wanted it or not. Shaking his head, Lucian set the knife and lemon on a cutting board and switched on the kettle.

"I'd make her a Hot Toddy," Galahad said.

"Already ahead of you on that." Lucian went to the liquor cabinet for his grandfather's bottle of whiskey.

"Make it stronger than usual. Be sure to tell her the drink will help warm her up and make her feel better. Then sit beside her on the sofa. Show her what you found on your grandfather's computer while easing closer, little by little."

Lucian snorted and cut the lemon in half. "Molly's going to notice if I move closer."

"Probably, but you'll already have won her over with your wit and charm. The whiskey will have kicked in, and she'll be relaxed and begging for you to take her in your arms and kiss her."

Lucian shook his head. "You think you've got it all figured out."

"It's a great plan. Admit it."

"It's a plan," Lucian said with care. "However—"

The humming noise of the hairdryer stopped.

"Get ready," Galahad said. "She'll be heading our way."

Molly set the dryer down on the bathroom

counter and ran her comb through her hair. She felt a whole lot better than she had ten minutes ago. After a quick shower to help her warm up, she'd dried her bra and panties as well as her hair with the dryer. While Lucian's T-shirt and sweatpants were too large for her smaller frame, they were soft against her skin and very comfy.

She wouldn't be wearing his clothes for long, though. As soon as the storm eased up, she'd be driving home.

Molly hung the towel and her wet clothes over the shower curtain rail, stowed the dryer back in the cupboard, and picked up her purse. When she stepped into the hallway, she saw Lucian standing in the kitchen. He'd changed his clothes in the time she'd been in the bathroom, but his hair still looked tousled.

"Feel better?" he asked.

"Much." She padded barefoot across the hardwood floor to the kitchen. Lucian had put the kettle on to boil, and an open bottle of whiskey sat beside two mugs on the gleaming granite counter.

Lucian's gaze wandered over her. "I like seeing you in my clothes."

She smiled, unable to tamp down her delight. "They're so comfortable, I might not give them back."

He whistled. "You're going to steal them? After I heroically rescued you tonight?"

Chuckling, she leaned back against the island opposite him. "Geez, you do get kind of dramatic."

"I *did* rescue you—" The lights dimmed then flickered. "Damn, I do hope we don't lose power."

"Has it gone out before during storms?"

"Yeah." The boiling kettle shut off, and Lucian poured water into the mugs. "This building has older wiring that can be unreliable." He handed her a mug. "We do have candles and flashlights, though, just in case."

Thunder crashed overhead, swiftly followed by flashes of lightning. As she wondered how long she'd be staying at Lucian's apartment, the drink's spicy scent wafted up to her. "Smells good. What is it?"

"A Hot Toddy."

"Yum."

"Are you hungry? I can fix some soup or heat up some of the stroganoff Cora brought me."

"I'm fine. Thanks, though."

Lucian gestured to the sofa. "Let's sit down, shall we?"

She crossed to the sofa and sank down onto the buttery leather. Lucian's grandfather obviously had expensive taste. Her mom's faded, sagging upholstered suite was pretty sad compared to these furnishings.

Lucian brought over his laptop bag and set it on the coffee table, along with his drink. He took out his computer and switched it on. Galahad, curled up on the nearby chair, watched them and purred.

After putting her purse down by the nearest table leg, she sipped the Hot Toddy. The blended flavors of whiskey, honey, and lemon warmed her tongue. The drink was delicious, but Lucian had been generous with the liquor. She didn't want to get tipsy. That wouldn't be clever. While Lucian seemed to be an honorable guy, she didn't know him all that well.

Also, once the storm had died down, she'd need to head home, and she didn't drink and drive. She'd just have to down the Hot Toddy slowly and, if necessary, not finish it.

If the clock in the entertainment unit was

correct, the paranormal society meeting had been scheduled to start a few minutes ago. "I hope I'll still get a chance to talk to Cora and the others about my mom."

"Don't worry. I'll make sure you do," Lucian said. "I have Cora's dish, which she wants back."

As he clicked open files on his laptop, she studied his profile: strong brow, chiseled cheekbone, unruly beard as dark as his hair. She didn't usually care for facial hair on men, but Lucian's enhanced his roguishness.

Her fingers tightened on the mug. What would it be like to love him and to be loved by him in return? Loneliness tugged at her, because she missed being in a relationship and being cherished by a partner. A different, keener ache stirred as well, one that reminded her of how feminine and powerful she felt wearing the antique necklace. How she missed kissing, touching, sex—

Galahad was staring at her; the same intense, knowing look that had unnerved her before. Her face heated, because he couldn't possibly know her thoughts, but still….

Thunder exploded outside. She jumped, sloshing her drink onto the sofa.

"Oh, no! I'm so sorry."

"It's okay." Lucian squeezed her arm. "I'll get some paper towel."

"I'll get it." Molly set down her drink and rose, even as the lights dimmed and flickered. "I'm guessing it's in the kitchen?" She started across the room.

"Yes, it's—"

A sizzling boom outside.

The room went black.

The room plunged into darkness, apart from the glow from the laptop screen.

"This night just gets better and better," Galahad drawled.

Molly sucked in a sharp breath. "Lucian—"

He stood, concern churning within him. She could get hurt trying to make her way to the kitchen. "Stay where you are, okay?"

"Yes."

Lucian recognized the thud of Galahad jumping down from the chair as he switched on his cell phone flashlight. Molly's eyes looked huge and round in the shadowy darkness.

"Take my hand," he said. "Come sit back down."

Her fingers slid into his. "We need to get paper towel first. I'll never forgive myself if I damage the sofa."

"Okay." He'd also seen regular flashlights in one of the kitchen drawers. He guided her to the kitchen and retrieved the flashlights. "One for you, and one for me." He handed her the larger one and several sheets of paper towel.

Molly switched on her flashlight and headed back to the sofa, while he retrieved his grandfather's box of candles and matches. As he returned to the living room, his flashlight shined on her, bent at the waist and swabbing at the leather. The cotton sweatpants stretched snugly over her rear: one of the most shapely bottoms he'd ever seen.

Lucian halted, his throat going dry.

"Kitty, you're getting in the way," Molly said.

The flick of the feline's tail alerted Lucian that the squire was on the sofa beside Molly and batting at the paper towel.

"Galahad," Lucian said sternly.

"Hey, if I'm lucky, she'll pet me or pick me up." The squire flopped onto his side to show his fluffy belly and swatted at her hand.

"You are cheeky tonight," Molly cooed, stroking the cat.

"Every day, babe." Galahad purred.

Confident Molly would move the feline if he became too much of a nuisance, Lucian put the box on the coffee table and set up some candles, their flickering golden light softening the room's shadows. After throwing away the paper towel, Molly came back to the sofa. Lucian sat and nudged Galahad out of the way so she could sit again.

"Yeah, I know. Three's a crowd." Galahad jumped to the floor.

"He does like to talk." Molly moved to sit down. "He'd get along well with my mother's cats— Oh!"

Galahad yowled and tore across the living room.

Molly dropped her flashlight, wobbled and then careened sideways.

Lucian's heart lurched. She was falling toward him.

On instinct, he reached to catch her. His arms slid around her, and as she fell, he guided her down into his lap.

Lying on her back, she blinked hard and stared

up at him, her head supported by his left arm. Candlelight shimmered on her hair spilling around her.

So lovely.

"Are you all right?" Lucian asked, his voice a husky rasp.

She nodded. "Galahad—?"

"He's fine."

"I think I stepped on him again," she said.

"Nah, she didn't," the squire said from over by the kitchen. "Things weren't moving fast enough, Lucian, so I helped you out."

Lucian clenched his jaw. Later, he'd reprimand the squire for such a risky and reckless plan.

But for now....

"Really, Galahad's fine." Lucian gazed down at her and unable to resist, he stroked her cheek with the backs of his fingers. He loved the softness of her skin against his.

Her lips parted on a quick breath. Her cheeks were flushed, either from the excitement of her near fall or the effects of the Hot Toddy. He stroked again, savoring the heat of her skin. Her lashes fluttered.

"Lucian—"

"Mmm?"

"I...."

The leather of the sofa creaked as he leaned down and pressed his lips to hers.

Sensation whipped through him: the whiskey taste of her mouth; the citrusy hint of her perfume; the silkiness of her hair against his wrist. One kiss wouldn't be anywhere near enough.

Her mouth opened beneath his, accepting his sensual invitation and responding in kind. He groaned, the sound rough with hunger. When their tongues brushed, his whole body ached with the need to touch and taste her.

Her hand sank into his hair and her nails lightly grazed his scalp, causing a sensual chill to ripple through him. As she pulled him even closer, the voice of reason intruded, warning him to slow things down. But, she moaned against his lips and kissed him deeper, tempting him to return her kisses with equal passion.

Hunger roared within him.

He wanted her.

He wanted all that she offered and that they could share together, here and now.

Reason gnawed, for while Molly seemed willing, she'd also downed the alcoholic drink he'd made for her. She might claim he'd made her the beverage to wear down her inhibitions and have his way with her.

A bitter taste gathered in his mouth, for he'd never dishonored a woman in such a manner. He'd not start now.

With a low groan, he broke the kiss.

Molly stilled, her mind muzzy and floating with pleasure.

Lucian had stopped kissing her.

No. *No!*

Disappointment settled within her. He'd straightened away, his features still taut with desire. But, as he stared down at her still lying in his lap, reticence shone in his eyes.

The exquisite anticipation that had hummed in between them had vanished.

No!

She wanted more. *Needed* more. She burned for him; yearned to finish what he'd kindled with his phenomenal kiss.

Never had she experienced such desire before. The intensity had shocked her, but even as she'd thought to stop the kiss herself, part of her had resisted.

Then, some kind of internal switch had flicked on. Her hunger had flared hotter, and with a helpless moan, she'd had no choice but to give in to it.

Is that why Lucian had drawn away? Had he realized she'd lost control and decided things were moving too fast?

Maybe they had been, but they were both adults...although she'd never had a one-night stand in her life. Now that she was thinking more clearly, she had to wonder how she'd forsaken common sense so fast.

Then again, she *had* been drinking; her lightheadedness was likely due to the alcohol. Was it possible Lucian had made the Hot Toddy strong to get her drunk? But, if he'd intended to take advantage of her, he wouldn't have stopped kissing her. He wouldn't be eyeing her with a guarded expression now.

Geez, she didn't know what to think.

Bracing her hand on the coffee table, Molly pushed herself up and off his lap to sit next to him. Tucking her legs up under her, she asked, "You okay?"

"I shouldn't have kissed you."

Her stomach knotted at the censure in his voice. Regret wove through her, because while the kiss had been impulsive, it had been wonderful—and she'd thought he'd been enjoying it as well.

"Wait." Sighing, Lucian pinched the bridge of his nose. "Let me try this again. I don't regret kissing you. I mean, for first kisses, what we just shared was pretty amazing."

"Yes," she murmured.

He gestured to her half-finished drink. "I don't want you to think, well, that I brought you to my apartment and made you that drink so I could seduce you."

She averted her gaze, because her thoughts *had* gone in that direction.

"I wouldn't do that. You have my solemn vow that I'm a man of honor."

Man of honor. Solemn vow. Such quaint, outdated phrases.

"I would never disrespect you or any other woman in that way, Molly."

"Good," she said, lowering her hand to settle over his. "And thank you. It's sweet that you're making sure I know that about you."

His gaze locked with hers. "Sweet?"

Maybe that hadn't been the right choice of word.

"I didn't tell you to be kind," he said evenly, "but because I want only the truth between us."

Her pulse fluttered. His words reinforced what she'd believed about him from their first meeting: that he was a good person. A man of integrity, unlike Howard.

"I want you to know you can trust me. Always. With anything."

"I want you to know," she countered, "that I

don't normally go to a guy's apartment and kiss him—not until I get to know him a little better than I know you." Heat burned her face. "Tonight, I...."

"You?" he coaxed.

"I'm not sure what came over me. I'm guessing the liquor is partly responsible."

"Since this is my apartment, I'd say the responsibility for tonight is entirely mine." He looked down at their joined hands. "Speaking of responsibilities, I should check on the store. Will you be okay here by yourself?"

Her disappointment drove deeper, but she managed a smile. "Sure."

"I shouldn't be long. Galahad will cry at the door until I return, so I'll take him with me."

"Okay."

He stared at her for a long moment then lifted his hand, raising hers along as well. Bringing her fingers close to his lips, he kissed her knuckles.

In one of the historical romance novels she'd read after her break-up with Howard, the hero had kissed the back of the heroine's hand not just to show his interest, but his determination to claim her. A tremor raced through Molly, because she had to wonder about the meaning of Lucian's kiss.

"I'll be back as soon as I can," he said, rising. "Help yourself if you'd like something to eat."

"Why did you stop kissing her?" Galahad demanded, as soon as they were out of the apartment.

Raising his hand, Lucian added to his earlier spell. Silver light glimmered around the doorway, along with hallmarks identifying him as the sorcerer who'd cast the enchantment, before the illumination became invisible.

Carrying his laptop bag, Lucian hurried to the stairs. "You know why I stopped. You heard our conversation."

"I heard it, but I don't understand why you didn't act on the kiss. She seemed willing."

"As I explained, the situation wasn't right."

"Is that Lucian speak for 'she didn't turn me on?'"

"Hell, no," Lucian muttered. When he'd kissed Molly, his jeans had grown so tight at the zipper, he'd wanted to tear them off, but the situation hadn't been right for that, either. While he hadn't mentioned his arousal to Molly, it had been a good reason for him to go to the shop and get himself under control.

"Let me get this straight. Because of your qualms—knightly honor and all—you're walking around unsatisfied and as grouchy as a bull with a toothache."

Pretty much.

Outside, twilight had fallen. Rain still fell in heavy sheets, but the thunder was less frequent and sounded farther away.

Lucian approached the rear door of the store. "I did what I thought was best."

"Yeah, well, let's hope she's still in the apartment when we get back."

"She will be. I cast a sleeping spell on her and strengthened the magical locks."

Lucian entered the shop. The storm had riled

up some of the dark magic collection. A cacophony of sounds greeted them: wailing, clicking, and thumping.

Galahad pressed his ears back. "Can you put a sleeping spell on me? Wake me when it's quiet?"

"You have a job to do. Go check the store."

"Aye, my lord," the cat grumbled as he darted across the shadowy interior. The shop wasn't usually dark in the evening, but the street lamps weren't working.

Lucian put his laptop bag in the storage room then using his flashlight, headed to the shelves holding the dark energy items. Among the antiques affected by the storm, the Lady of the Plate was moaning; a sound of agony. The scarab's wings flicked every few seconds. Judging by the intermittent *tap,* the finger of the murdered trapeze artist was moving in its box.

Lucian closed his eyes, focused his energy into a calming spell, and the noise-level in the store diminished. While the instruments in the storage room were quiet, and he hadn't received any alerts on his phone, he hooked up his laptop and reviewed the readings for the past couple of hours. No trace of the ancient magic.

How puzzling.

The storm would have provided the perfect conditions to empower the anomaly, but it hadn't appeared. Why not?

Lucian tugged at his beard. What piece of the magical puzzle was he overlooking?

"No problems in the store," Galahad called from the main room.

"Good."

As Lucian went to join the squire, headlights cut through the rain outside. A vehicle drove slowly down Whiskers Road.

"No one should be driving in these conditions," Lucian muttered.

The same instant, he experienced an odd feeling: like ants crawling across the back of his neck.

A Dealer was nearby.

A gray SUV came into view, slowed, then parked outside the shop.

The feline growled. "I have a bad feeling."

"Me too." Foreboding rooting in his gut, Lucian reinforced the protective spells on the shop and cast enchantments to disguise his and Galahad's physical presence. He moved backward, making sure he had a clear path to the storage room.

"Hide," he said to the cat.

"But, your spells—"

"Until we know what the Dealer's doing here, we'll play it safe. Those are the rules."

Growling again, Galahad hid under a chest of drawers.

Lucian stopped beside a tall wardrobe. Anticipation hummed in his blood. Motionless and silent in the quiet store, he was acutely aware of the sweat dampening his palms and the whisper of air as he breathed through his mouth.

He didn't take his eyes off the SUV, while he mentally analyzed what might happen in the next few moments. He couldn't use his magic to attack—not unless the Dealer struck first, there was no other way to spare innocents, or the situation was life-and-death critical. While he didn't agree with all of The Experts' rules, he'd sworn an oath to obey them, and so he would.

A man pulling up the hood of his raincoat got

out of the SUV. Lightning flickered. In its light, Lucian saw the vehicle bore no markings. The Dealer obviously hoped to appear to be a tourist or town resident.

While training with Julius in his teens, Lucian had learned that once, there'd been only one omniscient organization: The Experts. After a disagreement in the time of the Ancient Egyptians, The Dealers had split off on their own. While The Experts strove to protect humankind from dark magic, The Dealers used it to manipulate people and events. Their ultimate goal: to become Gods of a world they'd enslaved.

During the reign of the Pharaohs, The Experts had been associated with the symbol of the ankh. When The Dealers had formed their own organization, they'd claimed the serpent, especially the cobra, as their symbol. The Experts had adopted a key.

Through the centuries, The Dealers' influence had pervaded many societies around the globe. That meant not every instance of the serpent—in tattoos, jewelry, logos, and more—identified a Dealer. But, Dealers's serpents were always visible, symbolically representing the role of choice in corrupt magic: not just the choice of The Dealer who used it but those who yielded to it.

The man hurried through the rain to the front of the antique shop. He had something in his hand: A phone? That's what it appeared to be. He seemed to be scrolling, as though looking for specific information on the internet.

The man's gaze, though, kept darting into the store.

As the hood slipped back a bit, Lucian

committed to memory the guy's features: buzz-cut blond hair, rounded face, thin mouth.

The Dealer set his left hand to the glass and peered in. He looked right at the shelves of dark magic objects, and as he did, Lucian saw the cobra tattooed on his inner wrist, previously hidden by the raincoat's cuff.

The Dealer's phone—the magic-tracking device it really was—must have picked up the special collection. Knowing the downtown streets would be deserted, had he come to break in and steal some of the corrupted antiques?

He'd have detected the protections around the building that bore the hallmarks of William Lord, Lucian, and The Experts. Robbing the shop would be extremely risky and, quite frankly, stupid.

Unless....

Unless he hadn't come for antiques, but for something else.

*Some*one else.

Lucian's blood ran cold.

Since the Dealers had their own state-of-the-art detectors, they'd also know of the dark magic in Molly's late mother's home. Lucian thought of her asleep in the apartment. The spells he'd cast were strong, but he hadn't expected a Dealer, and there could be more than one.

He had to get back to the apartment.

The man straightened away from the window, slipped the phone inside his raincoat, and returned to his vehicle. Moments later, the SUV eased onto the road and disappeared into the darkness.

Galahad padded toward Lucian. "What did he want?"

"Molly, I think." Lucian sprinted to the storage room and retrieved his laptop.

"Molly?" the squire echoed.

"Later," Lucian snapped. "Come on."

The cat bounding ahead of him, Lucian exited the store. He scanned the parking lot for the SUV—the driver could have pulled around to the back of the building—but the vehicle wasn't there. However, the Dealer could have parked a block down and returned on foot.

Resolve tightened the knot in Lucian's belly as he raced to the apartment. The spells he'd placed were still in force. Still, he wouldn't be able to relax until he saw for himself that Molly was safe.

He entered the dark apartment. The air seemed close, stuffy, with the air-conditioning not running.

Crossing to the sofa, Lucian looked over the back. Molly lay on her side, eyes closed, her cheek resting on her slightly curled hand and her head pillowed by a decorative cushion. She even looked beautiful when sleeping.

He exhaled a harsh breath. "She's fine."

"For the moment."

"I will not let her get hurt. I swear—"

"Then you know what you have to do tomorrow, regardless of any qualms," Galahad said.

Yes. Tomorrow, without fail, he'd find the anomaly. Whatever it took, he'd get into her late mother's house and find it, for her sake as well as his.

His gaze traveled over Molly again, lingering on the wisps of hair trailing over her cheek and her slightly parted lips. A renewed ache gathered in his chest. He was going to have to betray her trust, but for good reason. Still, it didn't make what he had to do any easier.

Lucian set aside his laptop bag and once again, reinforced the spells on the apartment. Then he went to the linen closet and fetched a cotton blanket which he spread over Molly. She sighed, but didn't wake.

Galahad jumped up by Molly's feet. "I'll stay with her while you get some sleep."

"Thanks. First, I'm going to try and get a message to Julius."

"How, when there's no electricity? As far as I know, you don't have carrier pigeons. Birds aren't dumb enough to fly in this storm, anyway."

"Somewhere in the storage room, my grandfather has equipment to send Morse Code. I might try that." Lucian frowned. "I'll keep trying to send a text. Julius needs to know, if he doesn't already, that there are Dealers in Cat's Paw Cove."

Chapter Ten

Sizzling sounds and tantalizing smells coaxed Molly out of slumber. Eyes shut, her mind and body waking slowly, she savored the heavenly aromas: Brewing coffee, bacon—

Something soft brushed her mouth. The downiness was also purring. She opened her eyes to see golden fur—not the right color for one of her late mother's cats.

As the events of the previous evening came flooding back, she sat up, dislodging Galahad, who'd been curled up by her shoulder. A blanket fell away from her to land on the feline.

Lucian had covered her while she'd slept, and she'd been oblivious to him doing it. Normally she was a light sleeper. The Hot Toddy must have really knocked her out.

How sweet of him, though, to have made sure she was comfortable. Hopefully when he'd leaned over her to spread out the blanket, she hadn't been snoring, or even worse, drooling.

A scraping noise drew her gaze to the kitchen. Lucian stood at the stove, spatula in hand, while he watched whatever was cooking.

Her half-awake brain vaguely registered that for him to be able to use the appliance, the electricity had to be back on.

Lucian was half-naked. He wore dark gray pajama bottoms, but no top.

Oh, wow.

Her mouth went dry as her gaze skimmed over his impressive, sculpted back, down to where his waist disappeared under the waistband of his PJs. Her vivid imagination had teased her with an idea of how he'd look without a shirt; he'd resemble one of the muscular Highlanders or knights on the covers of her favorite romantic tales. But, what she'd imagined was nowhere near as awe-inspiring as seeing Lucian for real, his skin satiny and bronzed in the light streaming in through the kitchen windows, his honed muscles flexing when he moved.

How she wanted to trail her fingers over that gorgeous back—

Lucian glanced over his shoulder. "Good morning."

"Um…good morning," she managed to say.

She ran her fingers through her tangled hair then gave up. To try and make it presentable was a hopeless endeavor.

Lucian's attention returned to the stove. "Breakfast's almost ready. You hungry?"

"Starved." She stroked Galahad, now sitting in her lap. "Thanks for the blanket. I didn't expect to spend the night."

"Better that you did." Lucian didn't turn around. "I heard trucks driving by a while ago. Probably city crews checking for damage and clearing debris."

"What time did the power come back on?"

"Around three-thirty." He put sliced bread into the toaster. "Want butter on your toast?"

"Yes, please." She frowned. "I'm really surprised I didn't wake up when the electricity returned."

"You must have been tired."

"I wasn't, until right after you left. It was a bit strange. All of a sudden, I was exhausted. I lay down for a second, and that was it." She gently pushed Galahad aside and stood. "I'm being a terrible house guest. What can I do to help?"

"Get out the silverware? There are coffee mugs in the cupboard to my left."

She crossed to the kitchen, found the cutlery, and set two places on the kitchen table along with salt and pepper shakers and napkins. Then she got out white stoneware mugs decorated with the antique store's logo, into which she poured coffee.

She slid one mug down the counter toward Lucian. "Nice cups."

"They're a promo item my grandfather ordered a few Christmases ago. They were quite popular." Lucian gestured to the carton of half-and-half on the counter, letting her fix her coffee first. Chivalrous yet again. She murmured her thanks and, after getting her java to the salted caramel color she preferred, she leaned back against the counter and took a sip. Yummy.

And not just the coffee.

Lucian used tongs to take cooked bacon out of a pan and dry off the fat with paper towel then served up scrambled eggs and the toast. As he turned toward her, she glanced over what she hadn't been able to see before: his chest lightly dusted with dark hair, leading into six-pack abs that narrowed down—

She snapped her gaze back up before she could get herself into trouble.

Lucian handed her a plate.

"This is a feast. Thanks."

He smiled. "My pleasure."

"Do you like to cook?"

"I do, when I have the time."

She followed him to the table. "I know what you mean. Some days, when I get home from work, I'm too tired to make more than a salad for dinner."

"Where do you work?"

"I'm a teacher. Third grade."

"You enjoy teaching?" he asked, pulling out a chair for her.

Molly sat and waited until he'd taken his seat. "I do enjoy it," she said. "I love the kids. Most of them are hungry to learn. A few don't come from the greatest home situations, so it's hard for them to focus on their schoolwork."

Lucian nodded. "I expect you want to help them."

"I do. And I try. But there's a limit to what I can do."

He was silent a moment while eating a mouthful of eggs. "I have to admit, I was once one of those unhappy kids."

She paused, a piece of toast halfway to her mouth. "You were?"

His brows rose. "You're surprised?"

"Well, yes." He'd learned his chivalrous ways somewhere. "You seem well-raised, educated, highly intelligent—"

He grinned. "Go on."

Molly chuckled. "You like having your ego stroked?"

His stare sharpened a little and his smile turned sly. He seemed about to answer her question, but then shook his head.

"Why did you shake your head?"

"I was going to say something rude, but decided against it."

"You decided to be gallant, you mean."

"It seemed the wisest option."

"Wisest—?"

"For totally selfish reasons, I must admit."

She bit into the toast, and his gaze dropped to her mouth. When she licked butter from her lower lip, his eyes narrowed again and his Adam's apple moved with a hard swallow.

The way he was staring...like he'd wanted to lick the butter away himself. Her lower belly heated as she remembered his kiss.

"I liked kissing you yesterday," he said quietly. "If you become upset with me, I'm not likely to be able to kiss you again."

Her pulse jumped against her ribs at all that he'd revealed in those two sentences. He'd enjoyed kissing her. He hadn't found her kiss inadequate. "Lucian—"

"Before you say another word, I'd like to tell you something."

"Okay...."

"I don't talk about this much." He rested his knife and fork on the edge of his plate. "As I said earlier, I was a troublemaker at school. When I was twelve...." Anguish etched his features before he appeared to get his emotions under control.

"You don't have to tell me now," she said gently.

"I want you to know." He sipped his coffee then carefully set the mug down. "A few months after my twelfth birthday, my parents died."

"Oh, Lucian—"

"They were killed in a car accident in England."

"I'm sorry." She couldn't imagine the pain of losing both parents at such a young age and at the same time.

"My two younger brothers and I came to live with my grandfather. My siblings didn't like Florida and went back to England to live with my uncle." His mouth tilted at the corner. "I wanted to go with them, but my grandfather made me stay here."

She ate more of the delicious eggs. "Why?"

Lucian shrugged. "He saw potential in me, I guess, even though the last thing I wanted to do was learn. I was so torn up inside...."

"Did you go to counseling?"

"I did a few sessions, but didn't make much progress. I was too angry at the universe to want to talk about my feelings. My grandfather didn't make me go back. Instead, he made me work at the store after school and on weekends."

Molly nibbled on more toast. "You probably learned a lot about the business that way."

"I did." He chuckled. "Sometimes I got mad at him for insisting I come straight to the store after school, when my friends would go play football. One afternoon, in an act of rebellion, I didn't go to the shop. I went down to the boardwalk and hung out there, but

I was so emotionally messed up, I started sobbing. I thought about jumping into the water, even about letting myself drown, but then I felt a hand on my shoulder. I looked up and recognized one of the teachers from school." Lucian met Molly's gaze. "Your mom."

Molly's breath caught in her throat. "What happened?"

"She was on her way to her car after shopping at a boutique. She took one look at me, asked me to look after her purchase, and went to the ice cream shop. She returned with two gigantic waffle cones."

Molly laughed. "She loved ice cream."

"Strawberry was her favorite, I believe."

"Yes." Molly's eyes burned. During previous visits to the town, she'd had quite a few heart-to-heart talks with her mother over bowls of ice cream.

"That day, your mom and I ate our cones and watched the seagulls and waves," Lucian said. "She didn't push me to talk, just sat quietly beside me, and after a while, I started feeling better. She hugged me before she left and told me I could talk to her anytime. Just knowing she cared…. It meant a lot."

Molly smiled, because it had likely meant a lot to her mother to be able to comfort someone in need.

"She and I met at the boardwalk for ice cream five times," Lucian continued. "When we talked, it was about easy things, like our favorite books and shows on TV. As the days passed, my awful turmoil became more bearable. I always knew, though, that if I needed a friend, I could count on your mom."

"That's wonderful," Molly murmured. "Did you continue to keep in touch with her?"

Shaking his head, he picked up his fork. "A few

weeks later, I left town."

"Did you go back to England?"

"No. My grandfather ran out of patience with me. He enrolled me in a private training program."

"Oh."

"In Cat's Paw Cove, I'd been skipping classes. I got into fights. I broke into his liquor cabinet and got very drunk." Lucian's expression sobered as he finished a mouthful of eggs. "I didn't care about the antiques business, the store, or anything, really. I was out of control. Thankfully, my grandfather refused to let me ruin my life. He made a phone call and...I went to study with one of his associates."

"An antiques expert?" she asked.

"An expert, yes. I guess I'd describe him as a mentor."

Judging by Lucian's expression, the mentorship hadn't been easy. But, the tough program must have been what he'd needed, since he'd pursued a career in antiques and was on good enough terms with his grandfather to share his apartment and be in charge of his shop.

Lucian speared some bacon with his fork. "Back to your mother...." After eating the mouthful, he rose, the chair legs scraping back on the floor. "I can now show you what I intended to last night. If, of course, you're still interested?"

"I am." Molly finished the last of her scrambled eggs while he fetched his laptop. He pushed aside the salt and paper and set the computer where they could both see. "Now, let me just find them.... Ah. Here."

He pulled up a picture of an old pocket watch and link chain. Lucian opened another image: a snuff box.

"Why are you showing me these?" Molly asked, her curiosity growing.

"Your mother brought them to the store for evaluation some years ago." Lucian pulled up another photograph: six brass buttons that might have been cut off a garment. "My grandfather bought them from her. According to his notes, the items dated from the 1600s."

"Wow," Molly murmured.

"You mentioned before that your mother was researching your ancestors."

"Yes." Molly's pulse quickened. "These items could have belonged to my relative who arrived here on the Guinevere."

"Quite possibly," Lucian said.

"Did the items sell, or are they still in the store?"

"My grandfather sold them. Unfortunately, he didn't make a record of who purchased them."

She sighed. "That's too bad."

"I can give you copies of the pictures, though, if you'd like them."

"I would. Thanks." Molly grinned. "Maybe if I take the photos to a local fortune teller, she can tell me more about who owned the objects."

Misgiving touched Lucian's features. "Molly."

He didn't like the idea. Why not? Judging by what she recalled of their conversation at Devon Rex Desserts, he didn't believe in the paranormal. He likely thought the visit would be a waste of time and money. "I've never been to a fortune teller before," she said. "There are several in town. It might be fun."

"You'd trust what a fortune teller told you?"

Molly shrugged. "I guess it would depend what

she said."

Galahad padded into the kitchen, meowing. As Lucian reached down and scratched the cat's head, he said: "Fine. I'll get you the pictures today."

"Okay. Thanks—"

"I'll just have to figure out what to charge you."

"Charge me?" She ate her last bite of toast. "You mean for the ink and paper to print the pictures?"

He winked, and his gaze dropped to her mouth. "Just teasing. I won't ask you to pay for the printing."

"Well, that's nice of you, but why—?"

Lucian's arm nudged hers. "I want to kiss you again. If you owe me—"

"Don't I already owe you? I stayed overnight on your sofa and ate food from your fridge."

His eyes narrowed. "True. *And* I put your wet clothes in the dryer this morning. They should be done by now."

"Well, thank you."

When he looked at her in that predatory way, especially when he was half-naked, she could hardly breathe. Still, she managed to say, "Do you feel entitled to a kiss?"

"One kiss? No, not just *one*."

She laughed and swatted his arm.

"Ow."

Molly rolled her eyes. "That did *not* hurt."

"How do you know? You're not the one who got slapped—and on bare skin, too."

Molly made a disparaging sound, and Lucian chuckled. He loved the mischief in her expression. He shouldn't enjoy teasing her so much, but their lively banter had woken him better than the caffeine in his coffee.

As he held her gaze, uncertainty etched her face. She gathered her plate, mug, and silverware and stood. "That was very good, but I think I'm done with breakfast. How about you?"

"I'm finished eating." As he turned the laptop to face him and opened the email for Black Cat Antiquities, she carried their stacked dishes into the kitchen and started loading the dishwasher.

"Just leave them," Lucian said, skimming the messages. Two were queries from the website about appraisals. As he'd anticipated, there was an update from Julius. Lucian would read that email when she wasn't in the room.

At the sound of running water, he glanced at the kitchen. Molly had brought the pans to the sink.

"I'll do those later," he insisted.

"You made the meal. It's only fair I wash up."

"You're my guest."

"Yes, and because you've been so nice, I want to do my share."

Ah. "Does that mean you're hoping to be invited back to my apartment sometime?"

Molly smiled and bit down on her bottom lip. Heat swept through him, because he wanted to take her in his arms and kiss that gorgeous mouth. He'd make her wait a bit longer, though, before he kissed her again.

Water sloshed in the sink as she scrubbed a pan.

"If you really want to make things fair…."

"Yes?"

"You'll have dinner with me tonight."

Puzzlement entered her gaze.

"Is eight o'clock okay?"

She rinsed the pan, set it in the drying rack then shook her head.

"Is the time not convenient? Should we try earlier?"

"No, Lucian."

Frustration gnawed at him. "Do you have another commitment tonight?"

"My evening is free. At least, it *was*."

Bloody hell. "What——?"

"Don't get all grumpy." Mirth danced in her eyes again, and the tension within him eased a notch. "It seems to me that since you cooked me breakfast, it's only fair if I make you dinner."

Triumph burned in his gut.

"I see." He pretended to mull over what she'd said. With a sigh, she rinsed the last pan and put it in the drying rack.

"Lucian."

"Mmm?"

"Do you have plans for tonight?"

"Well, I was hoping to see this hot blonde I met recently."

Molly's face went pink.

"But, I think she's just claimed me for the evening."

She laughed. "You can't be talking about me. I'm not hot."

"I was, and you are."

"Hush."

"Nope."

"So are you available tonight?"

"For you?" he said. "Oh, yeah."

Tucking hair back behind her ear, Molly skirted the kitchen counter and approached the table. "I know you're working at the store, and I will be busy at my mom's house."

"Seven-thirty, then?"

She folded her arms. "How about seven?" When he nodded, she added, "If your offer still stands, I'd like you to evaluate a few things at the house."

Finally.

Lucian couldn't hold back a grin. "I'd be happy to."

"I'm coming with you tonight," Galahad said.

After tossing the clothes Molly had worn into the laundry room hamper, Lucian set his hands on his hips and studied the cat sitting a few yards away.

Molly had left a short while ago. Knowing he was going to see her again that evening had ignited a heady sense of anticipation within Lucian. If he kept his wits about him, he could accomplish a great many things that night—as well as enjoy his date with Molly. Because that's what her invitation was: a date.

Having the squire tag along? Not part of the plan.

Galahad's eyes gleamed in silent challenge.

"Bringing you with me isn't a good idea," Lucian said.

The feline's stare didn't waver. "You have no idea what you're going to find at the house. Also, a squire always accompanies his knight. That's the all-important rule. Remember?"

Lucian shut the laundry room door. "I remember. However—"

"Don't you dare. If you make tonight an exception and break your own damned code of honor, I will resign my post."

Lucian fought not to smile.

"I will run away, too."

Wincing, Lucian set his hand over his heart. "Ouch." The squire must really want to go to Molly's for him to raise not only the issue of honor, but to threaten to leave.

After more stony silence, Lucian sighed. "With respect, you can't resign. We're cursed to be together forever."

Galahad grumbled.

"Also, with respect, I'm the one in charge here. I decide—"

"Yeah, yeah. I'm fine with you managing my life most of the time. But, not tonight."

Such resolve hardened the squire's tone. Curious, Lucian asked, "Why is it so important that you come along?"

The feline's gaze flickered. "I just want to."

"No other reason?"

Galahad glanced down at his paws then back up at Lucian. "Fine. I like Molly."

"She *is* a nice person."

"I care about her. A *lot*."

"As do I," Lucian said, the truth of those three words resonating deep inside him. "I won't let anything bad happen to her."

"Me neither—especially after she and I slept together last night. *All* night long."

A ridiculous twinge of jealousy stirred. Lucian shoved it aside.

"I even gave Molly a good morning kiss on the mouth."

"Galahad!"

"So, I'm going with you," the squire said. "For Molly, if necessary, we will both kick ass."

Brave words, but Lucian had to wonder how, realistically, Galahad was going to kick anyone's ass when he didn't have feet, only paws. "Look, we have to be smart about tonight," he said. "It will seem odd if I turn up on her doorstep with you by my side. It's unusual. Molly might become suspicious."

The feline's tail twitched. "I'm sure we can think of a good explanation. Tell her I'm your therapy cat."

"Therapy for…?"

"Work-related anxiety."

Ah, the irony.

"Or, you could say I'm an adventurous cat that goes everywhere with you—like the ones we've seen on social media that climb rock formations and go hiking with their owners."

Lucian frowned. "I'm not sure—"

"Don't give me that look. If the dark magic flares up at Molly's house while you're there, I can help you. If the Dealer we saw yesterday happens to show up at her home tonight, I can help you. It's not only your duty to save a damsel in distress. It's mine too."

"True," Lucian said, "but we also swore oaths to be inconspicuous and intrude upon non-Magicals' lives as little as possible. Bringing you into the house might cause problems for Molly, since she shares it with her late mother's cats."

Galahad held up his right front paw. "I promise to be on my best behavior. No hissing. No fights. No stealing crunchies from their food bowls."

The squire sounded sincere, but Lucian shook his head. "That's not going to work. Unless…."

"Unless I don't go inside the house," the feline said.

"Right. You could keep watch outside."

The squire's demeanor brightened. "I'll be a spy cat. I might even cross paths with that special female kitty again."

Lucian nodded. "If the Dealer turns up, you can warn me and intercept him."

"What if you encounter the dark magic?"

"I'll open a door or window so you can get inside."

The feline's chin nudged higher. "We'll fight together."

"Together," Lucian agreed.

"I like our plan." Galahad purred and lazily stretched. "I'm going to have a nice long nap today, so I'll be ready for tonight."

Lucian ran his fingers through his hair, even as resolve coalesced in his mind. "I have something in mind for today, too."

Chapter Eleven

Molly drove through the green light at Sherwood Boulevard then turned left into the public lot opposite Sherwood House. After finding a parking spot with some shade, she switched off the engine and sat in silence while around her families unloaded from vehicles and tourists snapped selfies with the historic home in the background.

Sighing, Molly leaned forward to rest her forehead on the steering wheel. Why on earth had she invited Lucian to the house for dinner?

No point denying she had feelings for him. She enjoyed their flirty conversations and how he made her feel important and beautiful. When he looked at her with his smoldering gaze, her mind raced with imaginings of what could happen if she kissed him again. She'd want more than just a kiss. If her intuition was right, Lucian would, too.

She'd never been a casual fling kind of girl, though. A hopeless romantic, she could easily fall head-over-heels for Lucian.

Even as she'd silently reminded herself at

breakfast that she didn't want a relationship, she'd asked him to dinner—as if her mind and mouth were acting independently.

Crazy…but, she couldn't deny that at times in the past few days, she'd felt as though her thoughts hadn't entirely been her own.

Maybe all of the paranormal weirdness in the town had gotten under her skin.

Maybe she'd been possessed.

Molly snorted then straightened, pushing hair out of her eyes. More likely, she was exhausted from stress and grief. She'd feel better once she'd finished clearing out the house and it was on the market.

Having Lucian give her an in-home estimate of antiques she'd likely be selling was a step in that direction: A *necessary* step.

"Yes," she said aloud. Ignoring the puzzled gaze of the man who'd just gotten out of the truck parked beside her, Molly started her car's engine. Mentally putting together a list of what she'd need to cook dinner, she drove to the grocery store and did her shopping.

When she unlocked the front door to the house, all four cats greeted her with loud meows.

"Poor babies. You didn't get breakfast, and you're starving." After closing the door with her foot, Molly carried the bags of groceries to the kitchen. She fed the cats and put away the shopping then headed outside to check the house and yard for storm damage. Thankfully, apart from a few downed branches and shredded leaves, all seemed to be in good shape.

As she walked to the front porch to go back inside, a gray SUV stopped at the curb. She shielded her eyes to better see the magnetic sign on the side of the vehicle: Dennis Crow, Real Estate Agent.

A blond-haired man holding a stack of papers got out of the SUV. Even though the subdivision had a no-solicitation policy, she'd still found flyers for lawn cutting, tree-trimming, and other services tucked in the handle of the front door.

By now, local folks knew Molly intended to sell the home. If the real estate agent had come to leave a flyer for Molly in the hope that she might hire him, he was out of luck. She'd already chosen a realtor and didn't want to be drawn into a conversation with him.

Hoping Crow hadn't seen her, Molly hurried inside the house. When the front door shut at her back, she sighed in relief. If he came to the door, it would be a wasted trip, because she wasn't going to open it.

This afternoon, she'd planned to go through the kitchen cupboards. It was time to get to work.

Standing at his bathroom mirror, Lucian applied more hair gel with his fingers. He liked the shorter style the hairdresser at Claws-N-Coifs Salon had given him.

A short while ago, he'd also shaved off his beard. He hardly recognized his own reflection now. Getting rid of the facial hair, though, which he'd let grow from the day Stephanie had walked out, had felt a bit like a rite of passage; a fresh start.

Galahad, sitting on the counter, meowed. "Impressive."

"My hair gel skills?"

"The whole look. Molly's going to looooove it."

"Let's hope so." Lucian dried his hands on a towel and straightened his pale blue, button-down shirt, worn with his favorite dark-wash jeans. "Tonight we—"

His cell phone shrilled: The dark magic alarm.

Lucian grabbed his phone and read the incoming data. "It's almost a Category Three now."

"Three? *How?*"

"We need to get to Molly's."

"It's too early."

"I'll say I mixed up the time."

"Whatever. I'm ready to go." The squire jumped down from the counter.

Lucian headed to the living room. His keys were on the foyer table, next to the bottle of Cabernet Sauvignon and box of gourmet truffles he'd bought on his lunch break. Just as he reached to pick up the wine bottle, his phone rang.

Crap. He really didn't want to talk to Julius right now. But, The Expert would keep calling if he didn't pick up.

He answered. "Julius."

"The magic—"

"—is now a Category Three. I know. I was just heading out the door."

"Well, don't leave yet."

A muscle jumped in Lucian's cheek as he fought another growl.

"I have information to pass along to you," Julius said.

"Can it wait? I'm—"

"It'll only take a minute."

Struggling for patience, Lucian pulled out a

chair and sat at the kitchen table.

"It took some digging, but The Archivists found some very faint hallmarks. They managed to enhance one."

"And?"

"The magic's English."

A lot of ancient magic traced back to Lucian's home country. Since magic had existed there since the earliest days of mankind, English magic ranked with Ancient Egyptian as among the most dangerous.

Resting his elbow on the table, Lucian asked: "What era?"

"Sixteenth century, they think."

If Lucian's memory served him correctly, the first woman condemned for witchcraft in England had died in the mid-sixteenth century.

"But, we're still trying to make a final determination. The ancient power must be isolated and filtered out, which requires care. As I mentioned before, the data has been affected—altered, it seems—by modern contamination."

Lucian frowned. "Altered? How's that possible?"

"In very special circumstances, it can happen. There's a less than five-percent chance that's what we're dealing with, but The Archivists will work 24/7 until we have more answers. In the meantime, I'll contact some other Experts and send them to Cat's Paw Cove to assist you."

"No," Lucian gritted. "Not yet."

"You know the rules. It's protocol."

"I can still resolve the matter myself. If you send more Experts, the situation's going to get complicated." The last thing Lucian wanted was Molly getting pulled into the conflict between The Experts and The Dealers over a magical object she might know nothing about—not to mention the hassle of having colleagues underfoot.

"Look, after what happened in Boston—"

"Give me tonight," Lucian said. "Just another twelve hours. You can decide whether to send reinforcements after reading my report in the morning."

A pause. "All right. Let's hope you make headway this evening."

Lucian glanced at the time, relieved to see he wasn't due at Molly's house for another half-hour.

"I'll be in touch," Julius said then ended the call.

A short distance from their destination, Lucian stopped the Mini, leaned over, and shoved open the passenger side door.

Galahad leapt out onto the sidewalk.

"Be careful," Lucian said.

"Okay, *Dad.*"

"Dad?" Lucian snorted. "Don't get sidetracked. Go straight to Molly's."

"I will. Now, quit talking so I can go into spy cat mode."

The feline glanced to the left and right, snuck a short ways down the sidewalk then ran under a large bush. In his mind, was Galahad hearing the theme song of a secret agent movie?

Lucian shook his head then approached Molly's house. As he pulled into the driveway, he scanned the yard. All appeared perfectly normal, but that was an illusion. He'd muted his phone, but it was still receiving readings. The corrupt energy hadn't vanished this time, as it had done previously. He could sense its dark power inside the house.

After reinforcing the protective magical shield around himself, he got out of the Mini and retrieved the wine and chocolates as well as the sword he'd stowed in the car earlier. Since Molly had shown interest in his grandfather's blades, Lucian had brought a favorite from his collection to show her. He'd used the weapon in the past when battling dark magic. While he might not use the sword tonight, at least he had it at his disposal.

Lucian walked up to the front door, but as he raised his hand to knock, he saw a rolled sheet of paper pushed into the handle. He leaned the sword against the wall and took a quick look at the flyer. It advertised the services of a real estate agent; his business logo incorporated a cobra.

Damn.

If the Dealers had found Molly, why hadn't they already seized the object of dark magic? There had to be reason. Reining in his misgiving, Lucian shoved the paper into his pocket and knocked.

The door opened, releasing a waft of tantalizing smells, including sautéed garlic and simmering tomatoes.

With her hair curled back from her face, smoky eye makeup, and her curves accentuated by a figure-hugging black top and floaty skirt, Molly looked incredible—

The source of the corrupt power was *in front of him.*

Molly?

Oh, no. *No!*

She smiled. "Lucian."

He managed a smile in return. "Hi."

Lucian's gaze found her necklace. The jewelry oozed dark magic. The insidious power flowed like invisible smoke into the space between them.

He *had* to get the necklace, as soon as possible. But, he must be careful. The corrupt magic could injure or kill her or even destroy half of the neighborhood. That might explain why The Dealers hadn't acted: They'd avoid unwanted attention until they were prepared for it.

"Please, come in." Molly's high-heeled black sandals clicked as she stepped back, allowing him to enter.

He crossed the threshold. For now, like the Dealers, he'd be patient...until he could snatch the necklace from her.

"I come bearing gifts." He held up the items he'd brought. "I hope you like red wine and chocolate."

"I do. Those truffles are my favorites."

"Lucky guess on my part, then."

Molly shut the door and flipped the locks. Gesturing to the sword, she said, "Were you planning to hunt and slay our dinner?"

He chuckled. "No. I brought it to show you."

"It's one of yours?"

"Yes. I've had it a very long time." *If only she knew....*

"It looks old."

"It is. It was forged around eight hundred years ago."

"Eight *hundred*? Seriously?"

He nodded. "I can tell you more about its provenance over dinner."

"I'd like that."

So would he. Lucian's attention slid to her mouth; her lipstick was the crimson hue of Victorian garnets. "By the way, you look amazing tonight."

"Thanks. So do you. How about a drink?"

"Sounds good."

Molly motioned for him to follow her to the kitchen. As she walked, her flirty skirt swishing to and fro, two cats padded into the living room.

The gray tabby meowed.

"Who is *he*?" a woman said, her voice low-pitched and gravelly.

The ginger feline mewled.

"No idea," said another woman, who sounded younger than the first. "He's hot, though. Look how he fills out those jeans."

Lucian glanced about the living room crowded with stacked cardboard boxes, piles of books, magazines, and furniture. Who had just spoken? He didn't see any other people in the room, only cats.

"Hey, Molly?"

She glanced back at him.

"Is someone else in the house?"

"No, just us. Well, apart from Mom's cats." She motioned to the felines. "The gray one is Rose. The ginger is Marigold. I'm sure Petunia and Daisy will make an appearance soon."

The cats were directly between him and Molly now. If he didn't know better, he'd say they were assessing him, to see if they deemed him suitable for her. Their stares were very direct and aware...like Galahad's.

Shock raced through Lucian. Had he heard the cats talking? The only animal he'd ever been able to understand was Galahad, and their relationship was the result of unique, supernatural circumstances.

Galahad had met a kitty the other night who had talked, though....

The ginger feline meowed again. "Why would he ask if someone else is here?"

The gray cat's tail flicked. "How the hell would I know?"

"Could he have heard what we said?"

"Even if he did, he wouldn't understand us. He doesn't speak cat."

"Maybe he's different?" the other feline said, her tone conspiratorial.

Lucian resumed walking to the kitchen, where Molly was taking wine glasses out of a cupboard. No, he didn't speak the language of felines, so how could he understand Rose and Marigold? Had they somehow been affected by the magic of Molly's necklace?

Molly frowned at him and then the felines. "What is it with you, Lucian? No matter where you are, you get cats talking."

"Maybe they think I'm a hottie."

The orange cat's ears flattened.

Molly giggled. "Yeah, that must be it."

The gray cat growled. "He's definitely different."

"I told you he understands us." Marigold sighed. "I'm worried. This isn't right."

"Come on. Let's tell the others." The two

kitties scampered across the living room to an adjoining hallway.

Lucian set the red wine and chocolates on the nearest kitchen counter and leaned the sword against the wall, where it wouldn't be in the way. The kitchen, with its pale green tiles and older appliances, dated back several decades. A table with four chairs was set with a pair of green placemats, silverware, and a vase of pink roses that looked as though they'd been cut from the garden. A bottle of Cabernet Sauvignon sat open, breathing.

As Molly headed to the stove and snatched up a striped apron from the counter, she gestured to the wine on the table. "Since we're having beef, I opened red. I also have white chilled, though, if you prefer."

"Red's perfect. How about if I pour?"

"You would," said a woman's voice from across the room. "He plans to get her drunk."

"No!" Three meows sounded in unison.

Glancing in the direction of the meowing, Lucian saw four cats marching into the kitchen.

"Once Molly's plastered, he'll put his hand up her skirt."

"He'll take advantage of her, the bastard," another woman muttered.

Crossing to the table, Lucian struggled to stay calm. He did *not* appreciate what the cats had said about him. They'd attacked his honor, and he couldn't even defend himself against them—not without Molly thinking he was crazy.

The cats jumped onto a stack of cardboard boxes in the corner and lay down side by side, watching him.

"Look at that muscle ticking in his cheek," a

cat meowed.

"He knows *we* know what he's up to."

"We *are* just guessing. He might be a perfectly decent guy."

"He might. Or...."

"Or?"

"What if he's up to something else?" Rose's eyes narrowed. "If he can understand us, he may have magic."

"Girls! Hush." Molly stirred the steaming contents of a large pot. "Behave, or I'll put you out on the patio."

Cradling a stem glass in his fingers, Lucian poured some wine. "Maybe your cats are suspicious of people they don't know."

"That could be. One of my friends in Seattle has a Siamese that hides every time she has company." Molly raised the wooden spoon to her mouth to taste the sauce. When she licked her bottom lip, desire burned within Lucian. How he wanted to kiss her.

Obviously satisfied with the taste, Molly set down the spoon. Finished pouring the second glass of wine, Lucian handed it to her. Dark magic skated over his skin, and he fought not to shudder.

He raised his glass in a toast. "To a fabulous dinner."

"Cheers," Molly said before sipping her drink.

"He needs to leave," a cat groused.

"Shut up," another said. "If Molly puts us outside, we can't protect her. We already failed to—"

"If we force him to leave, we *are* protecting her."

"From him, but not that accursed necklace."

Ah. The cats knew about the corrupted magic.

Lucian downed a mouthful of his drink. Who knew what else he'd learn from the felines this evening?

Molly's skin tingled as she set down her stem glass. Lucian's gaze had dropped to the necklace again. How odd, when she'd been thinking of it at exactly that moment.

Truth be told, it had consumed her thoughts all day. As soon as she'd invited Lucian to dinner, she'd known she'd wear the necklace that night. Her whole body had grown warm with anticipation. While she'd sorted through the kitchen cupboards, her mind had kept straying to the jewelry and how much longer she had to wait before putting it on.

When it had been time to get dressed for dinner, she'd shut the cats out of her room and, finally, her skin still damp from her shower, had fastened the gold chain around her throat. As soon as the pendant had settled at the top her cleavage, a sigh had broken from her. It just felt so *good* to wear the necklace. It *belonged* there.

How and why did putting on a piece of jewelry evoke cause such feelings? Yet, even as she'd thought the questions, they were drowned by an addicting rush of desire.

Tonight, I'll make Lucian want me. He won't be able to resist.

She'd applied makeup in darker shades than she usually wore. Her outfit was bolder too, but she loved how the cross-over top put focus on the pendant.

The timer on the stove beeped. Drawn from her thoughts, Molly pulled on a quilted mitt, opened the oven door, and took out the foil-wrapped garlic bread. She pulled apart the edges of the foil to check the bread was heated through—unnecessary, since she knew it would be, but Lucian was leaning against the nearby counter, watching her.

"I couldn't help noticing your necklace," he said.

She closed up the foil. "Mmm?"

The cats were meowing again. Geez. What was going on with them?

Trying to steady her nerves, she stirred the sauce in the pot once more.

"I've never seen a pendant like the one you're wearing."

Panic flared. Why was Lucian interested in the necklace? Had he realized it was valuable? Was he going to try to convince her to sell it to him?

No. Lucian wasn't going to get the jewel.

It was *hers.*

Now.

Always.

Nudging her chin higher, she faced him. As his attention shifted to her mouth, desire stirred within her. Two steps, and she could press up against him, rise on tiptoes, kiss him—

"Where did you come by the necklace?"

Meow. Meow.

An inner cry of warning made her close her hand around the pendant. "I found it when going through my mother's dresser."

"The dresser that held the other jewelry you

brought to the shop?"

"Yes."

"The necklace wasn't mixed in with the other jewelry, though."

How had he known that? "No, it was in its own box."

His gaze flickered, as though she'd answered a question he hadn't yet asked. "What kind of box?"

Suspicion gnawed. Her protective hold on the jewel tightened. "Why so many questions?"

He smiled, but the mirth seemed forced. "I'm intrigued. Antiques are, after all, my specialty. If you'll indulge me? The box…?"

"Wood."

He didn't appear satisfied by her revelation; he sounded worried. "May I see it?"

Meow. Mrowrr.

A stronger flare of suspicion. "Maybe after dinner?"

He smiled, a roguish grin that made her stomach swoop. "Could I see the necklace too? It looks to be gold."

"I think it is."

"If I could see it close-up—"

Meow!

"Take it off, you mean? Hand it to you?"

"Yes—"

"*No!*" She couldn't explain the urgency of keeping the necklace from him. She just knew, instinctively, that he mustn't get hold of it—or its box. But, she could distract him with the thought that she'd concede another time. "I mean, would you ask me again later? Dinner's ready."

"Of course."

With a sigh of relief, she downed half of her wine in one swallow.

"You okay?" Lucian asked.

"I'm fine. It's just a bit warm in here. This kitchen isn't well ventilated."

Concern touched Lucian's expression. "What can I do? Turn down the air conditioning? I don't want you to suddenly pass out."

"No, no. That's not going to happen." She went to the sliding door off the kitchen. "Before we do anything else, I'm putting these cats outside. Go on, girls. Out!"

Lucian forked up more of the perfectly-cooked penne pasta smothered in a savory Bolognese. "This is an excellent meal."

Molly smiled.

He might have thoroughly enjoyed what he was eating, except that the necklace's magic taunted him from where she sat opposite him. Also, the unpleasant crawling-ants sensation had started at the back of his neck. A Dealer was nearby—perhaps the guy who had left the flyer on her door. He might not be alone.

Lucian's attention shifted to his sword. His warrior instincts urged him to grab it and draw it now. But, if he did that, he'd probably scare Molly, and he didn't want to give her a reason to end the evening early or call the police.

"I got the recipe for the sauce from one of my

colleagues," Molly was saying. "Her father's Italian, and.... What in the world?"

Following her shocked gaze, Lucian glanced over his shoulder. Twilight had fallen, but he could still make out the four female cats crouched at the opposite end of the screened patio. They stared intently at something in the yard: The Dealer?

Lucian's silverware clattered on his plate. He shot to his feet.

Molly startled, just as a golden cat jumped up against the screen then dropped back down to the ground.

Galahad.

Molly pushed her chair back. "I'd better go—"

"I'll go." Lucian strode to the patio door and opened it. She looked about to follow. "You've been busy today. Just stay there and relax, okay?"

"Okay." She frowned. "That ginger kitty looked like Gala—"

Lucian closed the door behind him.

The squire leapt at the screen again.

Rose growled. "If you don't leave *our* yard—"

"You gotta help me," Galahad wailed.

The gray tabby snorted. "Just because we understand you *doesn't* mean we have to listen to you."

"You should," Lucian said, reaching the four females.

Rose hissed. "The moron's joined us."

"Lucian," the squire gasped. "I tried to get your attention, but couldn't get *any* help."

Lucian met Rose's glare. "Just so you know, I also can understand everything you say. I don't intend to get Molly drunk. I'm not going to seduce her. I want to keep her safe."

"Why should we believe *you*?" Marigold said. "You want the necklace."

"Yes, to secure it."

"For all we know, you want the dark power for yourself."

Lucian clenched his hands. "My intentions are noble. I will gladly explain more later. Right now, Molly's in danger."

"Let us out of this enclosure—"

"No. Galahad and I will handle the threat. You keep Molly distracted."

"Bossy, isn't he?" Petunia groused, but to his relief, the felines didn't try to race out when he exited through a screen door into the yard.

He ran to the side of the house, Galahad at his heels.

"The Dealer," the squire said. "It's the guy who visited the shop yesterday."

Grass rustled underfoot. "Just him?" Lucian asked. "No others?"

"I only saw him."

When Lucian didn't immediately see The Dealer in the front yard, he continued on to the driveway. The blond man stood beside the Mini, toeing the right rear tire while taking on his cell phone.

Magic crackled to life in Lucian's palms. Even though he knew the man was the enemy, he must follow the centuries-old rules of confrontation.

"You," Lucian called. "Stop kicking my car."

The man glanced up. Recognition etched his features. Lucian hadn't ever been introduced to the guy, so The Dealer must have seen a photo of him, perhaps in a file he'd been given by his superiors.

The blond man swiftly raised his right hand. A

pulse of shrieking, black-colored energy shot toward Lucian. Not breaking his stride, Lucian thrust out his palm, blocked the magical bolt, and with a sideways swipe, diverted it. With a *thud-hiss*, the pulse hit an ornamental shrub. The stench of burning leaves wafted.

Scowling, the Dealer ended his call and shoved his cell into his back pocket. He raised his hand again, readying to fire another bolt.

Lucian halted. With a flick of his fingers, leaves, twigs, and dirt rose from the ground to form a barrier that surrounded him, Galahad, the Dealer, and the Mini. In the darkening twilight, the debris wouldn't be easily visible, but the blurring spell he'd added would keep people driving past or out walking their dogs from seeing the battle. The silencing spell would also muffle sounds.

"Lucian Lord," the Dealer drawled. "I was warned I'd run into you or your grandfather."

"I know why you're here, *Dennis Crow*. That's the name you're using at the moment, right?"

Crow smiled. "Why don't we make things easy for each other? Give me the dark magic object. Then I'll be on my way."

Lucian glowered. "Not a chance."

"I won't leave without it."

Lucian wondered how the Dealers were manipulating Crow: threatening to publicize a scandal from his past, perhaps, or hurt his children. Lucian would slay him if necessary; however, he also was honor bound to offer the opportunity to surrender. "Yield," he commanded.

"Nope."

"I won't offer mercy agai—"

Crow lifted his hand, another black pulse forming on his palm.

Light the color of chain mail armor flew from Lucian's fingers. The blast slammed into the Dealer's right shoulder. He cried out and staggered backward.

Black energy rushed toward Lucian. He dodged. The pulse screamed past the left side of his head.

A blur of movement snapped his attention to the Mini. Galahad was on the vehicle's roof and heading toward Crow. Lucian looked back at the blond man, lunged to avoid another strike. With a blast of silver magic, Lucian forced Crow to dart sideways, colliding with the Mini.

Galahad leapt onto the man's back and hung on by his claws.

Howling, Crow reached behind him to try and dislodge the feline.

Lucian raced forward. The blond man tried to fire another bolt, but Lucian locked his hand around the Dealer's throat. Crow choked. He tried to grab Lucian's arms, but Lucian tightened his grip until the Dealer stilled.

"How many Dealers are in Cat's Paw Cove?" Lucian growled.

Sweat beading on his forehead, his face scarlet, the man glared back, unyielding.

Lucian's hold tightened again. "How. Many—"

"You've already lost," Crow croaked. "Others are on the way."

"On the way? So you're a scout? Working alone?"

He heard the shriek of building energy.

"Don't," Lucian said through his teeth.

Crow's lip curled. As his hand aimed at Lucian's chest, Galahad scrambled higher, his claws sinking into the Dealer's shoulders.

Crow yelped. Lucian fired a shot of silvery light. The Dealer gasped as the energy slammed into his torso and immobilized him from head to toe. His eyes slid shut. Galahad jumped back onto the car as Crow collapsed on the ground.

"Ha! That showed him," the squire said.

"Julius will want to question him." After confiscating the Dealer's phone, Lucian took out his own cell and typed a quick text message.

Just as he hit send, he heard Molly's voice. "Lucian?"

He met Galahad's gaze. "She mustn't see you. Hide."

The cat leapt to the ground and darted under the car.

Lucian twitched his fingers, and the screen of leaves, twigs, and dirt fell silently to the ground.

"Lucian?" Molly said again. "Where are you?"

Chapter Twelve

Molly glanced around the yard again. As if the past five minutes couldn't get any stranger, Lucian had vanished. She didn't see his car, either. Had he driven away? That didn't seem likely, since his sword was still in her kitchen.

Confusion and disappointment tangled up inside her as she wiped her brow with her hand. While the sun would soon set, the humid air still held the day's heat. She'd wanted tonight to be uneventful, *normal*, so she could get to know Lucian better. Instead—

Her gaze landed on the ornamental bush's blackened leaves. Had it suddenly come down with some kind of leaf mold? She wasn't an expert on Florida plants, but the leaves appeared more burnt than diseased.

"Molly."

Startled, she glanced to her left, to see Lucian approaching. Then she inhaled sharply, because the Mini was parked in her driveway. She could have sworn the vehicle hadn't been there a second ago.

A man also lay on the ground. Twilight made it difficult to see, but he appeared to be unconscious. How had she missed him, too? Was she losing her mind?

She hurried to meet Lucian. His hair looked tousled, and a slight flush darkened his cheekbones. "What happened?" she asked, unable to hold back her shock.

"Everything's okay—"

"No, it's not. There's a guy lying in my driveway."

Lucian caught her arm and pulled her back toward the house. "You should go inside."

"Tell me what's going on."

"Trust me, it's better if you just do as I say."

No way. There was obviously more to the scene than he wanted to reveal to her, but this was *her* yard. "Is he hurt? Should I call 911?"

"He's going to be fine."

She struggled to ignore the way Lucian's touch made her feel restless and warm inside. If he wouldn't tell her what had transpired, she'd try a different approach. "He looks like the real estate agent I saw earlier today."

"Dennis Crow," Lucian confirmed.

"Why is he near your car? Did you two get into a fight?"

Lucian looked about to reply, but then a scraping sound drew her gaze to the driveway. Crow was pushing to his feet.

Lucian growled. He'd clearly expected Crow to remain unconscious.

Releasing her arm, Lucian stepped in front of her. He'd positioned himself between the blond man and her. Coldness pooled in the pit of her stomach. What did he think the real estate agent might do? Attack them?

Crow stood, brushing off his clothes.

His gaze met hers, and for some odd reason, she yearned to touch the necklace again. Even as she acknowledged the craving was different than what she'd experienced before—a colder, emptier longing— Crow glared at Lucian then ran down the driveway and was gone.

"I wonder…." she said aloud.

Lucian faced her. "What do you wonder?" He took her arm again and guided her toward the house. This time, she went with him.

"I think my mom's cats heard Crow. That's why they were acting so weird."

"Before dinner, you mean?"

"No, after you left the patio."

"Weird in what way?" Lucian asked.

"Well, I let them inside, and they went wild, racing through the house and up and over packing boxes. Rose even got on the kitchen counter and started knocking silverware onto the floor. She's never done that before."

Lucian chuckled.

"It wasn't funny."

"Rose is a pistol."

"How would you know?"

He smiled. "If I told you, I…. Well, let's just say she and I have a kind of understanding."

Molly mock-frowned at him as they started up the porch steps. "Not fair. You're going to have to tell me more."

His brows rose in challenge. "Am I?"

"Yep, if you want dessert."

Lucian washed down the last of his garlic bread with a sip of wine then sat back in his chair. "I could eat that meal every day."

Molly rested her head on her left hand. Her hair shimmered in the glow of the candles on the table between them. Thankfully, after escorting her inside, he'd managed to steer their conversation to cooking techniques and favorite restaurants, rather than on what had happened with Crow. "I'm just sorry I had to heat you up a second portion in the microwave," she said. "It never tastes the same reheated."

Shrugging, Lucian wiped his mouth with his napkin. "The microwaving didn't diminish the honor of dining in your realm, milady."

"My *realm*?" Molly rolled her eyes.

He grinned and gestured to his broadsword, still leaning against the wall. "I do have the right medieval weapon."

"You were going to show me your sword," she reminded him.

That was just too good to ignore. "I thought a bit of foreplay first was customary."

As he'd expected, she blushed. "Lucian!"

"I know. I may be a knight, but I'm also a bit of a knave."

She wagged a finger at him. "You're pretty bold to make assumptions about tonight."

His grin widened. "I'm pretty bold in general—

especially when I want something." Or some*one*. He didn't just want to get hold of the necklace. He couldn't get the memory of kissing her out of his mind. Even now, his blood hummed with awareness of her and the temptation she posed. He wouldn't leave her house tonight without kissing her again.

"I think you've had too much wine," she said in a teasing voice.

"Nah. I know my limit." Lucian picked up the half-empty bottle to pour more into her glass and then his.

Molly chuckled and her focus shifted past him to the patio. She'd put the four female cats outside again, and they lay near the sliding door, watching what was taking place in the kitchen. Lucian met Rose's hard stare; a warning that she was keeping an eye on him. Not much she could do, though, if he and Molly went into another room.

The clatter of dishes drew his attention back to Molly. She'd stacked his plate on hers and added their silverware before rising. "Would you like some coffee?"

"Sure. Thanks." He rose as well.

"I'm making decaf, by the way. In case you were afraid of being...awake all night."

From the mischief in her gaze, she'd meant the sexual innuendo.

He winked. "I don't mind being awake all night—"

"That's good to know."

"—although I didn't think you had *that* many antiques you needed me to appraise."

Molly laughed. "An all-night appraisal. Right, Lucian." Shaking her head, she set the plates by the sink and went to switch on the coffeemaker.

"Shall I load the dishwasher?"

"Don't worry about the dishes." She leaned back against the kitchen counter, her expression somber as she hugged herself. "Now will you tell me what happened outside? I would like to know."

Perhaps he could tell her just enough to appease her curiosity. In no way could he tell her the truth.

"Crow was in my yard. Why? What was he doing?"

Planning to steal your magical necklace.

"When I saw him," Lucian said, "he was talking on the phone while kicking my car."

She frowned. "Did he harbor a grudge? You'd obviously talked to him before."

"Not until tonight," Lucian said.

Puzzlement touched her expression. "But, you knew his name."

"I recognized him from real estate ads in the *Cat's Paw Cove Courier*. I confronted him, and he got belligerent. When he turned quickly to leave, he slipped on the gravel and fell. You found me soon afterward."

"Why was he on my property? I mean, he could have made his phone call anywhere."

"He mentioned flyers."

"Oh. I did see him with some earlier."

"He might have received a call from someone who'd seen the flyer. Maybe he'd heard you were going to sell this house and had gotten the call while on his way to speak with you."

Molly gnawed her bottom lip. "That makes sense."

Good.

"I wouldn't worry about Crow. With luck, he'll be too busy to visit you again."

She nodded, while the coffeemaker gurgled and steamed.

She still looked preoccupied, though—and Lucian couldn't resist a pang of jealousy that so much of her focus was on the Dealer.

Lucian crossed to her, set his hands on her upper arms, and gently rubbed, an offer of comfort. Sighing, she closed her eyes. Pleasure spread through Lucian, for he enjoyed touching her, longed to lean in and claim her lips. But, the necklace's corrupt power shifted and swirled between them like liquid poison seeking to find a chink in his protective armor and slip in.

Bloody hell, but the energy was insidious. *Ambitious*, even.

He'd heard stories of Experts who'd been corrupted by the objects they'd been sent to contain. No man was immune to dark magic, although Lucian had never encountered a power strong or complex enough to tempt him...until now.

He lifted his hands from Molly.

Her eyes opened. "How about dessert?" she murmured.

Both warning and desire shot through his veins.

"We'll move into the living room," she added. "It's more comfortable in there."

"Okay. I'll bring my sword."

"In case you have to defend my realm?" she asked coyly.

He chuckled. "Something like that. Can I help bring in the coffee and dessert?"

"You pour the coffee. I'll handle the dessert. Do you like Tiramisu?"

"Oh, yeah."

After serving up the java, he carried the mugs into the living room and set them on the coffee table then returned for his sword. As he laid the sheathed weapon across his lap, Molly walked in with two servings of dessert. "It's another recipe from my friend," she said as she sat beside him and set down the glass dishes. "Luckily, it has zero calories."

"I can't quite believe that."

Grinning, Molly said, "It's magic Tiramisu."

Lucian took a bite. As the mocha, chocolate, and mascarpone flavors melded on his tongue, he groaned. "That's *phenomenal.*"

"There's plenty more."

"Don't tempt me."

She brought a spoonful of the decadent dessert to her lips. As her mouth opened to take in the confection, he couldn't look away. He stared, captivated, while her lush lips closed around the spoon.

Desire roared within him. He wanted to haul her to him and devour the dessert's sweetness on her mouth; to claim her as his.

He could give her pleasure *and* get hold of the necklace...if he seduced her.

"So. My sword."

Molly giggled. The wicked voice in her head— the one that had urged her to tease him with her first bite of Tiramisu—wouldn't shut up. As she'd closed her lips around the spoon, she'd done as the voice had suggested and watched his gaze sharpen to a smolder and his breathing quicken.

Have another bite. Make Lucian wild for you, and he won't be able to resist you.

Even as the whisper goaded her on, another inner voice struggled to be heard. Molly was hardly a temptress. She'd never pursued a man in such a way before, so why did she think it was a good idea now?

You're not the woman you were months ago. You're single; ready for new challenges. Take a risk and seduce him.

She fought a shiver of anticipation.

A dull thud drew her attention back to Lucian. He'd set his dessert aside. With the hiss of metal against leather, he drew the sword from its scabbard. Light gleamed along the steel blade which he laid at an angle across his legs so the tip hovered over the coffee table.

"It's a beautiful weapon," Molly murmured.

"I think so, too." Pride warmed his tone.

"Has it been in your family since it was made?"

He nodded. "My ancestors wielded this sword in a great many skirmishes."

"In England, I'm guessing?"

"Many of the battles took place in England, but not all of them." As Lucian told her more of the history of the weapon, she finished her dessert. He was a talented storyteller. He really brought the past to life.

And his voice…. Rich, deep, and compelling, it caused goose bumps to rise on her arms. He'd make a wonderful audio book narrator of historical romances, although listening to his sexy voice might distract her so much she'd drive off the road.

"…and when my parents' estate was settled,

that's how it came to me." After turning the blade over to show her the other side, he returned it to the scabbard, so effortlessly, he'd obviously done that exact same movement countless times.

"You look pretty comfortable with that sword. Have you taken lessons?" she asked.

He propped it against the end of the sofa. "I've been told I have a natural talent."

"You really should have been born in the Middle Ages."

"I like being where I am right now."

A thrill raced through her.

"In fact," he rasped, "I consider myself *lucky* to be where I am right now."

Excitement raced through Molly, and their gazes locked. Held by his intense stare, she felt giddy, as though he'd chased her through a field and had caught up to her, and now intended to claim what was his.

Oh, how she wanted his kiss.

Don't give in yet. Tease him again. Make him crazy with lust.

As though aware of her thoughts, Lucian growled low in his throat.

The predatory sound made her eyelids flutter. Her hand closed around the necklace again, and she smiled, emboldened by the feel of the jewelry against her fingertips.

"You know, you seem different tonight," Lucian murmured.

"How so?"

"You're more...outgoing."

Was that his quaint word for provocative?

"Go on," she purred.

"Your eyes. They're brighter, somehow."

She winked, even as reason cried: *This isn't you, Molly.*

You're a more confident, sexier version of you now, the naughty voice countered.

"Your smile." With his right arm along the back of the sofa, Lucian leaned in closer. "It's more tempting."

"Is that so bad?" Where had that sultriness come from?

You.

Lightheadedness taunted Molly again, and she put her hand to her forehead, tried to mentally push aside the heaviness blanketing her mind.

"Molly."

She opened her eyes, knowing even before she did that Lucian had moved nearer. He smelled of a blend of lemon and spice. Her heart pounded, because all she had to do was lean forward and she could lose herself in kissing him.

Not yet. Torment him more, the inner voice urged.

No, this isn't you, the rational voice cried again.

"Molly," Lucian said.

"Mmm?" Was he going to be old-fashioned and ask permission to kiss her? That would be so Lucian. Another giggle welled in her throat, even as his fingers brushed her cheek, a touch so incredibly tender, she shuddered. His fingertips glided down to her jaw, under her chin, and as she inhaled on a rush of desire, he nudged her chin up. She had no choice but to look directly at him.

His brown eyes gleamed with suspicion, but also hunger.

You're the cause of that hunger. Enjoy your power over

him.

The voice of reason tried to speak up, but she ignored it and rubbed her cheek against his palm. His hand trembled slightly.

"Will you do something for me?" he asked softly.

"That depends."

Yes, keep tormenting him.

"Take off the necklace."

Do it, urged the rational voice.

"No," she said.

Wait. How had she answered 'no,' when she hadn't yet considered how to respond? But, her confusion was swiftly eliminated by a surge of desire.

"Take off the necklace, Molly," Lucian said again.

"Why?"

"As I mentioned earlier, I'd like to see it."

No. "I don't want it appraised. I'm keeping it."

"I'd still like to take a look at it. I can't when you're still wearing it."

Distract him. Use his hunger for you.

"Listen, if you take the necklace off—"

Pushing aside Lucian's hand under her chin, Molly shoved forward and crushed her mouth to his.

Chapter Thirteen

s Molly collided with Lucian and kissed him, his arms instinctively went around her. Momentum propelled him backward on the sofa. His head landed on a cushion.

His conscience reminded him she wasn't acting herself. But, his body eagerly responded to her hot mouth on his; her perfect breasts crushed against his chest; and her pelvis pressed to his groin.

He groaned. He'd secretly dreamed of having urgent, incredible sex with her. But to have her in his arms *for real*, kissing him like she wanted to tear off his clothes and be naked together, was almost more than he could stand.

She kissed him deeper. Her tongue delved into his mouth.

He groaned again.

Fire.

Every part of his being was aflame with hunger.

"Lucian," she moaned.

He struggled to think. As he fought for focus, he sensed the necklace between their bodies. The pendant touched his shirt. Dark power streamed over him; tried to break through his magic.

Molly kissed his jaw, his neck, his throat. "Come to my bedroom," she whispered against his skin.

"Molly—"

Her lips nibbled his. "I want you."

He definitely wanted her. Badly.

Did Molly really want him, though? Or was the corrupt energy manipulating her?

As though aware of his thoughts, she pushed up on her elbows on his chest. Her lower body shifted against his, and he shuddered at the delicious friction.

"Do you want me?" she asked, her voice throaty.

He loosened his hold on her waist. With both hands, he stroked her hair back from her face. "I do want you. Very much." But, there was only one sure way to know if Molly truly desired him: remove the necklace's influence.

He stroked her hair again. When she shut her eyes, clearly enjoying his caress, he continued, working his way lower each time. His fingers slid from the ends of her hair to her collarbone. If he could work his way inward, to the necklace's clasp....

Her eyes opened. Setting her hands flat on his torso, she started to move off him.

His hands settled at her waist again. "Don't move."

"Why not?"

"If you stay, you'll find out."

Her lips curved in a coy grin. "This is my house, so my rules. Let's go to—"

His hands slid up her ribcage. His thumbs grazed the undersides of her breasts.

Her lips parted on a gasp, and her head tipped back, her hair spilling about her shoulders. "You're not playing fair."

"I know." Triumph warmed him as he caressed her once more with his thumbs, and she gasped again. Dark magic from the necklace spilled over his hands.

Continuing his caresses, he shifted his hands higher, little by little, his thumbs grazing her beaded nipples through her top. A cry broke from her.

He dared to touch higher. When his fingertips brushed the satiny slopes of her shoulders, Molly opened her eyes and caught hold of his hands.

Had she guessed he was going to undo the necklace?

He held still, waiting for her next move. His breathing seemed loud to his own ears. Without a word, she slid off him, her skirt tumbling back down to her knees. She pulled him to his feet and linked her fingers through his. Their palms touched. Skin to skin....

He ached to caress her. He yearned to make her cry out with pleasure, to lose himself in their passionate lovemaking. He craved that a lot more than getting hold of the necklace.

No, his conscience said. *The dark magic is your priority.*

Even as he tried to rein in his desire, Molly pulled him down the shadowed hallway into a bedroom, lit by a lamp on the bedside table.

When she turned to him, her hair gilded by lamplight, he couldn't resist hauling her to him. He growled low, cupped her face in his hands, and kissed her hard. She leaned into him, matching him kiss for greedy kiss.

"Lucian...."

God, how he wanted her. Nudging her with his legs, he urged her backward toward the bed.

When the backs of her knees touched the mattress, she fisted her hand into the front of his shirt. She sat and scooted into the middle of the bed, while pulling him down with her. His body settled over hers; the perfect fit. Flushed and panting, she squirmed against him.

So beautiful.

Her eyelids fluttered. "Touch me," she whispered.

Get the necklace.

"How's this?" With a grin, Lucian trailed his fingers along her jaw.

Whimpering, she swatted his arm. "No."

Get the necklace.

"I'm burning," Molly pleaded.

"So am I." He kissed her. His fingers kept wandering, slowly, until they brushed the links of the chain around her neck. "Can we take this off? It'll get in the way, yes?"

Her eyes narrowed. Her lips parted, as though she was about to say no. Then she blinked and looked pained, as if she was refusing the urge to refuse.

Molly was fighting the dark magic.

Get the necklace! Now.

He tugged on the chain to bring the clasp into view.

"Stop," Molly snarled. She grabbed his wrist and dug in her nails. For barely a second, her gaze sparked—the same orange-yellow hue as fire.

What the hell...?

Lucian sent a pulse of magic, woven with a

sleeping spell, along the gold chain. Molly's eyelids drifted closed. Grabbing the clasp, he unfastened the necklace.

When his fingers closed around the jewel, its powerful energy whipped through his hand and up his arm. *Dear. God....*

He staggered away from the bed. The box. Where—?

His gaze landed on the dresser and the plain wooden box. That had to be it.

By sheer strength of will, Lucian crossed to the furnishing and dropped the necklace into the box. As he shoved on the lid, a vision flashed in his mind: A damsel screaming. A blazing fire. A woman chanting.

The lid closed. The images vanished.

What had he just seen? Anguish, horror, and remorse tangled up inside him. The overwhelming intensity of the emotions made him want to vomit.

His vision had to be linked to the necklace's evil magic. The scene, though, had felt intensely personal; as though he'd been there.

Had the magic accessed one of his past lives? Or had he experienced an event involving a previous owner of the necklace? Questions he couldn't answer, but must ask Julius.

Drawing in steadying breaths, he glanced at Molly. She lay asleep on the quilt, her lips slightly parted. She seemed all right, but was she?

Still fighting to recover from the ghastly vision, Lucian sat next to her. The mattress dipped at his weight, but she didn't stir. He gently raised her eyelids and checked her eyes, but they were their normal blue color. No sign of the fire-like spark.

He hadn't imagined it, but he also couldn't

explain it. He'd never seen anything like it.

At least he now had the necklace, and soon, it would be locked away forever. She'd be upset when she woke to discover that he'd left and taken the jewel, but he'd think of a reasonable explanation for his actions. He'd also ensure The Experts compensated her well for the necklace.

"I'm sorry for the sleeping spell," he said quietly. "I'll make tonight up to you, I promise."

Lucian rose and pocketed the box. If only he could be sure the dark magic hadn't hurt her—

A thudding noise reached him: the sound of paws pounding on glass.

"Luciaaaannnn." Rose's wail sounded distant. It would, though, since she was yelling through the patio door. How long had she been making that racket? She'd bring the neighbors over to check everything was okay, and Lucian would rather not have to deal with that awkward situation.

He hurried to the kitchen and opened the sliding door.

"Finally," Rose groused. The other three felines followed her inside.

"We wondered if we'd be out there all night," Petunia said.

"Without food, water, or even a litter box," Daisy added. "With our tiny bladders, that would have been *disastrous*."

"That's not the only thing we wondered." Marigold eyed him up and down. "You still have your clothes on. You don't look like you and Molly...um...."

"Because we didn't." Lucian locked the door.

Turning around, he found the four cats sitting

in a semi-circle, watching him.

"Why didn't you have sex?" Rose demanded.

Whoa. "That's none of your busin—"

Rose held up a paw. "Molly's like a daughter to us, so yes, it is our business."

"Maybe he was too stressed." Daisy's tone softened with sympathy. "Was that it, Lucian? Performance anxiety?"

"*No!*"

"What's that bulge in his front pocket?" Marigold asked. "It's obviously not, well, you know."

"It's the box." Rose growled. "He has the necklace."

No point trying to deny it. Lucian nodded.

Rose hissed, her hackles going up.

"As I told you before, it's my duty to secure the dark magic."

"How did you get the necklace from Molly?" The gray feline glanced about the kitchen. "Where is she now? Why isn't she here with you? Is she all right?"

He bristled at the accusation in Rose's tone. "Molly's fine. She's sleeping."

"Sleeping?" Marigold snorted. "Is that some kind of euphemism?"

"No—"

"She invites a hot guy like you for dinner and then goes to *sleep?* What woman in her right mind would skip sex to do that?"

"An exhausted one?" Daisy said helpfully. "She *has* been busy with the house."

"He used magic on her," Rose said flatly. "Didn't you, Lucian?"

Rose was now speaking to him as though he'd not only betrayed their beloved mistress, but had stolen every morsel of cat food in the house. He would not tolerate her insulting his integrity. "I did use magic," he said. "However, I only did what I deemed necessary. With respect, I *don't* have to explain—"

"You do," the feline cut in. "Your duty is important, but so is ours."

He should be in his car, driving to the antique shop by now. How tempted he was to turn on his heel and walk out, but his gut instincts told him she had information he needed to hear. "What's your duty, if I may ask?"

The four cats exchanged glances then nodded.

"We—the four of us—were born a very long time ago in Sherwood Forest in England," Rose said.

England, once again. Coincidence? Not likely. "I guessed you were Sherwood cats from your markings," Lucian said. "Some Sherwoods have magical abilities, right? Is that why when you talk, I can understand you?"

"There's a little more to our situation than that," Rose said. "Long ago, we were human."

"Women," Daisy added, "in case you were wondering."

No kidding.

"Yes, women," Rose continued, sounding impatient. "We were sisters by blood, and we were also witches. One day, a nobleman brought us a necklace he'd had made for his wife. He'd bought the gold from a peddler and had paid a jeweler to melt down the metal and create a necklace. But, the metal was cursed."

Lucian frowned. "What kind of curse?"

Marigold hissed. "An ancient one."

"A curse involving powerful evil magic." Rose sighed. "We created a special box and used spells to lock the necklace inside. But, when we tried to destroy the box, we were turned into cats."

"We still don't know how that happened," Petunia said.

"Or if we will ever be human again," Daisy added with a pitiful mewl.

"Then and there, we vowed to watch over the box and do our utmost to keep it from ever being opened. We were successful, too, until Molly found it and somehow got it open."

"We don't know how she managed that, either," Petunia yowled.

Rose shook her head. "I hope we'll find out one day. But, our vow to protect the box is how we ended up on the ship that sank near Cat's Paw Cove in the year 1645. The person who owned the box had decided to travel to the New World."

"That vessel was the Guinevere? The one that's now Shipwreck Museum?" Lucian asked.

"That's right," Marigold said.

Lucian's mind revived a past conversation. "Molly mentioned she had a relative on that ship."

"She did. We'd already guarded the box for hundreds of years before he inherited it, though."

"How many hundreds?" Lucian asked.

"Since the early Middle Ages."

He inhaled sharply.

"Ha! He didn't expect that," Petunia mewled.

"No, I didn't. I—well, the English knight I once was—was cursed by a sorceress in the late twelfth century."

"*What?*" Marigold and Petunia said.

Daisy gasped. "No!"

"Galahad may already have told you, but he

was my squire. When I was cursed, he transformed into a cat."

"Our situations are remarkably similar," Rose murmured. "How odd."

She was clearly still wary of him, although he could hardly blame her. However, he would like to start earning a bit of her trust. There might come a time when they must depend on one another.

"Do you think we were cursed by the same Magical?" asked Daisy.

"While it's possible, I'd say it's unlikely," Lucian answered. "According to The Experts, I killed the sorceress who put the curse on me and Galahad."

"Magic also isn't bound by death," Rose said. "As we cats have discussed before, the gold the nobleman had made into the necklace could have been cursed years or even centuries before. The curse lived on in the metal and, unfortunately, it retaliated when we tried to destroy it."

Daisy's ears flattened. "I suppose we're lucky we weren't turned into bugs—or horny toads."

"Horned toads," Petunia corrected.

With a low growl, Marigold rose to all four paws. "This is all very interesting, but Lucian still has the necklace *we* promised to guard."

"I haven't forgotten," Rose said with a predatory smile. "Luckily for him, he hasn't tried to leave."

As his gaze moved over the felines, Lucian uncurled his hands. The first stirrings of magic tingled in his palms. He didn't want to hurt the cats, but he had to fulfill his duty. "Look, I don't want to fight you."

"Give us back the necklace, then," Rose said.

"That, I can't do."

Rose and Marigold yowled.

"Oh, dear," Daisy meowed. "I hate catfights."

Petunia bared her fangs. "Can I bite him first?"

Lucian raised his hands, palms up. "I'm not your enemy. I, too, want to keep the dark magic from causing harm."

"So you've said. Why should we believe you?" Rose growled.

A reasonable question. "I'm not sure how to convince you, but I've told you the truth. I *have* to secure the necklace in my shop, as soon as possible."

Three of the cats stalked closer. He scrambled to think of a strategy that would keep the situation from disintegrating any further.

"You want what's best for Molly, right?" His gaze shifted from feline to feline.

Rose glowered. "What a ridiculous question!"

"Of course we do," Petunia said at the same time.

"Do you want Molly to wear the necklace again?" he asked. "Because you were protecting it before, and she managed to outwit you."

"Oh," Daisy mewled. "He's right."

"Shut up," Marigold muttered.

Daisy huffed. "I am not going to shut up."

"You're going to side with a stranger? A *man*?" Marigold said.

Daisy's furry chin nudged higher. "We need to look inward, be honest with ourselves—"

Marigold groaned. "Not that self-improvement crap again."

"—and admit we've done a rotten job of protecting Molly. We can't let her wear the necklace again. We just…can't."

Lucian heard dismay in the feline's voice. Warning tingled at the back of his skull. "What happens when she wears the necklace?" Had they also seen her eyes spark?

"No more questions. We've already told you more than we should have," Rose said firmly.

"The more information I can pass along to The Experts—"

"We don't serve them," the gray cat said from by Lucian's feet. "We're not going to get our Molly into any more trouble."

"I understand." Indeed, he did. The gray cat's reticence came from her love for Molly. Gentling his tone, he said: "You care about her. You want her to be safe."

"Yes," Rose said.

"That means your goal, and mine, are one and the same."

The faintest hint of acquiescence flickered in the gray feline's eyes. "You really can lock up the necklace where it can't influence anyone ever again?"

"I can."

"That sounds good. Then…we wouldn't have to worry anymore," Daisy said. "We'd be—"

"Free." Petunia sounded wistful. "Finally free of that responsibility."

"After eight hundred years, that would be nice," Marigold said, sitting on her haunches.

After glancing at her sister felines, Rose growled. "Well, then."

Lucian raised his brows. Waited.

"If you are the reincarnated knight you claim to be, you are a man of honor."

"Indeed, I am."

"I want your solemn vow," the gray cat continued in a gruff tone. "You will swear, on your honor, to get the necklace to The Experts and lock it away forever."

Lucian barely resisted a grin. Molly thought *he* was old-fashioned?

"He needs to do things properly. He should get down on one knee, like they did in the olden days," Marigold said.

"And kiss us on a front paw." Daisy looked down. "The right one, I think? Or was it the left?"

Petunia rolled her eyes. "You ninny, that's only if you're getting betrothed."

"I don't want man germs on my fur," Marigold meowed. "Can't we forego the kiss and just go with the vow?"

Good God. If he didn't take charge of the situation, they could argue for hours, and he needed to be on his way. "I will gladly get down on one knee to speak the oath." Lucian motioned to his sheathed sword. "How about if I swear on the same blade used to grant me knighthood in the reign of King Richard the Lionheart...if, of course, that's all right with you?"

Half an hour later, Lucian closed the loaded dishwasher at the apartment and started the machine— a perfectly normal chore he'd done every evening for as long as he could remember. But, tonight had been far from normal. At least his oath-swearing had gone well, the felines had let him leave without incident, and the box containing the necklace was now behind strong magical locks in the antique store's special collection. Crow's phone was also contained, until Lucian received instructions as to what to do with the device.

Crossing his arms, Lucian leaned back against the kitchen counter and glanced at Galahad, lying on the floor while grooming his tail. They'd completed their quest. Lucian had fulfilled his duty to The Experts. He'd thwarted a potential disaster and ensured peace reigned in Cat's Paw Cove...but somehow, he couldn't shake the feeling that the situation wasn't fully resolved.

Truth be told, he'd felt unsettled since seeing the vision. Maybe once he'd discussed it with Julius—he'd left a message and was waiting for The Expert to call him back—he'd be able to move on from what he'd seen.

Lucian's cell rang.

Finally.

He answered. "Julius."

"Where are you now?" the Expert asked.

Not even the slightest attempt at pleasantries? Lucian frowned. "I'm at the apartment. Why?"

"The necklace?"

"It's secured in the store. When will you pick it up?"

"Tomorrow. I'll call you when I get close to Cat's Paw Cove. Other Experts will be arriving tomorrow, too."

"Great." *Not.* "Look, I need to ask you about—"

"That'll have to wait."

Lucian's grip tightened on the phone. "It's important."

"So is my news. You need to be prepared."

The grimness of the older man's tone made Lucian straighten. "What do you mean, prepared?"

"The dark magic's Medieval."

Misgiving crawled through Lucian. "Early or—?"

"Late twelfth century."

A buzzing noise filled in Lucian's mind. "You mean...?"

"The same era as your original lifetime. Yes."

"How is that possible?"

"We're still trying to figure that out. But, the corrupt magic...may belong to her."

Her. The sorceress who'd cursed him.

Oh, hell.

"I killed Agnes," Lucian insisted. "You showed me the account in the archives."

"According to our records, that *is* what happened."

Lucian thought again of the horrific vision. Had he glimpsed the day he'd been cursed? It would explain why the images had affected him so much. "Send me what you have on Agnes. As you know, I have no memories of her or of that life."

"I realize that. Galahad, however, can help you remember."

Lucian's unease intensified. He glanced at the feline, who'd stopped washing. "Isn't that risky?" asked Lucian.

"Somewhat."

"Somewhat?" He hadn't forgotten Julius's warnings years ago.

"What are you talking about?" the squire asked.

"I'll send you the information you need shortly," Julius said. "But, considering the circumstances, I'm authorizing you to use the special collar."

Never before had Julius told him to use the Ancient Egyptian cat collar. Lucian had been given the exquisite object toward the end of his training and had been told it was only to be used in extreme circumstances. He'd shelved it in the antique store because he'd never imagined needing it.

"Talk to me," the squire said. "What's going on?"

Lucian's throat tightened. Galahad might be a pain in the ass, but he was also Lucian's closest friend. What if using the collar hurt the squire? Such focused magic, channeled through a small body, could mortally wound him.

"I'm sure you have reservations," Julius said.

"Hell, yeah," Lucian muttered.

"It's the best option."

"No."

"Lucian—"

"I won't do it."

"Yes, you—"

"There has to be another way. Check the archives. Ask other Experts—"

"I've given you an order."

Julius ended the call.

Anger burned, along with shock.

Galahad marched over and sat by Lucian's feet. "Talk."

He set aside the phone. "Julius ordered me to use the cat collar."

The squire's eyes widened. *"The* collar?"

"Yep."

The feline's gaze darted away.

"I don't...." Lucian tried again. "Have you ever worn the collar before?"

"It'll be my first time," the squire said. "But, there's a first time for everything, right?"

Lucian struggled and failed to find the right words. "I'm sorry. It's not what I—"

"I'll be fine. Go and get it."

Lucian nodded then went down to the shop and returned with the rectangular gold and lapis lazuli box decorated with the Eye of Horus.

He set the box on the kitchen table then removed the collar. The gold gleamed. Magic, shimmering like fine gold dust, flowed up his arm, swirled into the air, and surrounded him.

Resisting the enticement of the strong, ancient power, Lucian brought the collar into the living room.

"If I remember correctly, it's easiest if you lie down," Galahad said.

Leather creaked as Lucian reclined on his back on the sofa.

The feline jumped up beside him then sat in the middle of his chest.

Lucian grunted. "You're getting pudgy."

"Hush." Galahad's tail curled around his front paws. "Now, the collar."

Lucian carefully put the gold around the feline's neck.

As soon as the collar settled on Galahad's ruff, magic sparked against Lucian's fingertips. Galahad's eyes turned the same hue as the gold.

"Whoa. You okay?" Lucian asked.

The feline didn't answer. As though entranced, Galahad pressed both of his front paws against Lucian's forehead: toe beans to brow.

Golden light filled Lucian's mind. He gasped, but the magic held him immobile....

A knight wearing chain mail armor and a sword at his hip rode his horse down a forest road. His ginger-haired squire rode several paces behind. Night was falling, but they didn't have much farther to travel before they'd reach the knight's fortress. He smiled, for his betrothed, Brigitte, would be waiting for him. She visited often, but in less than a sennight, would become his lady wife. He couldn't wait for her to finally be his, in all ways.

The breeze rustled through the trees and stirred his shoulder-length hair. He glanced over his shoulder. "Galahad, when we—"

A woman screamed. The piercing sound came from the woods ahead.

The knight's hand flew to his sword. His gaze searched the shadowed trees.

Another scream.

"We must help that damsel, milord," the squire said.

"We will. Follow me." The knight spurred his mount into the trees.

Desperate sobs and shrieks drew the knight toward a thinning of the forest. In his childhood, years before the king had granted him these lands, he'd heard tales of the clearing. 'Twas said to be an ancient and haunted place; one where witches gathered to conduct rituals, cast spells, and do sacrifices.

"Please, spare me."

'Twas Brigitte's voice!

"Please. I beg you."

The knight jumped down from his horse and tore through ferns and low-growing bushes.

As he emerged in the clearing, he saw four men-at-arms

sprawled on the grass: Dead. The metallic stench of blood tainted the air.

Brigitte, weeping, stood bound to a post. Her long blond hair, wrenched free of its braid, tangled in the branches stacked up to create a pyre surrounding her.

A woman with copper-colored tresses and gold bracelets thrust a flaming torch toward the sky and chanted in an unfamiliar language.

Agnes.

Never would he have guessed the maidservant from his castle was a sorceress and a murderess.

"Agnes!" the knight yelled, striding toward her.

The squire caught up to him.

Seeing them, Brigitte cried out in relief.

"Lord Chadwick." The sorceress smiled—the same sultry curve of her lips as when he'd found her naked in his bed days ago. She hadn't been smiling when he'd told her to leave his chamber.

"Throw aside the flame," the knight commanded.

"I will not."

Anger clawed up inside him. "If you hurt her—"

"Why should I not? You have refused me, again and again," Agnes seethed, "because of her."

He had. He loved Brigitte and desired only her. He'd tried to be kind when rejecting Agnes, but she'd persisted. "As I told you," he ground out, "my heart belongs to another."

The sorceress smirked. "Not for much longer."

"Let me go," Brigitte wailed.

"You will be free, milord," Agnes said. "You will love me."

"Nay," the knight said. "I warn you—"

The sorceress threw the torch into the pyre.

Roaring, Chadwick lunged.

Dry kindling in the pyre burst into flame. Brigitte cried

out in terror.

"Free her," the knight yelled to Galahad. Raising his blade, he positioned himself between the sorceress and the squire.

Light akin to lashes of fire shot from Agnes's palms.

Shock tore through the knight—he'd never seen such light before—but with the flat of his sword, he deflected the flames. With an angry shriek, Agnes fired again. He swung his blade, dodged, moved ever closer to her. The pyre's blaze grew higher; hotter.

"The lady's free," Galahad shouted.

"Thank Go—"

Light slammed into the knight's chest. He flew backward through the air.

"Milord!" the squire cried.

Chadwick landed near the dead men. His head reeled. His nostrils burned with the odor of scorched cloth. It pained him to breathe. Over the ringing noise inside his skull, he heard the sorceress laughing.

Brigitte screamed again.

Resolve burned in the knight's blood as he staggered to his feet. He would save his betrothed. He'd die if he had to, to save her.

Palms up, Agnes focused on his lady love, crouched behind the squire. Brigitte was trying to draw a dead man's dagger.

As Galahad attacked the sorceress from the front, Chadwick ran at her from the side.

Hit by bolts of light, the squire screamed in agony and collapsed. The knight brought his sword down in a deadly arc. Spinning to face him, Agnes shot more light, but at the last instant, he tilted his sword. The light bounced off the weapon and plowed into her.

She jolted and fell to the ground.

"Beware," Brigitte cried.

"Aye." He stood over Agnes. Both hands on the hilt of his sword, he pointed it downward, between her breasts. One firm thrust, and he'd pierce her heart.

Fingers curled into the grass, she glared up at him. "You cannot kill me."

"Is that so?"

She didn't answer.

"I rule these lands. I can and will slay you."

Agnes's eyes narrowed. "Try, and I will curse you."

He ignored a flare of misgiving. "Yield. Refuse, and I will end your life."

Firelight glinted on her right bracelet. She was raising her hand to shoot fire.

He shoved the sword down.

"I curse you." Her voice caught, turned shrill. "You, your squire, your bloodline——"

Bone snapped. Blood spattered.

"——damned...together...forever."

A gurgling sound came out of her mouth.

Agnes twitched several times then went still.

He inhaled a deep breath and drew his sword free of her corpse. As he did so, bright light rushed out of her chest and momentarily blinded him.

As the light faded, he shook his head to clear his vision.

Brigitte stood close by, holding the dagger. Her clothes were scorched, and she no doubt had more burns than the ones on her arms. Her frantic gaze shifted from the sorceress to him. "Are you well?"

"I am." He yearned to pull Brigitte into his arms, to calm her and be absolutely sure she was all right, but he couldn't yet. He must deal with Agnes's body first. Then, the danger would be over.

"The light that broke from her." Brigitte trembled. "The curse——"

"Forget them. Never mention them again."

Her bottom lip quivered. "But—"

"No. 'Tis not safe to speak of such things. Do you understand?"

She nodded.

He sheathed his sword then leaned over the sorceress's corpse. Her bracelets were engraved with symbols he'd seen at ancient sites while he was on Crusade in Eastern lands. He reached to take the bracelets—the gold would fetch a good price—but a chill washed over his skin. He wanted naught to do with the evil bitch.

He picked up Agnes's body, strode to the blazing pyre, and threw her into the inferno. His shoulders lowered on a sigh of relief.

He wiped his hands on the grass and crossed to Brigitte. She ignored his bloodied garments and sank into his embrace. As he held her, gently kissed her hair that smelled of smoke, she wept against his shoulder.

Close by, a cat meowed.

"Milord," said the squire.

Chadwick stilled and drew his betrothed to arm's length. As he brushed tears from her cheeks, he asked, "Are you all right, squire?"

"I…am not."

Brigitte frowned. "Do you hear a cat?"

The knight's stare locked with the gaze of a ginger-colored feline standing where Galahad had fallen.

"Milord," the cat meowed. "The curse… 'Tis real."

The vision faded as a weight slumped on Lucian's chest. He opened his eyes to see Galahad, his eyes sliding shut, his head lolling.

Concern whipped through Lucian as he removed the collar and sat up, his right arm going around the cat. "Galahad?"

The squire's eyes opened a crack. They were no longer light gold, but their usual color. "Feel...weak."

"Let's get you a snack." Lucian carried the feline to the kitchen, set him down, and opened a can of duck dinner. "There you go."

The cat ate slowly. Lucian sat next to him to keep an eye on him.

His back against a kitchen cabinet, Lucian tried to make sense of what he'd seen. The vision he'd experienced in Molly's bedroom had clearly been a mental snapshot connected to the longer flashback he'd just experienced.

As a twelfth-century knight, he hadn't known what to call the symbols on the sorceress's bracelets. Modern-day Lucian knew, though: they were hieroglyphics.

When Agnes had died, her life force had somehow merged with the Ancient Egyptian bracelets, which someone—the peddler, perhaps?—had salvaged from the fire's ashes. The gold, infused with dark magic, had been melted down to make the necklace for the nobleman's wife.

Trying to destroy the necklace had caused the four witches to be turned into cats. Those cats had become Molly's mother's felines.

So, Molly's late mother's pets *had* been cursed by the same Magical as Lucian.

And Molly.... She'd also been affected by the same magic, although Lucian had resolved that problem by locking up the necklace.

How many other lives had the dark power influenced?

Why, also, did he still not have an explanation for what he'd seen in Molly's eyes?

Lucian dragged his hand over his jaw. Then, still sitting on the floor, he called Julius. When he got forwarded to voice mail, Lucian hung up and reviewed the three files Julius had emailed before calling his superior again. "I really need to speak to you," he growled before hanging up.

Then, he phoned Molly. He might wake her, but he needed to check in with her. When that call also went to voice mail, he left a message for her to phone him as soon as possible.

Galahad meowed at his empty plate. "Need...more."

Lucian spooned out a second can of duck dinner, left the cat to eat, and returned the collar to the antique store. When he walked back to the kitchen, the feline straightened away from his food dish.

"Ready for can number three?" Lucian asked.

"Nah." Galahad licked his lips. "I'm going to nap now. Tell me what you saw tomorrow, okay?"

"I will."

After Galahad curled up on the chair and fell asleep, Lucian went to bed. He left his phone on and put it on the nightstand before turning off the light.

Sleep, though, eluded him. His mind racing, his hands behind his head on the pillow, he stared up at the shadowed ceiling. His gut instincts warned him there could well be consequences of his actions today that he'd never anticipated—just like when he'd confronted the sorceress centuries ago.

Chapter Fourteen

ake up.

With a sigh, Molly ignored the whisper in her mind and snuggled deeper into her bedding. No reason why she couldn't spend five more minutes in bed. She was warm, cozy, had slept really well—

Wake up.

Eyes still closed, Molly frowned. The voice had been louder this time. It was definitely inside her head, not someone in the room speaking to her. She'd heard the same voice over the past few days, but it had mostly been interwoven with her thoughts, not independent and demanding.

What was happening now was…weird.

Get up. Now.

Suddenly feeling too hot—also weird, since she'd been comfortable until a second ago—Molly opened her eyes to see the sunlit bedroom. Memories of the previous night raced back to her, and she bit down on her bottom lip as she remembered leading Lucian into the room, him pushing her down on the bed. How she'd wanted him—

Find the necklace.

Molly sat up, the bedding sliding down to bunch at her waist, and glanced at the clock on the bedside table: 8:34 AM. Not only had she slept a bit later than usual, but she was still wearing her skirt and top from last night. Why hadn't she changed into her pajamas? Had she washed her face and brushed her teeth? She couldn't remember doing those things, and she never skipped them before bed.

Sweat beaded on Molly's brow as her hand, as though guided by someone else, reached up and touched her throat, confirming the necklace wasn't there.

What was happening to her? First, though, she'd better go and pee—

No. Find the necklace.

The words were accompanied by another hot flash and a flare of determination. Gripped by panic, Molly glanced about the room, looking for the jewel. What she wanted to do was go to the bathroom. What she actually did was look for the necklace...as though someone else was controlling her actions.

Yes.

"Yes?" Molly squeaked.

You and I are one now.

Molly shook her head. Could she be dreaming?

No. What she was experiencing felt too real to be a dream. "Who are you?" she asked. "What do you want from me?"

I want what's best for both of us. Get up. Look for the necklace.

Molly struggled not to obey. Her hand, clutching the bedding to draw it aside, shook as she willed herself to remain still.

I am far stronger than you. You can't resist me.

"I don't want you in my head!" Molly had to get help, but who could she talk to? Hers wasn't a normal problem, and it hadn't affected her until today.

Had something happened during Lucian's visit last night?

Lucian is the reason I am here.

"He is? Why——?"

I gave you the chance to obey me.

An orange-yellow haze clouded Molly's vision. Heat, like molten flames, shot through her veins. She gasped at the shocking pain. As a shriek burned in her throat, the agony cooled, as though the fire within her had burned down to embers.

The awful heat could rekindle at any time, though. So could the pain.

Now. Look for the necklace.

Molly wanted to disobey, but she couldn't bear to be in agony again. Trembling, she pulled back the bedding, slid her legs over the side of the bed, and went to the dresser where she'd left the box yesterday. Her phone was there, but the box wasn't. Maybe she'd put it away?

She searched the dresser, the room, and her bathroom, but the box and necklace weren't to be found.

Damn Lucian! He stole them.

"I did what you asked." Molly couldn't keep her voice from wavering. She mentally calculated how many seconds it would take to reach her phone, dial Lucian, and beg for help. She'd risk more pain——

You'll call Lucian when I say you can.

This couldn't be happening! But, when she tried to run to the dresser, her body wouldn't move.

The fiery punishment returned.

"Let me go," Molly screamed.

Not until I have what I want. Get dressed. We're going to pay Lucian a visit.

***

"I'll pose as a collector of antique jewelry." A ticking noise—a car's turn signal—sounded in the background of Julius's phone call. "I've brought credentials."

"You'll need them. Molly's not easily fooled," Lucian said while pouring himself a mug of just-brewed coffee.

"One of my assistants has updated the website on my business card and made sure there are breadcrumbs on the internet. Molly will have no reason to suspect I'm not who I say I am."

After sipping the stronger-than-usual java, Lucian glanced at the clock on the apartment's stove: 8:29 AM. If Molly wasn't already awake, she would be soon.

"Any word from her?" Julius asked.

"No." Lucian fought not to yawn. "I've called three times and left messages. She might still be sleeping." After being awake most of the night, Lucian would love to still be abed himself, but he had to run the shop—thus the strong coffee.

"Molly might be ignoring you."

Regret twisted Lucian's gut. "I know." He hated to think of Molly being angry with him.

"No matter. Once I reach Cat's Paw Cove, we'll take care of the situation and give her a generous payout," the older man said. "We can also use magic to alter her memories."

"I don't want to do that."

The distant honk of a car horn sounded on the line.

"With the necklace locked up and the dark magic contained, Molly will never be influenced by magic again," Lucian insisted. He bent down to pat Galahad who, thankfully, had suffered no lasting effects from using the collar.

"Let's see how things go when we visit Molly later today." The turn signal clicked again. "For now, stay at the store. Guard the necklace—"

The dark magic alarm sounded.

Galahad yowled. "It's only...what time?"

"8:34." Lucian skimmed the data on his phone.

"Similar signatures to before," Julius noted.

"Now it's...a Category *Four*," Lucian said.

"What?" The squire's mouth gaped.

Dread gnawed as Lucian set his mug on the closest counter. "It doesn't make sense. The necklace is locked away."

"Are you sure?" the older man asked. "It was secure last night. This morning?"

Lucian swore under his breath. He hadn't been down to the store yet. "I'll check."

"Do that. Report back."

Lucian downed the rest of his coffee. He raced for the apartment door, swung back to snatch up the sword he'd taken to Molly's, and then hurried to the shop.

A riot of sounds greeted him.

The Steiff teddy bear growled.

The desiccated finger was tapping in its box: Morse Code for SOS.

The wooden box containing Molly's necklace was still shelved and protected by magical locks—just as he'd left it yesterday evening.

"Is what's happening my fault?" Galahad meowed. "Because I used the collar?"

"I don't think so." With the cat running alongside him, Lucian went into the back room to view the latest readouts. While the data was similar to what he'd tracked to the necklace in Molly's late mother's home, he noted new elements.

He *hadn't* contained the corrupt power when he'd secured the necklace.

The magic had *evolved*.

Molly wasn't free of it after all. Was that why he'd seen the spark in her eyes?

Oh, hell

According to the data, the dark energy was on the move; heading for the town.

Lucian went back out into the main room, unsheathed the sword to lean it against the back of the counter, and reinforced the protections around the shop. Whatever happened within the next few minutes, Molly mustn't be harmed. For his grandfather's sake, Lucian also must minimize damage to the shop and its antiques.

Perhaps, if he was lucky, he'd be able to use his quick thinking and charm to defuse the situation. He'd start with diplomacy, at least.

Molly's car screeched to a stop outside. She got out, slamming the door behind her. As she rounded the front of the vehicle and headed for the shop, Lucian's throat went dry.

She looked incredible: snug black top, black jeans, black heels that made her legs look long and sleek. She'd left her hair loose, and it drifted on the morning breeze.

While the woman approaching the door was definitely Molly, he saw no warmth or sweetness in her expression. This woman had been wronged. Bitterness defined the set of her mouth.

The shop didn't open until nine o'clock, but Lucian didn't want their conversation to take place on the street, where passersby might overhear. He started for the front door, to let her in, but with a flick of her hand, Molly threw the locks. The door flew inward. She walked through the magical barriers as though they weren't even there and entered the shop.

Misgiving settled inside him like a block of ice.

He caught a hint of her perfume and...*darkness*. It swirled around her like an invisible cloak.

Yet, the energy wasn't extraneous, like a garment she could take off and set aside. It had become part of her.

Oh, Molly.

The finger continued to tap out SOS. Indeed, every antique in the special collection was reacting to Molly's s powers.

Lucian cast another, stronger spell to lock the front door and turn the sign from 'Open' to 'Closed.' He also cast a glamour across the front of the shop. To people walking past, the interior would appear blurry, the objects within indistinct enough to avoid stirring interest or suspicion.

Molly's head turned slightly, an acknowledgement of his spells. When he stepped back behind the counter, closer to his sword, her gaze locked with his.

"Good morning—"

"Where is it?"

Not even a 'hello.'

"Where's my necklace?"

Lucian braced his hands on the counter's edge. He and Molly had kissed last night, almost made love, but he saw no hint of affection in her eyes now, only rage. He silently cast a spell on her car; she wasn't going anywhere until he'd resolved what was going on with her.

She stopped in the middle of the store and set her hands on her hips—a posture that warned she was prepared to fight. "Give me the jewel."

He raised his hands, palm up. "I get that you're upset."

Her eyes narrowed.

"If you let me explain—"

"No. I want the necklace."

Orange-red light flickered in her eyes: a stronger spark than he'd seen last night.

"Lucian," Galahad growled.

"I saw it." Lucian didn't break Molly's stare. His mind, though, raced. "Tell me, does Molly want the necklace? Or do you, the Magical who has taken over her body?"

A humorless smile curved Molly's lips. Her gaze found the plain wooden box. "You should have just handed it over."

She raised her arms, holding them away from her sides.

A cry of warning flared in Lucian's mind. He instinctively reached for his sword.

With the sound of scrabbling claws, Galahad ran behind the counter.

A fiery bolt shot from Molly's right palm. *Bang-hiss*. The bolt left a sizzling, smoking hole in the wall behind Lucian. An etched Victorian mirror, which he'd put up yesterday, fell and shattered on the floor.

"I will ask one last time. Hand over the necklace."

"Ask as many times as you like," Lucian said. "You'll get the same answer: No."

Before the last word had left his lips, she fired another bolt.

Bang-hiss.

Bang-hiss, bang-hiss.

Plates smashed. Stemware shattered. Shards of porcelain and glass landed on Lucian's head and rained onto the floor.

As another stream of fire shot toward Lucian, he swung his blade. The bolt hit his sword and rebounded toward Molly.

She darted sideways. The bolt slammed into a carved chair and knocked it backward into a table.

"She's going to destroy the store," Galahad meowed.

"Not if I can help it."

"Want me to distract her?"

"Not yet," Lucian said. "I'd like to try to stop her attack."

"How? You can't just ask her to quit."

"Can't I?" Lucian held Molly's flickering, furious stare. "Can we not resolve this in a civilized manner? If you'd hold off attacking—"

She lobbed another bolt. Lucian ducked, but caught the crackle and stench of singed hair.

He straightened, fighting anger. "Think about Molly," he said to her.

"I have."

"You're willing to risk injuring her?"

A rough laugh broke from her. "Are you?" Fire

gathered in her palms as she pouted. "If she's hurt, Lucian, it will all be *your* fault."

"No, it will be yours."

She shot the fire toward him. Swinging his sword, he sent the blazing bolts racing back toward her. She tried to dodge, but her right heel caught in the rug on which she stood. With a shriek, she pitched sideways.

Lucian saw her falling toward an iron-bound wooden trunk. He cried out in warning, but she couldn't stop her fall. Her head hit the trunk, and she crumpled on the floor.

"Molly!" He raced out from behind the counter.

"Beware," Galahad howled. "It could be a trick."

Lucian's grip tightened on his sword as, angling the blade away from her, he knelt at her side. When he gently rolled her onto her back, she moaned.

Her eyes fluttered open. They were blue and held no trace of fire.

"Lucian." He heard fear in her whispered voice.

"Are you hurt?"

"Not important."

"Of course it's—"

"I'm sorry." Molly clutched his arm. "I can't stop her. She's controlling me."

"I know. I'm going to stop her. Tell me her name."

Molly grimaced, and her fingers dug into his arm.

"Molly," he said sharply. "Quickly. Tell me—"

Her back arched, and her eyelids squeezed shut

as she cried out in pain. Then, with a long, hissed breath, her body lowered to the floor again.

"Molly?"

Her eyes flicked opened. Once again, they glittered with orange-yellow flames.

Stop manipulating me! Molly silently cried. *Leave me alone.*

For an instant, after she'd hit her head, she'd broken free of the presence that had possessed her. But, as she'd gazed up at Lucian's worried face, her heart aching to see him so concerned, the controlling force had sent unbearable pain racing through her. She'd had no choice but to surrender to it. Once more she'd become a prisoner in her own body.

Lucian had clearly noticed she wasn't herself again. His gaze had hardened, and he'd scooted backward.

Molly pushed up on one arm, fire gathering in her hand. How strange that she couldn't feel the burning flame against her skin, but experienced full-force the emotions of the entity controlling her.

Why did the presence feel such jealous rage toward Lucian?

Molly's arm moved. She willed it to stop, tried to lower her limb to her side, to no avail. Fire from her palm whooshed toward Lucian. He dove sideways, slamming into the Edwardian chair. He grunted, a sound of pain, and the dark energy gloated.

Lucian scrambled to rise. "Tell me who you

are." He was standing now, his right hand flexing on his sword.

Molly silently wept, because the evil presence was enjoying the attack. It liked Lucian's torment and wanted to inflict more.

"You know who I am," the dark energy made her say.

"Do I?"

Lucian's answer infuriated the presence.

"I've known lots of women in my many lifetimes," he added.

Wait. What?

How could he have lived *many* lifetimes?

"I care only about your *first* life," the entity said.

Molly struggled to understand. She'd heard of immortals, even watched a popular series on TV about them, but they were just fictional characters. Weren't they?

Lucian's head tilted to the left, and she heard another man speaking; a voice she'd heard earlier before her thoughts had focused on the fight. She'd seen Galahad dart behind the counter, but a customer must have hidden there as well.

Unless…

No. Galahad was just a normal cat. He didn't speak as a human would.

Then again, antiques on shelves near Lucian that she hadn't noticed before today were moving around and growling, so nothing happening right now fitted her ideas of 'normal.'

"I do remember," Lucian was saying. "*Agnes.*"

The dark energy's smug satisfaction burned inside Molly. "Aye."

He scowled. "I killed you."

CATHERINE KEAN

"You slew my physical body, aye. With my dying breath, I cast a spell that bound my spirit to the gold I'd been wearing."

"So I was right about that," Lucian muttered.

"For centuries, I existed in a box," the sorceress continued. "Many people through the years tried to remove the lid and failed. Molly, though—your clever, curious Molly—managed to open the box."

I'm sorry, Molly silently sobbed. *So very sorry, Lucian.*

"Don't blame Molly for this situation," he gritted. "You tricked her."

"No. She chose her fate. She had free will through every step of my resurrection; right up until last night."

With sickening dismay, Molly thought of how wonderful she'd felt every time she'd worn the necklace. The addictive pleasure had been Agnes manipulating her.

"Molly didn't revive you just by opening the box," Lucian challenged. "Nor did your powers return by her wearing the necklace now and again."

"Quite right." The sorceress smirked. "However, the more she wore the necklace, the stronger I became. I also analyzed her conversations, what she watched on television, what she listened to on the radio, and I learned the modern language. It was easier than I'd ever imagined to become part of her."

A muscle ticked in Lucian's cheek. "How—?"

"She and I are highly compatible. You see, we share ancestors."

"Common DNA," he growled.

Oh, no, Molly silently moaned.

"Molly did, at times, resist me. Then last

231

night…." Agnes smiled. "The spell you used to put her to sleep? I used that magic, Lucian. *Your* magic. Thanks to you, I was able to take control over her."

Poor Lucian looked aghast, as though the sword he held had turned on him and run him through.

"Molly and I will be together now until the day she dies."

Oh, no. No!

"Using what Molly's mother learned about her ancestry, and the help of the Dealers who have already contacted me, we'll meet many more of our relatives."

"That's why you want the necklace," Lucian said. "You'll use the magic in the gold to gain control of those relatives."

The sorceress laughed. "Aye."

"I won't let you."

The sorceress sneered. Molly's arms rose, and even as she struggled not to obey, tremors of power rippled across her palms.

Lucian's left hand moved. Silver light rushed toward her and hit her stomach. She jolted, her body instantly numbed. She couldn't move at all.

Good. Now the sorceress couldn't hurt him—

The dark presence within Molly, though, merely laughed. Her skin tightened, as though she'd suddenly been encased head to toe in plastic wrap. With a fiery burst, the paralysis vanished.

Flames shot in steady streams from Molly's fingers. Agnes forced her to move forward, toward Lucian. He tossed aside his sword and used both hands to counter the fire with orbs of glittering silvery light.

With a thunderous *bang-hiss*, the table beside him exploded in flames.

Lucian lunged to the side, still shooting silver

light, but with a firm wrench of her hand, the sorceress sent him flying into the store counter.

Lucian! Molly silently shrieked.

He fell to the floor, gasping, the breath knocked out of him. No doubt he'd soon have bruises from the impact.

With the frantic scrabbling of claws, Galahad raced from behind the counter. "Get up," he shouted to Lucian. "You can't let her get the necklace."

Oh, goodness! The voice Molly had heard before hadn't been a customer's, but Galahad's!

Did *all* cats talk? If so, would she be able to understand her mother's kitties? Molly had no way of knowing because she hadn't seen them that morning. Agnes had made her leave the house without feeding them.

Clearly struggling to breathe, Lucian pushed up on his hands then twisted onto his side to shoot more silvery light. The bolts plowed into Molly. She staggered, careened into an oak side table. Despite throbbing pain in her hip, the sorceress made her keep walking. Only a few more steps, and they'd reach the shelf holding the plain wooden box.

"Don't," Lucian bellowed, on his feet again.

"Don't tell me what to do," the sorceress said.

He shot a stronger pulse of light that howled through the air. With a flick of Molly's hand, Agnes deflected the blast into a glass-front cabinet. Wood, china, and glass exploded. As Molly gasped in horror, Lucian cast a spell that contained the explosion and all of its tiny, deadly fragments.

The sorceress aimed Molly's hand at the still-burning table.

No! Stop, Molly silently pleaded. But, she

couldn't keep the table from sliding across the floor. With a dull thud, it hit Lucian and propelled him sideways. He slammed into the counter, trapped between it and the tabletop. With a jerk of her arm, the sorceress made the flames on the table leap higher, making it impossible to see him any longer.

Lucian! Molly silently cried.

How desperately she wanted to help him. Molly tried to run to him, but the sorceress sparked intense pain in her skull. Crying out in agony, Molly yielded.

Agnes made her approach the shelf. The box was easily within reach, but the sorceress didn't make her grab it.

Why not?

Molly's shaking hand rose, but on Agnes's command, she tapped patterns in the air that she'd never known or even imagined possible before now. Shimmering layers of colored light appeared in front of her, along with symbols: lions, initials, letters....

They were hallmarks. *Magical* hallmarks.

Several layers of light faded away. "So many locks," Agnes hissed, as Molly's fingers continued to move.

Molly prayed the sorceress wouldn't be able to undo all of the locks. How was Lucian? She couldn't see him, because of the direction she faced, but she could hear Galahad yelling his name and the roar of the flames.

What if Lucian was mortally injured? What if he—?

More layers of light vanished.

Oh, no. No!

Its wings buzzing, a scarab beetle rose from the

shelf of antiques and zoomed toward the ceiling. Other antiques were escaping, now that they were no longer contained by magical locks. Seeing them go deepened Molly's despair, because the antiques had been contained for a reason—and knowing what she did now about Lucian and magic, it would have been a good reason.

She gasped at more stabbing pain in her skull: The sorceress wanted her to take the box.

Molly reached for it. But, just as her fingers were about to close on it, sparks erupted, snapping and popping and swiftly spreading to surround the box. A row of hallmarks glowed inches from her wrist.

The sparks faded to reveal the box was encased in round links made of silver light. The patterning reminded Molly of…medieval chain mail.

"Lucian," the sorceress snarled.

When Lucian had talked about going all medieval on her, Molly really had thought he'd been joking. However, the sorceress *knew* this was Lucian's spell, because of its elements of *ancient* magic. If, as he'd said earlier, he'd lived many lifetimes, could one—or several—of them date back to the Middle Ages? How was that even possible?

The sorceress forced Molly to execute more patterns in the air.

Sparks zapped her skin, the sensation similar to snapping elastic bands. But, the hallmarks remained bright. The spell was holding steady.

Yes! Thank God.

"Try again," Agnes commanded, forcing Molly to convey patterns once more then draw lines and swirls in the air. But, the hallmarks didn't disappear. The spell didn't break.

With a furious shriek, the sorceress spurred Molly to face the burning table. Thick, black smoke rolled like fog along the ceiling. The flames, four or five feet high, consumed the furnishing.

No human being could survive such an inferno.

Yet, within the yellow-orange flames, she glimpsed silver light. *Lucian's* light.

Please be okay. Please.

"We're not done, Lucian," Molly heard herself shout.

Panting, darting back and forth by the claw-foot table legs, Galahad hissed at her. "Damn right. We *aren't* done."

"I wasn't talking to you, you stupid—"

Faint laughter carried from outside the shop. The stores on the street would soon be opening.

Molly sensed the sorceress's wariness; she mustn't be seen or discovered in the damaged store. Agnes wouldn't risk her plans being undermined.

The sorceress forced Molly to head for the rear door. Broken glass and splintered wood crunched under her shoes.

No! We can't leave yet. I have to know Lucian is okay.

The sorceress subdued her with more agonizing pain. "Bring me the necklace today, Lucian, or Molly dies."

Chapter Fifteen

Flames battered Lucian's magical shield. Scorching heat assaulted him. His head pounded as he struggled to remember the incantation that would move the table and douse the fire. He knew the words; he just couldn't pull them from his rattled mind. When the sorceress had thrown him against the counter, he'd hit his head, and now he had trouble thinking clearly.

"Come on. Focus," Galahad yowled.

Lucian's eyes streamed from the heat and smoke. He *had* to remember the spell. He had to save Molly.

Yet, handing over the necklace wasn't an option, either.

Seething anger and frustration broke from him on a roar. With his deepening rage, his thoughts coalesced.

He ground out the words of the spell, and with the squeal of wood on wood, the table skidded away across the planks. The flames extinguished. He exhaled a harsh sigh and canceled the shield.

The squire bounded over to him. "You okay?"

"I think so." Ignoring the aches in his limbs, Lucian raced for the rear door, flung it open, and scanned the parking lot for Molly, but she was nowhere in sight. He dragged his hand over his sweaty face, swore and kicked the pavement. He needed to find her, but he couldn't confront Agnes in the middle of town where she could jeopardize the lives of non-Magicals.

"Someone's trying to enter the shop," Galahad said from the doorway.

"Is it nine o'clock already?" Lucian hurried back inside. According to his phone, he didn't have to open for another five minutes. With the cursed antiques loose in the antique shop, and the floor littered with debris, it was a good thing his earlier spells remained in place. Whoever was now tapping on the door would have to come back later.

A droning sound cut into his thoughts.

"Um...Lucian?" The feline nudged his chin toward a spot behind him.

Glancing back, Lucian saw the scarab beetle diving straight for him; payback for it being confined to a shelf for years. Lucian lunged sideways, while the scarab swooped low then veered toward the ceiling.

Muffled growling came from a chair to his right. Shredding the padded armrest, the teddy bear looked at him, snarled gleefully, then went straight back to chewing.

Lucian surveyed the rest of the room. Luckily, none of the cursed antiques had escaped—and he'd make sure they never got out to wreak havoc in Cat's Paw Cove.

"We must go after Molly," Galahad said.

"We will. She's safe enough for now."

The cat's mouth dropped open. "You've got to

be joking. Did you breathe in too much smoke?"

Lucian's lips flattened. More than anything, he wanted to look for Molly, but he couldn't neglect other priorities. "Agnes won't seriously hurt Molly. Not until I hand over the necklace."

"You do recall what she's going to do with the necklace, right?"

"I do." Lucian raised his hand toward the scarab, scuttling along the top of an oil painting's gilt frame. With a twist of his wrist, he sent the scarab back to its shelf, quieted it, and quickly added magical locks. "You and I are going to stop Agnes for good *and* save Molly."

"We'll rescue her, just like we rescued Brigitte."

Lucian noted the wobble in the squire's voice. "Yes," Lucian said, even as he silently acknowledged what might be the only way to save Molly and destroy the sorceress: he might have to sacrifice himself.

After twenty minutes of chasing artifacts and securing them all back in their assigned spots in the collection, Lucian lifted his earlier spells and turned the store sign to 'Open." He went to fetch a dustpan, broom, and bucket.

Just as he was returning to the main part of the store, the bell on the front door jingled. Cora and a plump, gray-haired woman entered.

"This day just gets better and better," Galahad meowed.

"Good morning," Lucian called.

"Good morning. Our breakfast meeting finished early, so we thought we'd stop by." Cora's wide-eyed gaze traveled over the chewed chair, scorched table, and debris-covered floorboards. "What happened?"

"I had a problem to deal with earlier," he said with what he hoped was a reassuring smile. "It's mostly resolved now."

"What kind of problem?" Cora's companion asked, obviously intrigued.

"Lucian, this is Roberta Millingham." Cora gestured to the woman. "Remember, I told you about her?"

Lucian remembered. More recently, he'd seen her name in some of his grandfather's records. "It's a pleasure to meet you, Roberta."

The older woman blushed then gestured to the table. "Is it too damaged to be repaired?"

"I don't really know. I haven't had a chance to inspect—"

"I can recommend a restorer, if you need one."

"Thanks. I might—"

"He did some of the work on the Shipwreck Museum. Have you visited The Guinevere down at the waterfront?"

Lucian's grip tightened on the dustpan's handle. "Actually, that's one of the places I'd planned to visit—"

"The museum's been very busy since it opened. Lots of tourists. Visitors from all over Florida, too."

"Well, it's terrific it's so popular—"

"Yes. Most exciting. We'll soon be—"

"Roberta," Cora cut in. "Lucian hasn't told us what happened to his shop."

"Oh. Of course. I do get a bit excited about the museum. I just can't help myself. I know I shouldn't talk so much, but—"

Cora glowered.

"Right," the gray-haired woman said. "Lucian's

turn to talk."

"I had a problem with one of the light fixtures," he said, setting aside the items he was holding.

"Light fixtures?" Frowning, Cora took a step closer.

"She doesn't believe you." Galahad's head moved as he studied the antiques near him.

"I'm hoping insurance will cover the damage," Lucian added.

"How did the fire start? Are you all right?" Cora's features etched with concern, while her gaze fixed on the singed spots on his sleeves.

"I'm fine." Lucian sure as hell wasn't going to mention his headache.

His tail swishing, Galahad leaped up onto a side table.

"Were you hurt at all?" Cora cooed.

"Nope," Lucian said. "Not hurt."

Out of the corner of his eye, he saw Galahad padding over to a small lamp with a ruffled glass shade. Before he could say another word, the cat rubbed against the shade. The lamp teetered, almost enough for the base to fall over.

Lucian dashed over and snatched up the lamp.

"Your *cat* caused this morning's damage?" Cora's tone revealed both shock and outrage.

"Hey," Galahad drawled. "I was just demonstrating *one* possible scenario."

"I know," Lucian murmured.

Roberta squinted. "You *know* your cat caused the damage?"

Damn. "No. What I meant was—"

His cell phone rang.

Julius. Thank God.

"I must get that." He set the lamp on the counter and picked up his cell. "Sorry, Ladies, but this call's important."

Cora waved at him. "You go ahead. Roberta and I will clean up the mess for you."

Ring.

"Thanks, but that's not necc—"

"We insist." Cora shoved the broom into Roberta's hand. "We'll have this place tidied up in no time. I'll call Diane and a few others to help."

Ring.

"Really, I appreciate the offer, but—"

"You'll owe the Historical Society." Roberta smiled. "We're always short of hot...I mean, dashing heroes to dress in costume for special events.

Dress in costume?

Ring.

"Okay. Fine," he said.

Roberta and Cora squealed like teenage girls.

Crap. What had he just agreed to?

Mentally shoving aside his dread, Lucian hurried toward the rear of the store and answered the call.

Something awful was going to happen.

Something catastrophic.

Molly sensed the peril as keenly as she felt Agnes's determination to crush Lucian. If only Molly could figure out exactly what was going to occur. But, the sorceress had learned how to mentally block her. Every time she tried to access Agnes's thoughts, she was rebuffed, as if she'd walked into a solid mental wall.

Molly shivered. Existing now was like being confined to a tiny cell inside her own consciousness. She could still smell, see, hear, taste, and feel, but she was no more than a living puppet with an omnipotent master. Agnes had made it clear that Molly would never again be able to control her own body or the words that came out of her mouth.

Agnes had been horrible to Lucian in the antique shop. How desperately Molly hoped he was okay. But, he might not be.

He might also have decided he didn't want her in his life anymore. Lucian had far more reason to reject her than Howard ever had. Sadness wove into Molly's heartache, because she might never kiss Lucian again, never share breakfast with him, or tease him while his eyes softened to a smoldering, chocolaty hue.

Stop it, Molly. Don't dwell on such thoughts.

No.

She mustn't give up.

She couldn't.

She hadn't lost absolutely everything: She still had free will. She could still make her own choices, and she'd *choose* to do all within her power to help Lucian when he faced Agnes again.

Earlier, after running several blocks away from the antique store, the sorceress had used Molly's phone to hire an Uber. The car had arrived promptly, but Agnes had become annoyed with the young woman with spiky pink hair for not driving fast enough.

The driver, whom Molly had recognized as a

twenty-something cashier from a local store, had met her gaze in the rearview mirror. "I'm not going to go over the speed limit. Don't like it? I'll stop the car. You can get out."

Magic had kindled in Molly's palms, and terror had almost choked her, because she'd seen firsthand what Agnes could do with such powers. Families with small children walked the downtown sidewalks, and if the sorceress's actions should cause an accident or hurt pedestrians, Molly would be blamed. But, as though deciding to avoid trouble, the sorceress had fallen silent until the car had pulled into the driveway of Molly's late mother's house. She'd thrown a five-dollar bill at the young woman and gotten out of the vehicle.

Shaking her head, the woman had driven away.

Even as Molly had silently expressed relief that the driver was safe, a man rose from where he'd been lounging on the front porch: Crow.

He grinned, and Molly's sense of impending doom had deepened.

No! she'd cried. *I don't want anything to do with him.*

But, she might as well have been pounding her fists against a stone wall.

"We'll talk inside," Agnes made her say, while she unlocked the door and motioned for Crow to follow her.

The cats didn't come to meet Molly as they'd done every other time she'd returned home. After shutting the door behind the Dealer, Molly spied the four felines peering out from behind stacked boxes near the sofa.

"You were right earlier, Rose," Marigold hissed. "That's not our Molly."

Her late mother's cats *did* talk!

If only she could enlist their help, but being animals, they couldn't dial 911 or knock on neighbors' doors, even if those things could free her from her entrapment.

Truthfully, Molly didn't know what anyone could do to free her from Agnes's control.

"How could we have let such a terrible thing happen to Molly?" Daisy wailed.

Rose growled. "Lucian didn't keep his vow. He betrayed us."

No, Molly silently cried. *Lucian wouldn't do that.*

With a heavy sigh, Petunia covered her face with her front paw. "After centuries of keeping that necklace from doing harm, we failed, because of *him*."

Lucian isn't at fault for what happened. Molly silently wept. *I'm the one responsible.* But, even as she thought the words, she knew no one else would hear them.

The sorceress forced Molly to glare at the cats. "Stay out of the way. Try to interfere, and I'll kill you."

The cats drew back behind the boxes. One of them muttered, but too softly for Molly to hear.

"So?" Agnes asked, as she walked into the kitchen, Crow a few paces behind.

"Others are on the way," the blond man said.

Others? Who did he mean? How many others?

"We have an agreement, then?"

Crow smirked. "We do. It will be our pleasure to help you kill Lucian."

No! That must never happen.

"And grow my magic," Agnes added.

"You are already remarkably strong."

Anger crackled within Molly.

The Dealer dipped his head. "Of course, it will benefit us all for you to be stronger still."

The sorceress smiled then forced Molly to retrieve the folder of Historical Society notes which she handed to him.

He opened the file and glanced through the top papers. "We'll start with the Hendrickson relatives in Florida, as you suggested."

No. No!

"Good. We'll start as soon as I have the necklace. I told Lucian to bring it here. He might be stupid, though, and try to be heroic."

Crow's gaze wandered down Molly's body. "He'll do as you asked. He's smitten. He'll also believe he still has a chance to rescue her."

Chapter Sixteen

lmost a Category Five.

The danger was nearly beyond critical.

To non-Magicals, Molly's late mother's house would look no different than any other residence in the neighborhood. But, Lucian had seen the black, tornado-like funnel of magic swirling over the home long before reaching the area.

Crow's vehicle was parked one house down. Lucian pulled into the curb. Better not to use the driveway and risk getting blocked in by other vehicles. A grim smile touched his mouth, because such thoughts implied he'd actually survive the coming battle and would, at some point, be leaving.

After switching off the engine, he turned to Galahad, who hadn't said a single word since leaving Cora and Roberta at the store, but had stared out the window the entire drive.

The cat returned his gaze. "Lucian…."

There were things Lucian had wanted to say to the lad, but now that the time had come, he didn't want to add to the strain Galahad was clearly feeling. Instead, he reached over and scratched the cat's neck, the way the feline liked. "You've been an excellent squire to me. Thank you."

"That sounds like goodbye."

It likely was.

The feline rubbed his whiskered cheek against Lucian's hand. "I couldn't have asked for a better owner."

Aww, how nice—

"So, you'd better go kick ass."

"I intend to."

"Good, because if you let that bitch win, or if you die, I'll never forgive you. Got it?"

Lucian's eyes burned as his thoughts slipped back to his conversation a short while ago with Julius. The Expert had ordered him to kill Molly. Slaying her might not eliminate Agnes's life essence, or force the sorceress back into the necklace, but would at least temporarily stop the threat she posed—until The Experts figured out how to eliminate her.

The thought of killing a woman who meant a great deal to him made Lucian want to throw open the car door and retch.

Yet, the Molly he'd grown to love might not even exist anymore. Agnes could have already wiped out every trace of her.

Damn Agnes.

Damn the gold that had allowed her to survive in that damned bloody box.

And damn bloody DNA.

He shoved the car door open. The storm over the house, lit by flashes of lightning, howled like thousands of souls in Purgatory.

Shrugging off a ghastly chill, Lucian got out.

Galahad clambered onto the driver's seat. "I'm

coming with you."

"No. Stay here." Leaning in, Lucian grabbed the box holding the necklace from the console between the front and passenger seats.

"I'm going." The cat jumped out before Lucian could shut the door. "A squire always stays with his knight. I'm with you until the end."

"All right," Lucian said gruffly.

For an instant, the magical chain mail he wore gleamed like iron links. While the enchanted armor was invisible to non-Magicals, Agnes would see it. She'd know he intended to fight with the conviction and honor he'd not once forsaken, before or after her curse.

Lucian reinforced the protective spell around Galahad.

The feline swished his tail. "Lead on, my lord."

With the cat running at his side, Lucian crossed the lawn to the house. The rotating winds, narrowing over the house, didn't affect the building or ground; but, Lucian had no doubt that if Agnes wanted, she could make the tornado wreak havoc or pull him up into the tempest. The fact that she hadn't done those things told him she wanted a face-to-face battle—just like when they'd fought centuries ago.

The front door opened. Crow stood on the threshold.

The crunch of gravel warned Lucian of a vehicle pulling into Molly's driveway. Snatching a glance, he saw the truck belonged to a yard maintenance company. Its logo cleverly disguised a serpent. No doubt more Dealers would be arriving at any moment.

Lucian reached the porch and stopped a few

paces from Crow.

"The necklace," Crow said.

Lucian gestured to the box in his left hand.

"Prove it's in there."

"It is."

"*Prove*—"

"I can't. I don't have the DNA to get the box open. Do you?"

The Dealer's hands opened, as though he intended to attack. Then, perhaps receiving a non-verbal order, he nodded once, stepped aside, and gestured for Lucian to enter the house.

Every one of his senses on high alert, Lucian stepped over the threshold. His whole body screamed a warning, because the magic he sensed was unlike anything he'd ever felt before: as cloying as toxic perfume, and as seductive as illicit dreams.

Galahad darted into the living room.

The four female cats peeked out from behind some boxes.

Daisy meowed. "Look who has arrived!"

"Liars!" Rose hissed. "Traitors."

Galahad approached the other felines. "We're here to help."

"Now I *know* we're going to die," Marigold yowled.

"Chins up, Damsels. We're not dying without a fight," the squire said. "Let's think how we can help Lucian."

Magic kindling in his palms, Lucian headed toward the flickering light coming from the hallway near Molly's bedroom.

Fine hairs on the back of his neck stood on end. The power emanating from that room…. It glided like wicked fingers over the magical armor surrounding him.

"Luuciaaan."

The sultry way Molly had drawn out his name—the way she'd addressed him in his fantasies— caused sweat to bead on his brow.

He reached the doorway. Her head propped up by one arm, Molly reclined on the bed.

Aww, h-h-hell.

His throat went dry as his gaze traveled over her lacy black bra, black thong, and black stockings with seams down the back. He'd imagined her in lingerie, all vixen curves and shapely legs. *Perfection.*

But, with Agnes manipulating this scenario, she would be.

She smiled and crooked a finger. "Come closer."

"No." Lucian fought not to remember the little sounds she'd made when they'd kissed; how much he'd desired her...as he did now.

Yellowish-red light burned in Molly's eyes. "Are you teasing me?"

"Nope." Forcing out the lie, he said, "I'm not interested."

Giggling, she trailed a finger down her cleavage to the front fastening of her bra. "I know you want Molly."

"Molly, yes. *You*, Agnes?" he ground out. "Never."

The smile on her face hardened.

"Is Molly still alive?" he demanded.

"She is for now. How much longer...? Who knows?"

That meant he still had a chance of rescuing

Molly. "Let her go."

"No."

"Let her go, and I'll give you what you want." He tipped his head toward the box he still held.

Her eyes sparked. "The necklace is mine anyway."

"Not yet it isn't."

Before he'd finished the last word, her fingers twitched. The box jolted in his hand, as though she'd cast a spell to take from him. But, the sparkling mesh of silvery chain-link light surrounding his body glowed, held strong, before becoming invisible again.

"You won't get it that way," he said.

"Maybe this way, then?" She thrust her hand toward him.

He lurched as an invisible noose locked around his neck. His protective spell, though, kept the noose from tightening. Through the silvery light around him, he glared at her.

Her smile broadened. "Oh, Lucian. You might as well give up now."

"Why would I—?"

She murmured words that sounded like Latin. The dark magic abruptly thinned, became no more substantial than lengths of thread. Warning flared, even as the threads wove into the light around him, looped around the chain links...and under them.

No!

The threads converged at his neck and braided into a rope. Fighting not to panic, he reached up to grab the noose, but his fingers closed on air. The noose, though, remained in place. Tightened.

"How arrogant of you, to think I wouldn't break through your spell."

Somehow, she'd found the origins of his incantation. Fear knotted his gut, because that knowledge had been archived by The Experts long ago and stored in a secret location. How, then, had she gotten hold of it?

The mattress creaked. She sat up then swung her legs over the bed. "Now," she purred. "Kneel."

"No," he bit out. Despite the increasing pressure on his throat, he raised his hands and fired silvery light toward her.

She laughed, as though he'd missed her by a long shot.

The magical noose tightened again.

He tried to swallow, and his vision blurred.

He sensed her leaving the bed. Lucian fired more bolts, but darkness, akin to a cloth hood, slipped down over his face, leaving him blind.

His rasped breaths taunting him, he turned his head, barely hearing her footfalls an instant before her fingers trailed down his chest. Her touch burned like fire on bare skin.

He lashed out, but heard her dart away, unharmed. Her laugher mocked him.

"Still, you haven't dropped to your knees."

She'd moved behind him. The noose around his throat tightened. He struggled to inhale a breath, or even the barest fraction of a breath.

His head swam.

Voices reached him from the living room: another man's and Crow's.

Lucian ground his teeth. He had to break free. He had to—

Burning pain seared down his back, and he couldn't hold back a cry of agony.

"Kneel."
Damn Agnes.
Damn the gold.
Damn bloody DNA.
Fury hot in his veins, he sank to the floor.

Fight, Lucian! You have to fight!
Watching in anguish as he collapsed to his knees, Molly silently sobbed. His face was a ghastly reddish-purple color. Veins bulged in his neck, and spittle gathered in the corners of his lips. But, he was far from defeated. His eyes blazed with anger.
Fight, Lucian.
How she wished she could break Agnes's hold on him. Molly could see the magical hood and the noose, a coil of wispy blackness wrapped around his neck, but even as she tried to command her own hands to move, she mentally smacked into a barrier.
How could she help Lucian when she couldn't even control her own body?
She had to find a way.
Molly's mind raced. The sorceress had *some* need for her, otherwise she wouldn't still be alive. So, what was her purpose? Why was she important?
"Now," Agnes made her say. "Before I take the necklace and then kill you, I'm going to give you one last choice."
Sweat trailed down the side of Lucian's face into his hairline.
Close to his ear, the sorceress said, "If you want

Molly, you can have her."

He made a startled sound.

"Accept she's part of me. Accept both of us."

He blinked, wavered on his knees.

"I know you're tempted," the sorceress goaded. "I can sense how much you care for her. *Want* her."

Lucian's gaze sharpened.

"Give in to your desires. Forsake The Experts, and take what *you* want," the sorceress coaxed.

His lips moved. But no sound emerged, and his eyes began to slide closed, as though he was on the verge of passing out.

His free hand fluttered, indicating the noose was preventing him from answering.

Molly sensed the sorceress's suspicion, but after a second, she cast aside the hood and loosened the noose, allowing Lucian to heave in a breath.

"Your answer," she snapped.

Lucian dragged in another breath. "Just so...we're clear...."

"Aye?"

"If I agree...then in future...when I kiss Molly—"

"You'll be kissing me as well."

He swallowed hard. "When Molly and I...pleasure each other—"

Molly's heart squeezed.

"You'll be loving me as well." The sorceress skimmed her fingers along his shoulder.

"Loving." Lucian's voice sounded stronger now.

"That's right."

"I don't think so." Lucian touched the noose.

On a bright spark, it vanished.

He pushed Agnes backward, dove, and rolled.

With a shriek, the sorceress regained her balance and fired blasts of flame.

Bang-hiss!

Lucian dove again.

Bang-hiss!

The bed caught on fire.

He shoved the box into his front pocket; shot silver light at Agnes. She countered with more fire.

Bang-hiss!

Scorch marks blackened the carpet and walls. With a *whoosh*, the drapes at the window erupted in flame.

Fear raced through Molly. The whole house could go up in flames.

As smoke darkened the air, Molly desperately tried to think of a way to hamper Agnes.

Lucian lashed out again.

The sorceress ducked then twitched her fingers. The box holding the necklace flew from his pocket.

Agnes caught it.

She smiled. "Now I can kill you."

Lucian gritted his teeth. He was running out of options.

Where were Julius and the other Experts? They should have arrived by now.

Over the crackling of flames, he heard Galahad

in the living room: "Go!"

Crow and the other man yelled.

"What the—? Ow! Get the cat—"

A flash of light.

Lucian initiated his shield and diverted Agnes's attack. But, even as he did so, fire burned through the barrier, rendering it useless.

He ended the shield, lunged sideways, and fired a strong bolt of his own. Hit in the ribs, the sorceress staggered. Flames from her fingers streamed through the doorway.

Judging by the smoke in the hallway, the fire was spreading to the rest of the home. Perhaps, if he could keep the sorceress inside, the building would collapse in on her. She'd burn to ash, just as she'd burned long ago. With the necklace in the box, her spirit might not be able to return to the gold.

It's a chance I must take. Forgive me, Molly.

He fought a pang of remorse and aimed several blasts of light. Two of them hit the sorceress. Lurching, she slammed into the door frame.

One well-directed strike, and he might render her unconscious.

He wiped away sweat running down his face.

I'm sorry, Molly.

He thrust his hand to deliver the blow, but suddenly, couldn't move. Glancing down, he saw a black magic rope coiling around his legs and up his thighs, binding him.

With punishing force, he was thrown back against the wall. The ropes whipped up to pin his arms to his sides. He gasped, trying to put air back into his lungs, as the rope encircled his neck then stopped.

The sorceress walked to stand in front of him.

He swallowed hard. His eyes burned from the heat and smoke.

"Enjoy your last breaths, Lucian."

He blinked to clear his vision. He could still hear fighting in the living room; wished he could see Galahad one last time.

And Molly.

His Molly.

His gut twisted. If only he could see her, reach her, through the hold Agnes had upon her.

"You're crying?" the sorceress taunted.

"No. The smoke's bothering me."

She stroked her fingers down his face, the way he'd touched Molly before. The anguish within him deepened.

Her hand trembled slightly. "You cared a lot for Molly, aye?"

He narrowed his eyes, for the bitch was obviously going to maximize his torment.

But, if he could keep her talking, allow the fire to weaken the structure of the house to the point of falling in upon them both....

"Of course I cared," he ground out.

"Poor Lucian. Did you hope for a future with her?"

"Yes." His tone became a rasp. "I...would have married her."

The sorceress's hand jolted, as though his statement had surprised her.

Her gaze flickered for barely a second before the merciless stare returned. "You're not the kind of man who wants marriage."

"She's not like any other woman I've known."

Again, her hand shook.

How curious that his words affected her so much.

Unless....

He silently pleaded for Molly to hear him. "Molly deserves to be cherished," he said. "To be loved."

The sorceress lips curved into a gloating smile. "You loved her, Lucian?"

"Yes, I did."

He loved her.

Lucian loved her.

Molly wailed. It was too much to bear. He loved her, and she was trapped in her own mind, forever isolated, forever helpless—

No! Not helpless.

She still existed.

She could still think, feel....

Rage and dismay warred inside her. No! No longer would she tolerate this imprisonment—

The sorceress's hand shook again...as it had several times in the past few moments.

Each time, Molly had resisted.

Each time, her heart had cried out for Lucian.

"I didn't realize I loved her until now," he was saying. "But, I did. Still do."

Oh, Lucian.

Love for him glowed brightly within her...and the walls of her prison moved a fraction outward.

Stop, Molly, Agnes warned.

No. She'd never quit loving Lucian...because she did love him. She loved the mischievous way he smiled...

Stop!

Loved the way he laughed, the way his eyes crinkled....

I warn you, Molly...!

No! No more.

No, no, *nooooooo...*!

The word became a shrill scream. It filled Molly's mind, broke from her, the sound full of fury and resentment.

The walls around her shattered on a blinding explosion of light.

Chapter Seventeen

Lucian opened his eyes.

Blistering heat and a crackling roar assaulted his senses.

He blinked several times and realized he was lying on his side, his cheek pressed against carpet. No longer was he restrained by magical bonds.

Remembering the flare of light, he pushed up on his elbows. He was still in Molly's bedroom. A short distance away, not far from the bed that was engulfed in flames, Molly lay on her back, motionless, her eyes shut. The box containing the necklace lay beside her.

The blinding light had to have been some kind of powerful spell. If Agnes had hoped to kill him, she'd failed.

She might try again, though.

What had just happened could also have been some kind of trick.

Or not.

He muttered a quick incantation to hinder her magic, should she try to attack him. Crawling on his belly to avoid the worst of the smoke, and keeping watch for any clue that she wasn't really unconscious, he approached Molly.

Her eyelids didn't flutter. Her features remained slack.

Lucian cautiously touched her arm.

She sucked in a breath, as though waking from sleep. Her brow creased.

"Molly," he said, wiping his streaming eyes with the heel of his hand.

She moaned softly, but didn't answer.

His gut instincts told him she wasn't acting. Those same instincts also didn't sense the sorceress's presence.

Worry gripped him, because dark magic didn't just disappear. Where had it gone? And why was Molly barely responsive?

Judging by the smoke and flames, there wasn't much time left to get out of the house. He'd been willing to sacrifice himself, but his heart told him to get her and himself out.

Over the noise of the inferno, he caught the wail of sirens. Whether or not help would reach the house in time, though....

Lucian shifted to a crouch and grabbed the box. He went to lift Molly into his arms, but paused at the thought of others seeing her in her lingerie. He crawled over to the closet, pulled a silky bathrobe off a hanger, and pushed her arms into it, then tied it closed.

After lifting her into his arms, he stumbled out into the hallway. With each indrawn breath, his lungs filled with more of the acrid fumes.

Coughing, he hurried into the living room. "Galahad," he yelled.

Through the smoke, he saw Crow and several other men sprawled on the floor. Galahad, batting the front door handle with his paws, dropped down to the planks.

"Lucian." The squire wheezed. "You did it! You beat Agnes."

"I'm not sure—"

"Is Molly okay?" Rose asked.

"What caused the light?" Marigold meowed.

"Questions later. We need to get out of here," Lucian said.

"Yeah." The squire yowled. "Can't...breathe...."

Lucian wrenched open the door and hurried down the porch steps. A small group of spectators, tending to several men lying on the sidewalk, glanced at him.

"Go, Damsels," Galahad yelled from inside the house.

"Not without you," Daisy said.

"I'm right...behind you."

Wailing sirens sounded from close by.

Drenched in sweat, Lucian dragged in breaths of clean air. He took Molly a safe distance from the house and laid her on the grass then coughed until he was almost hoarse. His throat and lungs felt like old parchment.

Fire trucks pulled up, followed by ambulances. Seeing him, paramedics jumped out of the nearest vehicle and rushed to him and Molly.

He pointed to the blaze. "People...inside. Living room," he croaked.

Firemen raced toward the home. Thankfully, all five cats had made it out safely and were huddled together on the lawn.

Lucian declined medical treatment. "Take care

of Molly. Please."

"Lucian."

Julius.

Glancing toward the road, Lucian saw the older man, wearing a police officer's uniform, walking up from the sidewalk.

Damn. He wanted to check on Galahad and keep watch on Molly, because when she revived, Agnes might as well. But, he couldn't ignore his superior.

Yet, as Lucian dried his face with his scorched shirt and acknowledged what his senses were telling him, he realized a number of Experts were close by. If Agnes stirred, he'd have a small army to help him.

Lucian followed Julius to a far enough distance that their conversation wouldn't be overheard by gawking neighbors. "You look like hell," Julius said. "You okay?"

He must look awful, for Julius to express concern. "I'll be fine."

"That's Molly, I'm guessing, being checked over by the paramedics?"

Lucian nodded. "Agnes—"

"We'll handle her from here."

Handle her? Coldness gripped Lucian. He'd never see Molly again. "No. You can't—"

"We must."

"*No.*" Lucian's voice hoarsened. "Something happened inside."

"I know. The readings were highly unusual."

"It was a spell, I think. Afterward, I couldn't sense Agnes anymore."

Julius shook his head. "Agnes isn't gone. Molly will still be under her influence."

"Are you sure—?"

"Dark magic adapts. It doesn't just vanish."

"That's what you taught me, but—"

"Even if by chance Molly's no longer possessed, she knows you have magic." The Expert's piercing stare didn't waver. "We won't tolerate that."

Lucian's very soul bled. He'd done his best to keep his magical abilities from Molly, and he'd failed— just as he'd failed to keep the ancient magic from growing strong enough to control her. He was a failure all around. Whatever the consequences of his actions were, he'd accept them with honor and courage. But, he wanted to say goodbye to Molly. "At least give me a chance to talk to her," he said.

"Why? What can that accomplish?"

"Let me talk to her," Lucian said, more firmly. "It's not a lot to ask."

The older man's lips flattened. "Very well, but I'll take the necklace."

Lucian had forgotten he had the box. He handed it to The Expert.

Across the lawn, a cat yowled: a reminder that he'd wanted to check on Galahad.

"If you will excuse me—"

"The others in the house?" Julius asked, before Lucian could walk away.

"Dealers. Galahad and the female cats fought them."

"Apparently, the men on the sidewalk just collapsed. They're Dealers too."

"Collapsed?" Lucian wondered about the full impact of the flash of light, just as he heard an eerie howl. Rose and the other female cats were pacing...by Galahad, motionless on the lawn.

"*No*," Lucian choked out.

"Wait—" The Expert's cell phone rang. When he scowled and answered, Lucian raced across the grass and dropped down beside the squire.

Grief almost smothering him, he stroked his hand down the feline's back.

The cat's eyes didn't open. His chest rose and fell, though, with steady breathing.

Had he suffered internal injuries while fighting Crow? What if he'd inhaled too much smoke?

"Galahad," Lucian said.

"He was so gallant," Daisy meowed.

"*Was?*" Oh, no....

"He was a fine young cat," Petunia wailed.

"Please." Lucian ran his hand down Galahad's back again. "You have to be all right."

The feline's eyes opened a crack. His lips barely moved; the tips of his fangs were just visible.

Lucian leaned in closer. The squire could be dying. These could be his last words.

"*Go—*"

"Yes?" Lucian soothed.

"Away." As Lucian startled, the squire muttered, "You're ruining my moment."

"Your moment?"

"Yeah. Being lauded as a hero."

The four female cats, meowing plaintively, seemed unaware of the conversation between Lucian and the squire, who'd once again shut his eyes.

Shaking his head, Lucian sat back on his heels. If Galahad was well enough to entertain such foolishness, he must be all right.

His heart ached, because that just left Molly.

Time to go say goodbye.

Molly woke with a gasp. "Lucian!"

The sounds of men shouting to one another, the rumble of engines, and the ashy odor of smoke bombarded her senses. Recognizing the roughness of grass against her skin, she sat up, coughing hard. Her stomach hurt, and her head swam.

"Don't move too fast," a male voice said: a paramedic, who'd crouched on the grass beside her.

"Lucian," she said again, unable to control her panic. Dismay gripped her as, her eyes streaming, she took in the burning home. Flames were visible through the front windows and on the roof, while smoke spewed toward the sky.

Thankfully, her mother's cats seemed unharmed. What about Galahad, prone on the grass? What about Lucian?

Last she remembered, they'd been inside. She'd been about to kill Lucian. Not her, exactly, but Agnes.

Molly's gaze found Lucian talking with a gray-haired police officer.

Thank God he was all right, but....

She frowned. Blinked. What exactly was she seeing?

"The dark-haired guy carried you out of the house," the paramedic said, reclaiming her attention.

"I don't remember." Molly coughed again. She recalled acknowledging her love for Lucian, the rising intensity of her feelings, and the brilliant light, but then nothing until she'd awakened moments ago, wearing a bathrobe she couldn't remember putting on. She sweltered, but was grateful not to be wearing only lingerie in front of the gathered crowd. Some of the onlookers were taking pictures that might end up on social media or in the *Cat's Paw Cove Courier*.

As she glanced at Lucian again, guilt gripped her. She'd been horrible to him, whereas he'd been kind and selfless. She hadn't been in control of her body or actions, however, when she'd meant to kill him. The sorceress had. But, Agnes wouldn't be a threat any longer.

"Let's check your vitals again," the paramedic said.

"I'm fine." She really did feel okay, apart from a sore throat and some sore spots from Agnes fighting Lucian.

"It won't take long."

With a grudging sigh, Molly relented. She did, after all, need to figure out what she'd say to Lucian when they next talked.

While she answered a few questions for the paramedic, firemen brought Crow and the other Dealers, who were still unconscious, to the ambulances. She'd avoided looking at Lucian—she'd worried she'd catch his gaze—but as the paramedic finished up, her skin tingled with awareness.

Lucian approached. His hair was a sweaty mess, his clothes were burnt in places, and he looked exhausted, but to her, he'd never looked more handsome.

Tears brimmed as Lucian nodded to the paramedic, who picked up his bag and went to help the others tending to Crow. Lucian sat down beside her. He smelled strongly of smoke: a scent that reminded her of the danger he'd confronted to save her life.

She longed to throw her arms around his neck and tell him, with passionate kisses and tender caresses, how sorry she was for all that had happened between them. She loved him, so very much. Her heart almost couldn't hold all of the love she felt for him. But, after all she'd done, how could he ever want her?

Tears slipped down her flushed cheeks.

He obviously noticed, because he set his fingers under her chin and gently, firmly, forced her to look at him.

His wary gaze searched hers. "How are you?"

She knew what he was really asking: whether she was still possessed by Agnes and trying to deceive him, or whether she was her true self again.

However, with so many other people around, she could hardly tell him the evil sorceress from the Middle Ages, who'd possessed her through a gold necklace, was no longer able to wreak havoc. The paramedics might decide she needed to be hospitalized.

"I mostly feel like myself," she said.

"Mostly?" The suspicion in his eyes didn't diminish.

She had to make him understand she was herself again; that she'd never knowingly hurt him or anyone else ever again. How, though?

Lucian's hand settled over hers. "You were a damsel in distress earlier." His intense gaze continued to search hers, as though to confirm she was indeed herself. "I had to save you from the fire."

"You went all medieval knight to the rescue, once again."

"I will every time. That's who I am."

She thought of the silver bolts he'd shot from

his hands and the talking cats. Rose was busy scolding the squire for his "dramatics." Galahad, thankfully, was sitting up now.

Some of the paramedics and police officers nearby, several of them watching her.... If what she suspected was true, they had magical abilities. So did the gray-haired man Lucian had spoken with earlier.

How was she able to perceive magical powers? She hadn't been able to do so before the sorceress inhabited her body.

Panic fluttered, because she needed to understand the changes in herself. Lucian, with his magical expertise, might clarify things for her.

If he was willing.

He might not want anything more to do with her.

Their conversation now...might be his goodbye.

She set her other hand over his; she couldn't bear for him to walk away. "Can we talk?"

"We're talking now."

"Can we go somewhere a bit more private?"

He glanced at the gray-haired policeman and after a couple of seconds, looked back at her. "Okay. Can you stand?"

"I think so." She pressed her heels to the ground and he offered her his hand to help her to her feet. The robe gaped in front, and she grabbed it with one hand to hold it closed—a bit pointless when Lucian had already seen her almost naked.

His gaze rose from her clenched fingers. A muscle leapt in his jaw.

They walked across the lawn to the fence dividing her mother's yard from the neighbor's. "This is far enough," he said.

She faced him. Despair and remorse welled up inside her. "Lucian...."

He squeezed her hand.

"I'm sorry." Her voice wobbled. "I'm so sorry for what Agnes did to you."

"Molly—"

"She's not in control any more. I am."

His expression grim, he shook his head. "That's unlikely, I'm afraid."

"I swear, I am ninety-eight-percent myself."

"The remaining two percent...?"

"Not cause for concern."

His stare sharpened. "How can you be certain?"

"I just am."

"How about explaining to me? *How* is she no longer controlling you?"

"I...I'm not sure. But, in the house, she was hurting you. She intended to kill you—"

"Yes."

"—and I couldn't let her. I got upset. I knew, without the slightest doubt, that I... love you."

"Love?" he murmured.

Molly nodded. Tears streamed down her face. "I thought I would explode with love for you. Agnes tried to stop me from acknowledging my feelings, and...I couldn't take her telling me what to do anymore. Something inside me snapped. Then, the light."

Lucian's eyes widened. "That light...spell...."

"*Spell?*"

"Yes, spell...was you."

Chapter Eighteen

olly's expression held both astonishment and fear. "To cast a spell," she said carefully, "I'd have to have magic."

Lucian wondered how best to answer, but he'd already revealed the truth. "Yes."

A cry broke from her. He sensed the instant her legs buckled and stepped forward to catch her in his arms and draw her against him.

He never wanted to let her go; wanted her in his arms like this every single day for the rest of his living days. But, that might never be.

Out of the corner of his eye, he glimpsed Experts rushing toward them, but he signaled for them to stay away. He wasn't in danger; Molly posed no threat.

"I have magical abilities now," she whispered against his neck. "Because of Agnes."

"Mmm." He savored Molly's warm breath on his skin. He didn't want to scare her, but the fact she had powers made her even more of a concern to The Experts.

"That would explain…."

He moved her to arms' length and tried not to notice the lacy top of her bra revealed by her robe. "Explain what?"

She gnawed her bottom lip as her gaze darted to the ambulances and fire trucks. "Those men. I can tell the ones who aren't really firemen, police officers, or paramedics." Her breath hitched. "Or even neighbors."

His heart sank. "Tell me what you see," he coaxed.

"It's like...a thin, shimmering light around them."

"A kind of aura?"

She nodded. "They're different colors."

Damn.

"The gray-haired man you were talking to earlier.... His light's strong." She looked back at him. "You have an aura too. It's silver, like the light you shot from your hands."

Dismay tangled up inside Lucian. He'd wondered if she'd remember seeing him use his powers at the antique store and in the house. Clearly, she did.

What a bloody mess.

With a heavy sigh, he drew her back into his embrace.

"I have to know, Lucian. You have magic. Do you see the auras too?"

"I do."

"The colors—"

"They vary, depending on the place and time in which the person got his or her magic."

"Why is yours silver?"

He tightened his hold on her. "I got my magic in the Middle Ages. I was—"

"A knight?"

"Yep."

"Oh my God. Galahad?"

"He was my squire. We've both been reincarnated a number of times."

"Just like my mother's cats?"

"Just like your mother's cats."

Molly was silent a long moment. He sensed her struggling to comprehend all that she'd learned in the last few moments.

"Can my magic be taken away?" she asked quietly.

"Honestly, I don't know."

She shivered. "I don't want it!"

"I understand, but—"

"What am I going to do?" Desperation sharpened her voice. "Those men, the ones watching us...."

She knew.

"They're aware I have powers. They're going to take me away, aren't they?"

Lucian kissed her hair. "I'm afraid so. Your powers must be—"

"I *won't* go with them."

Admiration wove through him at her defiance, but she needed to hear the truth. "You won't have a choice."

"I want to be with you." A sound like a sob broke from her. "I love you—"

"—as I love you." Lucian slid his hand up to cup her face and then kissed her. Her mouth, hungry for him, opened beneath his. For a blissful moment, he allowed himself to feel nothing but the pleasure of their kissing.

As their kisses slowed, she moaned. "They can't make me go with them."

"Regrettably, they can." Resentment gnawed, because he'd never forget the day he'd been forced into the service of The Experts. But, this was the twenty-first century, and the love he'd found with Molly was a true love worth fighting for.

After more than eight hundred years of obeying The Experts' rules, surely he'd earned the right to ask a favor or two.

Molly rubbed her lips together and glanced at Julius again, who was speaking with several paramedics. Crow and the other Dealers appeared to be waking. "Is that gray-haired man the one in charge of the Magicals?"

"He is. His name's Julius." Resolve tingled in Lucian's veins. "Come with me."

"Why? What——?"

He kissed her and linked his fingers through hers again. "I believe there was a very good reason we found each other in Cat's Paw Cove. We're going to make The Experts believe it, too."

Hugging herself, Molly looked at the smoldering remains of her late mother's home. The firemen, having done all they could, were reeling in their hoses. The ambulances had left hours ago with Crow and the other Dealers, who'd seemed disoriented and unable to remember the events of the past few days. According to Julius, reports had come in of

Dealers in various Florida counties—people suspected of having contact with the sorceress—collapsing and suffering memory issues. At least none of them would be fulfilling Agnes's desire to hunt down Molly's relatives.

She heard the familiar sound of Lucian's Mini and glanced toward the road. He waved to her through the windshield, parked, and got out. He'd changed into a snug pair of jeans and a black, button-down shirt, and his hair looked wet from showering.

Earlier, a neighbor Molly had chatted with a few times had invited Molly into her home for a shower, change of clothes, and a sandwich. The borrowed turquoise top and floral-patterned skirt were a bit loose, as were the sandals, but they were much more practical than the bathrobe.

Lucian strode to her, pulled her in close, and kissed her. "Okay?"

Molly snuggled against him. "Mostly." Once the fire had extinguished, she'd see what could be salvaged. According to Rose, the cats had pushed the historical society folder into some flames and watched it burn, which, in truth, was a relief. Insurance and other paperwork needed to be finalized, but she wouldn't dwell on those things right now.

"Your cats are settling in well at the apartment. Galahad's taking good care of them."

"Thank you. And thanks for letting us stay with you, until...well, for now."

His eyes narrowed slightly, but he kissed her again. "My pleasure. Ready to go?"

She swallowed hard as her gaze returned to the house. "All those memories...."

"We'll make new ones. Together."

"Yes," she murmured. "We will."

A nervous tingle raced through her as she recalled her and Lucian's conversation with Julius. The older man had been rather intimidating, especially when he'd asked her to sit in his air-conditioned patrol car—which wasn't really a police vehicle at all—and had questioned her about the sorceress and how Molly had locked Agnes away in her mind. He'd also explored her mind using strange instruments and magic.

He'd confirmed the sorceress was indeed confined by an extremely powerful spell. There were few records, apparently, of Magicals with Molly's ability.

"You're exceptional in many ways," Julius had said with the faintest smile.

Lucian, sitting beside her in the back seat, had squeezed her with his arm around her waist.

"That's nice of you to say, but honestly, we all owe a great deal to Lucian," Molly said. "If I hadn't met and fallen in love with him, I wouldn't have been able to defeat Agnes. She might never have been stopped."

Julius scowled. "We don't know that."

"We do," Molly insisted.

"It's obvious you view Lucian as a hero—"

"Because he is." Molly couldn't resist a proud grin. "He's one of the most honorable, selfless people I've ever met." Lucian made a strangled sound, as though embarrassed by her words, but she pressed on. "Every day, with his magic, he protects this town, its residents, and its visitors. I'm going to use my magic to help others, too."

Julius's brows rose.

"Does that mean...you'll be staying in Cat's

Paw Cove?" Lucian asked.

"I just might." She smiled. "I've found a great reason to stay."

He smiled back. "I know you enjoy teaching, but I could use your help at the store. My grandfather has talked several times about retiring—"

"If that's a job offer, I accept."

"Perfect. You're hired." Lucian leaned in and kissed her.

Julius muttered under his breath. "Hold on, you two. Agnes, and therefore Molly, must be constantly monitored."

"Easily done," Lucian said, "if Molly's working alongside me."

"She's only just discovered her magic," the older man countered. "She must learn how to use it, control it—"

"I'll teach her."

"As you are aware, Lucian, it's not that simple. There are procedures—"

"Here and now, I pledge my skills, my magic, my life, to the Experts." She held out her hand, palm up. "Need me to swear an oath with my own blood? I'll do it."

The gray-haired man rolled his eyes. "We haven't required that since the Dark Ages."

Her pulse skittered. "So? Does that mean you'll accept me?"

She waited, hardly daring to breathe.

"It means," Julius finally said, "I'll discuss the arrangement with my superiors and The Archivists."

But, after consulting with his peers, Julius had said 'yes.' Before getting out of the patrol car, Molly had vowed to serve The Experts. She'd recited the same oath that Lucian had made over eight hundred years ago.

As the afternoon breeze tousled her hair, Lucian pushed strands back behind her ear. "Why don't we go back to my place? I'll pour us some wine, and I'll cook dinner, too."

"That sounds wonderful." Weariness seeped into her as they walked to the car.

When Molly and Lucian entered the apartment, all five cats, curled up together on the sofa, looked up at them.

"Poor Molly. She looks exhausted," Petunia said.

"As she would be, after all that's happened today." Daisy pushed up to all four paws. "We should go ask for snuggles. That will help her feel better."

"That's sweet of you, but don't get up," Molly said. "I'm fine. Really."

Rose's mouth gaped. "She can still understand us?"

"Yes, Rose," Molly answered. "I can still understand you."

Lucian shut the door. "I did bring you cats up to date on the details. Remember?"

"Rose had a senior moment," Petunia said.

"Another one," Marigold noted.

Rose huffed. "I can't be expected to remember *everything*."

"Ladies," Galahad meowed. "If Molly doesn't need snuggles, I'll take 'em." He rolled onto his back, paws up. "Who's first for cuddles?"

Shaking his head, Lucian took Molly's hand again and led her to the kitchen, where he poured them both glasses of white wine. "Bring your drink," he said

279

then motioned to the spare bathroom. "I expect you'd like to freshen up. Take all of the time you need. I just have to run down to the shop, but I'll be back soon."

"Okay."

With a grateful sigh, Molly washed her face and tidied her hair. Feeling better than ten minutes ago, she stepped out into the hallway with her almost empty wineglass.

"She's coming," Rose whispered.

Daisy giggled. "How exciting."

Frowning, Molly walked into the living room. "What's going on?"

"Nothing," Galahad said, a little too quickly.

The mischief in Lucian's expression, though, told her that wasn't true.

"Would you mind helping me in the store?" he asked.

Her stomach clenched. She'd promised to help The Experts. This could be her first task for them. "Does it involve magic?"

"A kind of magic, yes," Lucian answered.

They left the apartment. The five felines, she noted, were close behind them.

"Shouldn't they stay in the apartment?"

"Your cats haven't seen the store yet. Galahad offered to give them a tour."

"Oh. Okay."

Lucian let them into the shop, which was remarkably tidy. If Molly hadn't been involved in the recent battle, she'd hardly have believed a glass-shattering, furniture-scorching fight had taken place. Well, except for the burned table. She was glad to see the thoughtful note, taped to the tabletop, that provided the contact information for a restorer.

"When did you clean up the debris?" she asked.

"Cora and her friends handled it for me," Lucian said. "Remind me to get Cora's dish back to her in the next day or two, will you?"

He led her to the front door, opened it, and ushered her outside.

Molly squinted against the late afternoon sun reflecting off the store fronts.

"Lucian...?"

He pulled her to the right a few steps. "About here, I think."

"I only see sidewalk."

He smiled. "Not just any sidewalk. This is where you and I first met."

Hearing a thudding noise, she glanced up, to see Galahad on his hind legs, just as he'd done when she'd almost dropped the box of antiques she'd brought for appraisal. Her mother's cats stood lined up beside him.

"How adorable," she murmured.

Lucian moved to stand beside her. "I'll never forget the day we met."

"Neither will I." Meeting Lucian had changed her life forever, and for the better.

He dropped down on one knee on the concrete.

Her pulse fluttered. "Oh, goodness—"

Lucian took an object out of his pocket: A vintage ring box.

Tears filled her eyes, and she pressed her hand to her mouth.

Lucian opened the box to reveal a square-cut diamond surrounded by smaller diamonds on a white gold band. "This antique engagement ring was given to a woman by a man who loved her very much. They had a long, happy marriage," he said.

"Oh, Lucian—"

"That's what I want for us. A long, happy marriage built on love."

She trembled.

"I realize we haven't known each other for long, Molly, but will you—?"

"Yes."

"Hey, I didn't finish my question."

"Well, you weren't going to ask me if I wanted another glass of wine."

Lucian chuckled. "Not yet, I wasn't. But, I must be gallant and propose properly." He cleared his throat. "Molly, will you marry me?"

"Yes." She waited while he slipped the ring on her finger. "It's a little large," he said, but we'll get the band adjusted." As he rose, he asked, "Do you like it?"

"I love it." She melted against him and kissed him; slow, deep kisses that promised she'd love him forever…because she would.

"Aww," Molly heard Rose say through the glass.

"We *must* help with the wedding plans," Petunia mewled.

"And choosing the dress," Daisy said.

"Veil, too," Petunia agreed.

"Do they let cats into bridal shops?" Rose asked.

"Geez," Galahad muttered. "They haven't even finished their engagement kiss."

Daisy sighed dreamily. "They look perfect together."

"They do." Rose agreed.

Lucian broke the kiss, and Molly blinked up at him, her heart still soaring.

His mouth curved in a sly grin.

"What?" she murmured.

"I'm going to go all Medieval on you now."

"What does that—?"

He bent and slung her over his right shoulder.

"Lucian!"

Ignoring her spluttering, he went back inside the shop and locked the door. "Give the ladies the full tour, will you?" he said to Galahad before heading for the apartment.

Jostled against Lucian's back, her hair hanging down over her face, Molly heard Daisy sigh again.

"That love they share? That's its own kind of magic."

"Not just any magic." Galahad purred. "*Hot* magic."

Want more Cat's Paw Cove?
Turn the page for an excerpt from *A Witch in Time* by Catherine Kean and Wynter Daniels

In a violent storm in 1645, Colin Wilshire's Barbados-bound ship is swept off course. He's sure he and his pregnant bride are fated to drown when he's tossed into the sea. He wakes in a strange land and is saved by a blue-haired angel.

Twenty-first-century witch and cat rescuer Luna Halpern has fallen for more than her share of unsuitable guys—including one with a long-distance fiancé, and another who was more interested in other dudes than in Luna. Finally, a safe, drama-free guy is interested in her, and she's confident that she'll muster up an attraction to him. When she stumbles upon a handsome, mysterious man who speaks oddly, seems not to know where he is, or even what century it is, her first instinct is to help him.

Certain he's either stuck in a crazy dream or in limbo between life and death, Colin stays close to Luna. As his feelings for her grow, he's forced to choose between his obligations in the past and his hopes for the future.

Available now in eBook, print, and audio.

Chapter One

*L*una opened her eyes and gazed up at an ominously black sky. Shivering against the damp wind, she tried to get her bearings.

Where am I?

And why was the ground moving? Not moving exactly, more like rocking. She inhaled and detected the salty smell of the sea. Propping herself up on her elbows, she scanned the surroundings. She was alone on the deck of an old-fashioned ship, like the one they'd raised from the harbor—which had been turned into the Shipwreck Museum.

The floorboards creaked nearby. Then she saw him— a man, leaning on the railing, facing the water. In the darkness, she could only make out his silhouette—a little taller than her brother Leo, and more broad-shouldered. The man's long hair blew around his face and neck, and his loose white shirt billowed in the wind. Gripping the railing, he turned his head her way.

Luna gulped, but knew immediately that he didn't see her. Still, she couldn't stop staring at him. He was...ridiculously handsome.

Only in my dreams....

She studied his strong jaw, chin, and cheekbones. His dark brows knotted. Until his eyes found Luna's, and his gaze trailed down her body, heating her skin as if he'd actually touched her.

Tendrils of desire spread through her.

Ding, ding, ding.

The unwelcome noise yanked her from the dream.

No! She hadn't even gotten to kiss him.

Ding, ding, ding.

She grabbed her phone from the nightstand and shut off the alarm. Squeezing her eyes closed, she tried to return to the ship, to the man.

A rough, wet tongue licked her chin.

"Meow?"

Luna groaned. "You're a poor substitute for my dream guy, Hecate."

The white cat with facial markings like a black mask around the eyes climbed onto Luna's chest and purred. And she knew from experience that Hecate wouldn't leave her alone until Luna fed her.

"Okay, fine." Luna eased Hecate off of her as she sat up in bed. It was almost 4:30, and she had to be at the café in half an hour to start the morning baking.

After pouring food into Hecate's bowl, she stumbled into the shower. Before she left for work, she knocked on the guest room door to wake her brother, who was staying with her after an epic fight with his girlfriend of the month. "Time to get up, Leo."

He grumbled something unintelligible.

"See you at seven," she said. "I fed Hecate. Don't believe her if she acts like she's hungry. And remember, Jordan and I will be leaving the café before nine for the Founders' Day event, so don't be late."

"Mm-hmm," he mumbled.

Founders' Day, ugh! It was going to be a long day, as it always was. But this year, aside from the crowds, period re-enactors, and all the vendors at the park to commemorate the seventeenth-century shipwreck that had led to the founding of Cat's Paw Cove, there was the additional draw of the preliminary opening of the Shipwreck Museum. Luckily, Cove Cat Café was only a ten-minute bike ride from her cottage near the beach—a little less at this time when the streets were virtually deserted. As she pedaled past Wilshire Park, the clock in the tower struck five.

She turned off of Whiskers Road into Calico Court then locked her bike on the rack next to the café door and let herself inside. When she switched on the lights, she glanced through the large window that separated the coffee shop from the cat room. A grey tabby yawned before returning to his nap. None of the other cats stirred.

Luna got right to work, baking enough cookies, pastries and miniature quiches for both the café and their Founders' Day booth. Three and a half hours flew past.

By the time Luna parked the work van behind their booth at Boardwalk Park, most of the other vendors were already set up. Good thing she had Jordan there to help her this year. Luna had a feeling that her very talkative friend and employee would make the day fly past.

The blonde chirped about her boyfriend, Sawyer. "...And he made the most amazing dinner last night." Jordan sighed. "I feel like the luckiest woman on the planet."

"That's great, sweetie." Luna climbed out of the van.

Jordan met her at the back of the vehicle. "My first Founders' Day." She helped Luna transfer cats from small carriers into the large pen at their booth on the boardwalk. "And the fact that it's such a special one—with the opening of the Shipwreck Museum—makes it even better! I'm so excited."

"Mm-hmm." Luna wished that she shared her friend's exuberance for the annual event. She probably should have asked her brother to handle the Cove Cat Café's vendor booth at the celebration, but Luna had always been the one to do it. Besides, she really was looking forward to the time with Jordan. In the short time she'd known the young woman, they'd become close friends. And Jordan's gift of communicating with animals had made the cat adoption part of the café run so much smoother. Hopefully, Jordan's bubbly personality would save Luna from having to engage with everyone who wanted to play with the cats, or hopefully, adopt one or two. Luna's naturally shy nature wasn't suited to working crowded festivals.

Who am I kidding?

The real reason she now hated Founders' Day had nothing to do with the hard work and long hours. But this year she had a plan. This morning she had cast a spell of protection around herself before she'd left the café. Too bad she hadn't thought to do that in years past. She'd have saved herself a whole lot of misery.

"Are you worried about the café?" Jordan asked. "I doubt it'll be busy today. Most of the town will be here. Leo can handle things there."

"I know." Luna had every confidence that her brother would be fine running the place by himself. So why was her stomach tied up in knots? Twice in the past three years, she'd met guys she'd ended up dating at Cat's Paw Cove's biggest yearly event. Both of those relationships had ended badly. But how could she have known that Glen had had a fiancé in New York? He certainly hadn't shared that information with her at any point in the four months he and Luna had dated. Until the woman had shown up at his door sporting a suitcase and a canary diamond.

Then at last year's Founders' Day, Tim had approached the Cove Cat Café's booth and played with every cat in the pen. By the end of the day, he'd convinced Luna to go out with him, against her better judgment. He'd been so handsome and sweet. She should have known that he'd been too good to be true. The jerk had strung her along for three months before admitting that he preferred men. He'd merely been "trying to be straight" for his very-conservative parents.

Yeah, she had a knack for choosing the most unavailable guys. But this year she was safe. She was taken, sort of. As soon as she really gave herself over to the idea of dating Chuck, everything would be fine.

If only she could shake off that witchy premonition that something was going to happen today that would rock her world. No, it was probably just the fact that she hadn't slept enough. She couldn't get that strange dream of being on an old-fashioned ship off her mind. And that insanely hot guy she'd seen there. Must have been because of that news story she'd seen on CPC-TV last night. Several members of the Historical Society had spoken about the restoration of the Guinevere. Luna had paid closer attention because the reporter had interviewed one of Luna's regulars from the café, Roberta Millingham.

The sheriff approached the booth and smiled at Luna. "Good morning," he said. "Hi, Jordan."

"Hey, RJ," Jordan replied.

The sheriff stepped closer and lowered his voice. "I'm speaking to all the vendors before the festival kicks into high gear. I'd like you to let me know if anyone asks a lot of questions about the museum."

"What's going on, RJ?" Luna asked.

His lips flattened to a tight line. "I'm sure you've both heard the rumors that there's a secret treasure hidden somewhere on the ship. And believe me, I'm sure it isn't true. The restoration team has been all over that vessel. Ninety percent of it is completely restored. If there were any treasure to be found, they'd have come across it by now. But, there are still folks out there who think they can find what everyone else has missed."

"We'll call you if we hear or see anything suspicious." Jordan set a basket of cat toys for sale next to the bakery case chock full of Luna's homemade pastries and cookies. "How about a coffee, on the house?" She nudged Luna. "I'm sure my boss is down with that."

Luna grabbed a paper cup. "Absolutely. No sugar, extra cream, right?"

"You know me, Luna. Thanks." Sheriff Higgins grinned. "I hope you've got enough supplies for an army. I heard that ticket sales for today surpassed last year by more than fifty percent."

"Oh, great." Not! As she handed the sheriff his coffee, she glimpsed a crowd of festival-goers, some dressed up as pirates, headed her way. Swallowing, she mentally reinforced the protective shield around herself.

Atlantic Ocean, near St. Augustine, Florida
1645

"They're moving away," the ship's captain said, his spyglass trained on the vessel on the horizon.

Standing on the deck of the Guinevere beside the captain, Colin Wilshire released a sigh of relief, but the sound was snatched by the wind. The gentle sighing of the breeze had increased to an eerie whistling a short while ago when storm clouds had blackened the mid-afternoon sky.

Lightning flashed in the distance, accompanied by peals of thunder that were growing louder. The tempest was headed straight for them.

The storm must have convinced the other vessel—the captain believed it was a pirate ship—to change course.

Still frowning, the captain lowered his spyglass. Glancing over his shoulder, he shouted orders to his crew already working to adjust the sails. Other crewmembers on deck were tying ropes around barrels and nets to secure them.

Fifteen years older than Colin and with graying brown hair, the captain had made the journey from England to Barbados and back again four times. Before leaving the Port of London, he'd gathered all of the passengers together and had warned them of the risk of being attacked by buccaneers. Since families with young children were booked on the sailing, he'd felt an even greater responsibility to deliver the warning.

With Spanish galleons weighed down by riches traveling the waters, and the British also eager to claim a share of the New World's treasures, pirate attacks were a constant threat. The captain had offered to refund passengers' money if they decided they'd rather not make the sea journey, but no one had accepted the offer.

"It's good news, surely, that the pirates turned away?" Colin curled his right hand on the weathered rail and fought to keep his balance as the Guinevere rolled upon strong waves.

The captain shook his head. "Once the tempest is over, the pirates will be back."

"Perhaps their ship will be damaged in the storm. They might no longer be able to attack."

"It's possible." As Colin's hopes lifted a fraction, the captain added grimly, "Unfortunately, the marauders know these waters better than my crew and I. They know the islands and protected coves where they can drop anchor and wait out the storm. They know the reefs that can pierce a ship's hull. They'll let the wind and sea batter us. Then they will come for us."

Crikey. The situation couldn't possibly be so dire. "Can't we also seek shelter at one of those islands or coves?"

"And make it easy for the pirates to entrap us or force us aground? You must not have heard what pirates do to their captives."

Colin had indeed heard some harrowing tales. His cousin, Matthew Wilshire, who'd invested in a small shipping fleet that sailed from London to the Caribbean, had told him the stories after Colin had confided that he was going to leave England. "I wouldn't want anything to happen to you or your lovely wife," Matthew had said, his unusual, pale blue eyes lit with concern. "If I were you, I'd stay in England. I beg you, think about it."

Colin had, over many sleepless nights. Kept awake by his racing mind, he'd sat at the desk in his late father's study and had put quill and ink to parchment—rather ironic, when his sire had always considered Colin's creative pursuits a waste of time. Colin had finished the drawings of his latest invention; sketches he'd intended to show investors. He needed funds to not only make the wheeled contraption, but begin paying off his late father's secret, outstanding gambling debts. Colin had inherited them along with the bankrupt family estate and letters bearing King Charles I's official seal that demanded immediate payment of overdue taxes.

While Matthew had offered to loan Colin some money if he'd stay in the country, Colin couldn't accept. His cousin's finances were already at risk from investing in the fleet. Colin's sense of pride also wouldn't let him become indebted to anyone else, especially a widow with a limited income—his reason for refusing Evelyn's plea to borrow money from her mother. In the end, Colin had decided his only option was to use the savings he'd reserved for his inventions and flee. Perhaps in Barbados, once he and Evelyn were settled, he could look for investors.

In truth, Colin was already a hostage: of his late sire's financial ruin. Could being a prisoner of pirates really be as bad—or worse—than what he'd been facing in England?

As though following Colin's thoughts, the captain's scowl deepened. "The lucky captives of pirates are ransomed. The unlucky ones are sold as slaves or tortured for any bit of information that can be bartered for the buccaneers' gain. And the women...."

Colin thought of Evelyn in their cabin below deck.

"The women are used day and night until the pirates grow bored of them. Then they are sold or slain. Not, I vow, a fate you'd wish upon any of the fairer sex, let alone your wife who is carrying your babe."

"No." Imagining Evelyn facing such horrors made Colin's gut clench. While they hadn't wed for love—their fathers had arranged a marriage between them—he'd known her since they were children, and he cared about her. He had a responsibility to her, and he'd honor it until his dying breath.

If pirates did end up attacking the ship, he'd do all he could to protect her. Guilt grazed his heart, because it was, after all, his fault they were sailing to Barbados. His fault they were on the run and practically penniless. His fault she was lonely and miserable, as she'd reminded him every day since they'd left port.

As the wind rose to a hiss, and the Guinevere tilted hard to the left, Colin struggled to stay upright. Stinging raindrops began to fall from the heavens.

The helmsman, gripping the ship's wheel, shouted down to the captain then motioned to the water.

Colin glanced in the direction the helmsman had pointed, but could see only sea spray and churning waves.

"Go below," the captain said to Colin.

"Tell me how I can help." Colin didn't have much experience with ships, but since the Guinevere had set sail, he'd learned to tie knots, the basics of reading charts, and had fixed a window in the captain's cabin. "I realize you and your crew have sailed in storms before—"

"This is no ordinary storm."

The captain's words echoed Colin's own sense of dread. He'd experienced some strong thunderstorms in his lifetime, watched one recently from the leaded windows of the manor house he knew he was going to have to abandon. Yet, he'd never seen clouds as ominous as the ones overhead.

"Go below," the captain said again. "Stay with your wife."

Colin swiped away rainwater running down his face. "If you need my help—"

"I will call—"

The ship lurched to the left again. Men yelled over the hissing wind, while the soles of Colin's leather boots slipped on the deck and he careened into a post, pain jarring through his shoulder.

He steadied himself, to see the captain staggering toward the helmsman.

A wave crashed over the side of the vessel. Cold water sprayed over Colin, soaking his white linen shirt, and he gasped before grabbing hold of ropes nearby and making his way to the door and the cramped stairway that led to the cabins below.

As the ship groaned like a rusted gate, he stumbled down the hallway to his and Evelyn's room at the far end. Beyond the closed doors he passed, he heard frightened moans, worried voices, and crashes of objects hitting the floor. He'd met the Bells and Harrisons and most of the other passengers, and they were clearly terrified. There were cats on board too; Sherwoods, the captain had called them, a breed that had mask-like markings around their eyes. Two felines were huddled by his and Evelyn's cabin.

Colin thought to knock on the doors and

quickly check on the people inside—the captain and crew needed to focus on the ship, not the passengers—but when he heard a cry from the direction of his cabin, he hurried to see to Evelyn first.

He knocked twice then opened the door. The heat and stuffiness of the dark room hit him, along with a sour smell. Evelyn was clinging to the edge of the bunk, doubled over, her left arm wrapped around her belly. As the ship swayed and the door slammed inward against the cabin wall, she looked up. Tears streamed down her ashen face and onto her gown that even before the storm had badly needed washing.

"Colin—"

She threw up. As he stumbled into the room, following the cats that had darted inside, he saw more vomit on the floorboards. A pang of sympathy ran through him, because she'd already suffered for weeks from severe morning sickness. From the day they'd set sail, she'd been seasick. Being on the storm-ravaged boat must be utter hell for her.

Breathing hard, Evelyn dragged the back of her hand over her mouth. "I...can't stop...."

"It's all right." He managed to shut the door; the cats were now under the bolted-down chest of drawers, where they were welcome to stay. He lurched over to the bunk and on the way, snatched up their spare, clean chamber pot that had been sliding across the floor.

Evelyn squeezed her eyes shut. When she opened them again, tears welled along her bottom lashes. "We're going to die, aren't we?"

"Come now." He handed her the chamber pot, sat beside her, and put his arm around her waist. As he gripped the bunk to try and maintain his balance, he said, "The captain and crew—"

"They can't outwit nature." Her brown eyes blazed as she gestured to her rounded belly. "No one can."

He swallowed hard, wishing she hadn't brought their innocent, unborn babe into the discussion. Neither of them had expected her to get with child so soon after they'd married. It had happened so quickly, she must have conceived on their wedding night. But, a child—any child—was a miracle.

Colin very much looked forward to being a father. He'd vowed to be a far better parent than his own sire had been. Perhaps, if the child were a boy, he'd also be interested in inventing things. Surely Evelyn was excited to be a parent, despite their current predicament.

He stroked Evelyn's hair that was a rich brown color, like polished oak. She'd pinned it up earlier, but now most of her tresses tumbled to her lower back. "I spoke with the captain moments ago," Colin said. "We must trust his experience with storms—"

The ship rocked, and she groaned.

"—and you must trust me," he said.

She glared.

"Trust that I will protect and provide for you, as a responsible husband should." He sincerely meant those words. When Colin had asked about safekeeping important documents on the journey, the captain had told him that the Guinevere's former owner had been a smuggler; there was a secret cavity in the cabin Colin had booked. Colin had brought all of his sketches, protected by layers of canvas and stored inside a watertight wooden tube. After finding the secret spot concealed by crown molding, he'd hidden the tube in it.

Once they reached Barbados, he'd work hard to support Evelyn and not only the child they'd soon have, but any other offspring.

Moaning, she bent over the chamber pot.

He held her hair back from her face until she'd finished vomiting. Then he pulled the linen pillowcase from her pillow and handed it to her to wipe her mouth. He would have offered her water to rinse away the taste of bile, but the pitcher had fallen off the iron-bound trunk they'd used as a table and had shattered.

"I wish we'd never left England." Her words ended on a sob.

"Evelyn, we've talked about this."

"Don't you *dare* tell me to be quiet."

Colin gritted his teeth. "I wasn't going to. But—"

She averted her gaze. Her spine stiffened, and misgiving rippled through him. She was withholding something from him. Something important.

He gently squeezed with the arm around her waist. "What is it?" When she didn't answer, his misgiving deepened. "Are you hurt? Were you injured while you were alone?"

"No," she bit out.

He fought a welling of panic. "The babe. Is it all right?"

"As far as I can tell, it's fine." Tears dripped onto her bodice.

With an eerie creak, the ship listed to the right. She clutched the sloshing chamber pot with white-knuckled hands as he steadied them both.

The vessel finally leveled. The cabin, though, seemed to be growing smaller, closing in on Colin.

Sweat trickled down the back of his neck to blend with the seawater soaking his hair and shirt.

"I was going to wait to tell you," she said.

Bloody hell. He struggled to keep his voice steady. "Tell me what?"

She drew a sharp breath. "It's…it's about—"

A muffled *thud.*

The ship juddered.

As he and Evelyn were thrown several yards across the room, shouts and screams sounded down the hallway. The chamber pot flew from her hands and broke, its contents spreading over the floor.

"What's happened?" Evelyn cried, pushing up on one elbow.

"I don't know." She'd landed on her belly. His heart hammering, Colin struggled over to her. "How are you? Is the babe—?"

"We're all right," Evelyn said.

A muffled *crack*; the sound of splitting wood. Another *thud* that jolted the deck above their heads.

More urgent cries.

"I must go," Colin said.

"No." Wild-eyed, Evelyn caught his hand. "Stay with me. Please."

"I must do my part."

Her fingernails dug into his skin. "You'll abandon *me*? Our *child*?"

"No, I'm going to try and save you and everyone else on the ship. I promise, I'll return as soon as I can."

Read the rest of Luna and Colin's story in *A Witch in Time*, available now in eBook, print, and audio.

About Catherine Kean

C atherine Kean is an award-winning, Kindle Unlimited All-Star author of medieval romances whose creative muse has coaxed her to also write in other romance genres. She wrote her first medieval romance, *A Knight's Vengeance*, while her baby daughter was napping, and now has a backlist of over 22 published books.

Catherine's novels were originally published in paperback and several were released in Czech, German, and Thai foreign editions. She's won numerous awards for her stories, including the Gayle Wilson Award of Excellence. Her novels also finaled in *InD'tale* Magazine's RONE awards, the Next Generation Indie Book Awards, the National Readers' Choice Awards, and the International Digital Awards.

In 2019, she co-founded CPC Publishing with author Wynter Daniels and is busy writing books for the Cat's Paw Cove Romance series.

When not working on her next book, Catherine enjoys cooking, baking, browsing antique shops, shopping with her daughter, and gardening. She lives in Central Florida with two spoiled rescue cats.

Catherine loves to keep in touch with her readers!

Newsletter sign-up

https://landing.mailerlite.com/webforms/
landing/g8a7w8

Website

www.catherinekean.com

Facebook

https://www.facebook.com/Catherine-Kean-
Historical-Romance-Author-196336684235320/

BookBub

https://www.bookbub.com/profile/catherine-kean

Goodreads

https://www.goodreads.com/author/show/
695820.Catherine_Kean

Amazon Author Page

https://www.amazon.com/Catherine-
Kean/e/B001JOZEMU/

Also Available from Cat's Paw Cove

Artist Samantha Cartwright arrives in Cat's Paw Cove for a visit with her great Aunt Emma, hoping to get clarity about Emma's cryptic prediction. Instead, Sam finds out she must mind her aunt's metaphysical shop while Emma is away on vacation. The temporary job proves impossible for Sam because unlike Emma, Sam possesses no magical powers. Lucky for her, tall, dark, and handsome help enters the shop just in the nick of time.

Eli Kincaid managed to get on the bad side of a ruthless loan shark. Now his life depends upon his ability to con an innocent woman out of the only thing of value she owns—a precious jewel she inherited. If he can get close to Sam, maybe he can figure out where she's keeping the gem. What he hadn't counted on was falling for his mark. Can he escape the web of deception and protect Sam as sinister forces close in on both of them?

Available now in eBook and print.

Also Available from Cat's Paw Cove

BESTSELLING AUTHOR
WYNTER DANIELS
Her Homerun Hottie

Cat's Paw Cove

Event Planner and earthly Cupid Tori Sutherland enjoys nothing more than playing matchmaker for lonely hearts. Too bad Tori will never find her own happy-ever-after because the only guy she ever loved moved on years ago.

Heath Castillo managed to escape his dysfunctional family for a career in major-league baseball. His only regret was not acting upon his desire for his best friend. When an injury threatens his livelihood, Heath has no choice but to face the ghosts of his past.

When long-buried passions ignite, Heath and Tori consider taking a chance on love. But will the forces that kept them apart in high school destroy their budding romance before it even begins?

Available in eBook and print.

Also Available from Cat's Paw Cove

Eight holiday tales set in the magical town of Cat's Paw Cove:

Familiar Blessings by Candace Colt
To repay an old man who brought him out of war's dark shadow, a former Army Ranger delivers a cryptic letter to a gifted medium in Cat's Paw Cove. If what the letter says is true, the reluctant medium and skeptical Ranger must travel back to 1720 to save a young boy from the gallows.

Christmas at Moon Mist Manor by Kerry Evelyn
Lanie and Matt Saunders return to Cat's Paw Cove two years after their first disastrous Christmas there. When a mysterious kitten leads Matt back in time, can he right the wrongs of the past and give his expectant wife the perfect Christmas?

Charlotte Redbird, Ghost Coach by Sharon Buchbinder
With the help of hunky real estate agent, Dylan Graham, life coach Charly Redbird and her new kitten have found the perfect home next to a cemetery. Charly gets a new client right away, who happens to be

her neighbor—and a ghost. What could possibly go wrong?

Gnome For the Holidays by Kristal Hollis
When an empath who's failed at every relationship impulsively kisses an enchanted garden gnome, he magically turns into a real man. Together they must find his one true love and end the curse by Christmas or he'll be forever alone and trapped within his stone prison.

Ring Ma Bell by Debra Jess
In 1979, Michael Bell fell in love with high seas radio technician Dvorah Levi's voice as she guided him to safety, but their marriage was cut short by a bullet. Forty years later, Dvorah still mourns him. Can a special holiday and a magical Sherwood cat bring him back?

Purrfectly Christmas by Mia Ellas
Faerie Sormey Johnson moved to Cat's Paw Cove to live a quiet life as a human until a sexy werewolf deputy needs her help tracking down a murderous monster. When Sormey offers herself as bait, the cost may be more than she bargained for.

Collywobbles for Christmas by Sue-Ellen Welfonder
The fate of star-crossed lovers falls into the magical paws of a time-traveling kitten determined to right an ancient wrong and claim the greatest Christmas gift of all - love.

New Year's Kiss by Darcy Devlon

In order to overcome a family curse, Griffin Brooks, the town's hotshot assistant fire chief, must earn his true love's trust. Trina Lancaster knows she can release Griffin's curse, but will her magical family baggage be a deal breaker?

Available now in eBook and print.

Also Available from Cat's Paw Cove

What if Mr. Right was really Mr. Wrong?

Former ugly duckling Sydney McCoy yearns to break into television. And the hottest guy she works with—TV sports personality, Chip Haggerty —could be her ticket to the airwaves. Too bad that Chip hardly knows Sydney is alive. Worse, she has no clue how to speak Chip's sports-oriented language.

Up-and-coming real estate agent Levi Barnett is desperate to convince the owner of a hot downtown property to sell so the company Levi works for can redevelop the site into a multi-million-dollar complex. When he literally crashes into a woman he knew in high school who could champion his cause, he'll do anything to get Sydney's help. All she wants from him in return is help communicating with her office crush. No problem! But when Levi starts to fall for the beautiful Sydney, he wonders if he's making the worst mistake of his life by being her would-be Cyrano de Bergerac.

Available in eBook and print.

Also Available from Cat's Paw Cove

Abby Blessing is cursed. Every time she says the word "love", there's an unexpected power failure. She's tried everything— hypnosis, Reiki, meditation, crystals, vitamins, a Keto diet. Nothing works. Back in Cat's Paw Cove for a short visit, she's resigned to live a secluded life.

Beau Grayson, the sexiest and best electrician in town, is a technical genius with a magical gift to talk to cats. But around beautiful women, he's as tongue-tied as King George VI and has zero ability to manage his office. When an out-of-town chain threatens to force him out, Beau has to step up his game.

With her uncanny organizational skills, Abby agrees to help Beau. But her curse and his inability to solder three words together around her doom any chance for romance.

The only one who believes they are a perfect match is Scarlett, a tortoiseshell cat with a real "Tortitude". Does she have enough kitty magic to bring these two humans together for the happy ever after they deserve?

Available in eBook and print.

Also Available from Cat's Paw Cove

Once upon a time, Rachel Saunders told Javier Consuelos she was truly, madly, deeply in love with him. And he ran.

Fifteen years later, Javier still regrets breaking Rachel's heart, but watching her succeed as a corporate attorney confirmed he did the right thing. A long way from his troubled childhood, he's cooking for celebrities and giving back to the community that believed in him.

But Rachel has had a tougher fifteen years than she's let on. When she's offered an opportunity to start over, she realizes her dream job will put her in constant contact with Javier. Distraught, Rachel flees to Moon Mist Manor on Guinevere Island to connect with her long-time feline adviser, Ameerah, who has always steered her in the right direction.

When Javier unexpectedly shows up to make amends this Valentine's Day weekend, and with no vacancies in town, the trio are stuck together. That is, until mischievous visitors threaten to overtake the island. Can Rachel and Javier overcome magical forces and their painful past to save the resort and get a second chance at love?

Available in eBook and print.